Praise for Krista Davis'
Bestselling Domesti

"Reader alert: Tasty descriptions may
spark intense cupcake cravings."
—*The Washington Post*

"Davis . . . again combines food and felonies
in this tasty whodunit."
—*Richmond Times-Dispatch*

"Loaded with atmosphere and charm."
—*Library Journal*

"A mouthwatering mix of murder, mirth, and mayhem."
—Mary Jane Maffini, author of *The Busy Woman's Guide to Murder*

"Raucous humor, affectionate characters, and
delectable recipes highlight this unpredictable mystery
that entertains during any season."
—Kings River Life Magazine

Praise for Krista Davis's *New York Times*
Bestselling Paws & Claws Mysteries

"Wagtail Mountain will appeal to animal lovers
and mystery lovers, alike."
—Kate Carlisle, *New York Times* bestselling
author of the Bibliophile Mysteries

"Davis has created another charming series."
—Sofie Kelly, *New York Times* bestselling author of
the Magical Cats Mysteries

Please turn the page for more praise for Krista Davis.

Color
Me
Murder

Krista Davis is the author of

The Pen & Ink Mysteries:

Color Me Murder

The Domestic Diva Mysteries:

The Diva Cooks Up a Storm

Color Me Murder

KRISTA DAVIS

KENSINGTON BOOKS
www.kensingtonbooks.com

KENSINGTON BOOKS are published by

Kensington Publishing Corp.
119 West 40th Street
New York, NY 10018

All Kensington titles, imprints, and distributed lines are available at special quantity discounts for bulk purchases for sales promotion, premiums, fundraising, educational, or institutional use.

Special book excerpts or customized printings can also be created to fit specific needs. For details, write or phone the office of the Kensington Sales Manager: Kensington Publishing Corp., 119 West 40th Street, New York, NY 10018. Attn. Sales Department. Phone: 1-800-221-2647.

Kensington and the K logo Reg. U.S. Pat. & TM Off.

eISBN-13: 978-1-4967-1641-5
eISBN-10: 1-4967-1641-8
First Kensington Electronic Edition: March 2018

ISBN-13: 978-1-4967-1640-8
ISBN-10: 1-4967-1640-X
First Kensington Trade Paperback Printing: March 2018

10 9 8 7 6 5 4 3 2

Printed in the United States of America

Dedicated to
The Cake and Dagger Club

ACKNOWLEDGMENTS

I owe an enormous debt of gratitude to my editor, Wendy McCurdy, and my agent, Jessica Faust, for giving me the opportunity to write this book. I can only hope that this story is what they imagined.

Huge thanks also to Ritu Ghatourey, who so kindly gave me permission to begin this book with her wonderful quote about people and crayons. It couldn't be more perfect.

When I was doing some research I landed upon The House History Man blog (http://househistoryman.blogspot.com). Paul K. Williams researches old homes, creating a genealogy for the house. It was from his blog that I learned the fascinating information that Emily Branscom shares at her book signing. My heartfelt thanks to Mr. Williams for allowing me to use this information in *Color Me Murder*. Any mistakes are my own.

And finally, I need to thank my family and friends for always being so supportive.

Sometimes you have to see people as a crayon. They may not be your favorite color, but you need them to complete the picture.

—Ritu Ghatourey

CAST OF CHARACTERS

Florrie Fox
    Mike Fox—Florrie's dad
    Linda Fox—Florrie's mom
    Veronica Fox—Florrie's sister
    Peaches—Florrie's tabby cat
    Frodo—Mike and Linda's golden retriever

Professor John Maxwell—adventurer and Florrie's boss
    Delbert Woodley—Professor Maxwell's nephew
    Liddy Woodley—Professor Maxwell's sister

Mr. DuBois—Professor Maxwell's butler

Helen Osgood—Color Me Read employee

Bob Turpin—Color Me Read employee

Regular Patrons of Color Me Read
    Professor Goldblum
    Professor Bankhouse
    Professor Zsazsa Rosca

Norman Spratt—crazy about Florrie

Jim—homeless man

Jacquie Liebhaber—Professor Maxwell's second wife

Lance Devereoux—Delbert's roommate

Scott Southworth—Delbert's roommate

Sergeant Eric Jonquille

Detective-Sergeant Guy Zielony

Cody Williamson—security expert

Chapter 1

"Florrie? Is that you?"

I had just stepped inside the front door of Color Me Read, the bookstore I managed. The owner, Professor John Maxwell, bounded down the stairs. During the four years I had worked at the store, Professor Maxwell had arrived early to contemplate curious matters of history and missing treasures. Sometimes he slept in his office or arrived in the dead of night to pursue some theory in his vast library of uncommon books.

He rubbed his salt-and-pepper beard with one hand. Along his sideburns, his hair turned snowy white. But black pepper crept back in and nearly took over on the top of his head. I guessed him to be about sixty-five. His bronzed skin was as wrinkled as the old maps he constantly perused. I had tried to sketch his face at home, but he would have to model for me to get those creases exactly right. The skin just under his eyebrows had drooped, covering the outer edges of his upper eyelids. The effect was enchanting. His violet eyes were spirited but kind, as though he had discovered secrets as yet unknown to mankind, like a wizard. I had seen a photo of him as a young man and there was no doubt that women must have chased him. Even now, he exuded a powerful presence.

"Florrie! My little artiste. Have you found a place to live yet?"

For years I had rented a tiny apartment in Reston, Virginia, but I longed to live closer to work in the Georgetown neighborhood of Washington, DC. I had looked around but rent in the city was high, and I had blown past my roommate years. I looked at every miserable, tiny studio as it came on the market but the dark, dreary holes in the wall were expensive and far too depressing for me. "No. Do you have a lead?"

"How would you like to live in my carriage house? It's an easy walk to work and quite private."

I didn't know what to say. "That, that would be great," I stammered. But a cloud of doubt descended on me fast. "How much is the rent?" Georgetown prices were well beyond my means.

Professor Maxwell's mouth shifted, and he scratched his head. "My sister is pressing me to let her son live in the carriage house behind our family home. I am very sorry to say that her son is a thoroughly odious young man whom I detest. I won't charge you so much as one penny of rent if you'll do me this favor."

Sold! Professor Maxwell had taught history for several decades. I assumed he had interacted with enough young men to know whereof he spoke. But I couldn't quite believe my good luck. "Are you sure? It doesn't seem right to freeload."

"Nonsense. It would be a personal favor to me. And frankly, it would be better for all of us if you lived closer to the store. Snow days, late events, and such, you know."

"I have a cat," I said doubtfully. Peaches was like a baby to me. I wouldn't dream of moving without her.

"No problem."

"Okay!" How could I pass up an offer like that?

"Wonderful." He smiled, clearly pleased, and turned to go. He didn't even take one step before he turned back to me and raised his forefinger. "But there is one caveat."

Uh-oh.

"You must have it looking like you live there by six this afternoon."

It was nine thirty on a Saturday morning, and I was scheduled to work until five.

As though he read my thoughts, he said, "I'll cover for you. Get going!"

I rushed out the door before he could change his mind. It wasn't until I was on Interstate 66 frantically calling my sister and parents for their assistance that it dawned on me that I had never seen the carriage house. It could be as dreary as the other rentals I had hated.

My father offered to procure a small U-Haul. My mother and sister agreed to meet me at the apartment. By noon, it looked like my home had been ransacked. We sat on the floor to eat Chinese takeout.

My father, who usually approved of my life decisions, shook his head. "I can't believe you would take the place without seeing it first. It must be a dump. Maybe I should check it out before we go to the trouble of hauling everything over there."

My sister, Veronica, protested vehemently. "This is so exciting. It's just like Florrie to move into a home she has never seen. No one else would ever do that. She's such a free spirit."

I had never understood how Veronica and I came out of the same gene pool. A long-legged natural blonde, my sister looked just like my mother had in her youth. Mom was pudgier now but they were both energetic, long-legged extroverts. They had been homecoming queens and popular cheerleaders. I, on the other hand, was quiet and had been accused by my mother more than once of being *retiring.* I much preferred to pull out my sketch pad and draw, or curl up with a good mystery. I wasn't anti-social but some days I liked my cat, Peaches, more than most people. Unlike Mom and Veronica, I had long brown hair and could reach five feet two inches if I tried to stretch a bit.

"I don't know, Mike," said Mom. "The Maxwell family goes back generations in Washington and the house in which the professor lives is on the historic register."

"How do you know that?" I asked.

"Everyone who grew up in Washington back then knew about the Maxwell family. John was quite dashing and frequently in the news. I remember when his little girl was kidnapped. It was huge news in Washington. Such a sad story."

"Did they find her?" I helped myself to more lo mein.

"It was so long ago. Seems like they didn't. She was with another little girl at a birthday party. The kind of safe place where parents drop off their children all the time. Parents all over Washington were having second thoughts about where they left their children."

"Weren't original carriage houses for horses?" my father asked, clearly not listening to Mom's story.

Mom cringed a little when she said, "I suppose it could be like an old stable."

My father, the sensible one, offered again to check it out and report back. "It's probably a studio above a garage."

There really wasn't time for that, though, and we needed Dad to help us move the bulkier items like the sofa and mattress. In the end, it took longer to pack my art supplies than my clothes.

At three o'clock, with Peaches secure in her carrier, our motley caravan set off for my new home.

A uniformed butler met us at the driveway to the white brick Maxwell mansion. He gestured for us to drive through and past the main house to a one-and-a-half-story building painted vibrant Key West pink.

When we stepped out of our vehicles, the butler introduced himself as Mr. DuBois. A petite man, he appeared older than Professor Maxwell, but he stood quite straight and held his chin high. A man with dignity. He shook each of our hands and welcomed me. "Thank you for rescuing us, Miss Florrie. I fear Delbert, the dreaded nephew, would likely have slit our throats as we slept."

My mother gasped.

The excitement drained out of me. What had I done? Mostly, I was angry with Professor Maxwell for not having mentioned that his nephew might be violent. It wasn't too late to turn around and go back to Reston and the security of my old apartment. Or I could sleep over at my parents' house.

My father wrapped a protective arm around my shoulder. "I hope you jest."

Mr. DuBois did not smile. "I would sooner have the Joker living in the carriage house." He cast a scowling glance at Peaches in her carrier. "I abhor felines, yet I'm willing to deal with yours in order to avoid Delbert the devil. Take care to keep your cat in your quarters."

Mr. DuBois led us to a white door flanked by bluish-green shutters. A brass mail slot reminded me of a mouth in the middle of the door and two small quarter round windows peered at us like eyes.

My dad whispered to me, "I'll stay over with you until we straighten out this Delbert problem."

"Dad! I'm sure that was an exaggeration." At least I hoped it was. Any fears I had burst like overfilled balloons as soon as I stepped inside.

The living room and kitchen had been combined into one large space. On the side away from the main house, the wall was fitted with six sets of eight-foot-tall French doors. A stone fireplace was flanked by what appeared to be ancient and perhaps original columns crafted from finely hewn giant tree trunks so big that I wouldn't have been able to circle one with my arms. The ceiling over the living area was lofted and held up by wooden beams of the same bleached pine shade as the columns and the hardwood floor. I turned slowly, taking in the built-in bookcases that surrounded the fireplace and lined the long wall that faced the main house. The kitchen had been updated with silver-white granite countertops and a substantial refrigerator. The baker in me noted the exquisite oven and cooktop.

Beyond the French doors lay the most amazing part of all. I drifted toward them for a better look. The property had been enclosed with a high wooden fence that barely peeked through a carefully planted forest. Trees, bushes, and flowering vines had grown together so tightly that it was like a private garden in the woods. Slate stones formed a dining patio and a pergola offered shade over it. Narrow slate paths led to far corners and in the middle of it all, the sun caught flashes of goldfish as they swam in a pond.

"I'm sorry, Mr. DuBois," I choked. "There must be a mistake."

"Not at all. Now, may I lend a hand with unpacking so you will be settled before Delbert and his mother arrive? It would be best if the U-Haul were not here then. Professor Maxwell's sister can be quite disagreeable."

By five in the afternoon, the living room and kitchen brimmed with my belongings. The bookshelves had been filled, a bit haphazardly because of our hurry, but my art collection punctuated the spaces between books nicely. My bed had been set up in the single bedroom upstairs over the kitchen, and we had even tossed some clothes into a hamper to make it look lived in.

My father and Veronica took off to return the U-Haul. I had just put on water for tea when my mom screamed.

Chapter 2

I looked up just in time to see a portly woman and a man retreat from the French doors and disappear around the side of the carriage house.

Mom's face had gone pasty. "Did you see them? They cupped their hands against the glass and peered in here. Oh, Florrie." She shook her head. "I don't know what kind of mess is going on in Professor Maxwell's family, but maybe you should make other arrangements. I won't sleep a wink knowing that you're here by yourself."

I had to admit that I harbored doubts, too. But I had known the professor for five years and it wouldn't have been at all like him to put me in peril. "Why would Professor Maxwell offer me the carriage house if he thought it would be dangerous?"

Mom swallowed hard. "Some people always put themselves first."

I gazed around the beautiful room. The thing was—I wanted to stay. I wanted to walk two blocks to work. I wanted to be part of the Georgetown scene. And most of all, I wanted to sketch in the serene garden. Why did it have to turn out this way? Feeling melancholy, I poured tea for both of us. I had just handed a mug to my mom when someone knocked on the door.

"Don't answer it," she hissed.

"Mom!" I approached the door slowly, which made no sense but seemed like the right thing to do. As I drew closer, I saw Professor Maxwell standing outside. "It's okay, Mom. It's the professor."

I opened the door and Professor Maxwell stepped inside. "Ah! Linda Fox," he said to my mom, "how lovely to see you." He pecked my mother on both cheeks in a very European way. "I have come to apologize for the rude behavior of my sister and her offspring. They had no business sneaking around the carriage house. Alas, I obviously anticipated that they would not believe me when I said I had a tenant. I expected their boorish manners would lead them to poke around. My sister knows better than that, but I fear her husband has taught her and their son his coarse ways."

"Mr. DuBois said your nephew would kill you in the middle of the night." My mom looked him straight in the eyes when she spoke. I had no idea she had that kind of moxie.

To my utter surprise, Professor Maxwell burst into laughter. "That DuBois. Always prone to drama. I'm sorry if he frightened you." He lowered his voice as though he was confiding in us. "He watches entirely too many true crime programs on TV. DuBois sees murder everywhere. Frankly, my nephew Delbert barely has the grit to tie his own shoes. I have tried to take him with me on trips, but he's uncomfortable if he's more than a mile from a Starbucks. Must have gotten those genes from his father. He's a con artist, for sure, but not violent. In any event, as my sister and her son were thwarted in their plan to appropriate the carriage house, they have now departed to inspect other lodging. You needn't worry about them. DuBois refuses to cook for them, so I shall entertain them in a restaurant this evening. Now that their plans have been dashed, I trust they will be on their merry way after dinner."

"So it's safe for Florrie to stay here?"

At twenty-eight, I felt foolish when I heard my mother ask that question as though I were a child. Nevertheless, part of me was glad she inquired, as I wasn't sure I'd have been bold enough to ask such a thing of my employer.

"Of course. Color Me Read would be a disaster without Florrie running the show. She's like a daughter to me. I would never put her in a dangerous situation. DuBois showed up the moment you arrived, right?"

"Yes," I said.

Professor Maxwell grinned. "DuBois has been with my family a very long time but he's a bit of a worrywart. Not much happens here without his knowledge. I tease him about being part hawk. He'll know if Florrie so much as sneezes. I dare say that with DuBois on top of things, we're safer here than at the bookstore."

"That's a relief. It's such a beautiful spot. Florrie's sister is sorry there aren't two bedrooms."

Frankly, *I* was relieved about that feature. I looked forward to drawing in the peaceful backyard. Considering our differences, Veronica and I got along very well together. But I cherished my quiet time and Veronica was always lively.

"I'm very sorry if DuBois frightened you. He's a splendid man. You'll grow to like him, Florrie."

My father returned just as the professor left. They shook hands and spoke a minute before Dad barreled into my new quarters. "I hear that was all nonsense about the nephew. You know the professor better than any of us, Florrie. What do you think? Do you want me to stay overnight?"

I could tell he wanted to go home and sleep in his own bed. I assured Dad that I would be fine and sent my parents on their way.

No doubt exhausted by the move, Peaches, a tabby with markings all colors of chocolate and an exotic smattering of peach, had curled up in her favorite plush leopard print bed. One paw draped across her eye as though she meant to block out the world.

I checked the large atomic clock that reset itself daily and was always correct. Fifteen past six. The store would be open until ten to catch the evening crowds of browsers. I had been scheduled to work and felt like I should go in for the remainder of the day.

I dashed up the stairs and hopped in the shower, glad to freshen up after the move. The shower helped me find a second wind after the busy day. I stepped into a skirt printed with scenes of Paris in shades of turquoise and matched it with a square-necked white top and white sandals.

In spite of Professor Maxwell's assurances about dreadful Delbert, I checked to be absolutely certain that all the French doors were locked. Satisfied that Peaches would be safe, I locked the front door and walked the two blocks to the store. I felt thoroughly spoiled to be living so close.

The second I entered the front door, Helen Osgood descended upon me.

"Where have you been? I've been filling in for you all day!" She tapped the golden watch on her wrist. "I have plans tonight." She stopped being agitated for a moment and beamed. "That cute guy I like so much was here again today."

Behind her, Bob Turpin, who was always starting a diet the next day, turned his eyes up to the ceiling and stuck out his tongue. It was all I could do not to laugh.

Helen hurried behind the register and retrieved her purse. She tossed her glorious mane of rich copper hair over her shoulder. Helen was frustrated by her job at the bookstore. I had trouble relating to that, but I noticed that she didn't read much. She had become the store expert on children's books, though, and had even instituted an hour on Saturday mornings when she read to children. She seemed happiest when she was surrounded by kids.

"The next time you decide to take a day off, give a person advance notice, okay?" she grumbled.

I decided it was best not to tell her what I had been doing. I wasn't sure why, but it felt like the prudent thing to do. "I'm sorry, Helen. Professor Maxwell said he would fill in for me."

"He's been here all day, driving me nuts. There's a guy in a blue shirt looking for you. See you Monday." She flew out the door, and at once the atmosphere in the bookstore was calm and more pleasant.

Bob sighed and shook his head. "I don't get it. What's attractive about wearing your hair short on the sides and full of gel to make it stand up in the middle? That guy she likes looks like a skinny bird with a crest."

I glanced up at his sweet pudgy face. Bob's dark brown hair fell relatively flat against his head. "Bob Turpin! I believe you have a crush on Helen."

His face flushed raspberry, and he studied his shoes. I didn't want to put her down to discourage him, but I figured it was fairly hopeless. "She'd be lucky to have you."

"You think?" he asked eagerly.

"Any girl would be lucky. Now, I'd better find that guy in the blue shirt."

"Good luck. It's not like it's a color many men wear." He plucked at his own light blue shirt.

I laughed at him and peered into the front room, which had a fireplace and cushy leather sofas. So I was looking for a guy in a blue shirt. Navy blue? Denim blue? Sky blue? To my dismay, I found him right away.

Norman. Ugh. My skin prickled at the sight of him. I had dated Norman Spratt very briefly. His parents were friends of my parents, and they all dreamed of us as a fabulous couple, including, apparently, Norman himself. I wondered if he liked me because no other women had ever been vaguely polite to him. Maybe I was the only one who had ever agreed to a date.

Norman had a master's degree in turf grass management. Now, I had no problem accepting a need for people who knew how to grow a perfect golf course or make sure stadium fields were healthy. But hearing about grass growing was more boring than watching grass grow. At the ripe old age of thirty, Norman had a round head, sparse hair, and a flaccid beer belly that would have been more interesting had it actually been the result of drinking beer. Poor Norman was simply a bore.

I wasn't particularly dynamic myself, so it pained me to be shallow, but a two-hour date with Norman dragged by like an eighteen-hour flight and was equally exhausting. In the world of colored pencils, Norman was walrus pink. In fact, he was shaped somewhat like a walrus now that I thought about it.

"Florrie!" Norman smiled at me, and the other man peering at coloring books whipped around and stared me.

"Are these really your books?" asked Norman.

I was proud of my adult coloring books. I had started drawing doodles with crayons as soon as I could hold one. *Color it in,* everyone had instructed me, but I was always more interested in adding details to the pictures. I nodded shyly. "Yes."

"They're really cool. I knew you liked to draw but this is actually pretty impressive."

I thought he meant that as a compliment, not the backhanded slap it was. I sighed. "Thanks. Is there something I can help you with?"

Norman flushed. "I miss seeing you. What time do you get off? Maybe we could have drinks."

Nooooooo! Oh no. How was I going to get out of this? "I'm closing the store tonight, and it has been an exceptionally long day for me. It would be too late, and I'm bushed."

"Tomorrow? How about brunch?"

Torture! Maybe his lack of experience with women meant he didn't understand a brush-off? I tried not to shudder at the thought of brunch with Norman. The long silences while he gazed at me—ugh. There was only one thing to do. The one solution that had worked for me before. "Norman, I'm sorry, but I'm seeing someone else."

The coloring book slid out of his hands and whopped against the floor.

"Are you sure? Your mom told my mom that you weren't dating anyone."

"I think I would know."

"Yes, I suppose you would. Well, if it doesn't work out, give me a call, okay?"

I had already told one lie. Another one would spare his feelings. "Absolutely."

I felt incredibly guilty as I watched him trudge away like I had filled his shoes with wet cement. With mixed emotions, I picked the coloring book up off the floor and put it back on the shelf. I didn't want to hurt the poor guy, but I was not going to put myself through the torment of another date with him. His mother would simply have to find him someone else.

"So you're the Florrie I've heard so much about," said the other man who had been looking through coloring books.

His statement took me by surprise. Why would he have heard about me? He didn't look familiar. Slender with cognac brown eyes, he had a striking square chin and prominent cheekbones that I itched to sketch. His brow bone jutted out just a bit along his eyebrows. Surprisingly, his unique features fit together in an interesting, if not entirely trustworthy, appearance. I didn't recall seeing him in Color Me Read before. "How can I help you?"

"You drew these, right?"

"Yes, I did. Is there something in particular that you're looking for? We have a wide assortment of coloring books for adults and children if those aren't your style."

"Thanks. These are exactly what I wanted. They don't look too difficult to do."

"Coloring is easy. Just follow your imagination about color choices. There's no wrong way. It's very freeing."

"I'm not going to color them. I plan to make my own."

"Oh! Are you an artist?" I asked.

He snorted. "No way. But anyone could do this."

I was taken aback. Maybe my drawings weren't going to hang in the Metropolitan Museum of Art but they were intricate and detailed. I had no illusions about my own capabilities, but I spent considerable time on my drawings. I didn't really know how to respond, but choked out, "Good luck to you."

I walked away in haste, right into a gentleman looking for a Churchill autobiography. I led him upstairs to our history room. Because of our location in Washington, DC, we carried a vast selection of books that were of interest to the historians, professors, and the international population in the community. He thanked me and was immediately lost in the books on the shelves before him.

On my way back, I thought I heard someone on the third floor in Professor Maxwell's office. I walked up the stairs. The door was open just a hair. Hinges squeaked when I pushed it.

The man with the dramatic features who had been interested in coloring books was seated in Professor Maxwell's desk chair. A sand-colored map was spread out before him.

I did my best to be polite. "Excuse me, sir, but this office is for private use only."

He barely glanced at me. "It's okay."

"I'm sorry, but I'm going to have to ask you to leave. This is the owner's private office." I opened the door all the way and pointed at the sign on it that said PRIVATE USE ONLY.

He laughed. It was a gesture that usually brightened faces and made people appealing. On him, it was scary. All those sharp, interesting features morphed like a sarcastic caricature.

He didn't budge, nor did he look at me. It was as though I was talking to the walls.

"Sir! Please."

I heard footsteps on the stairs and hoped Bob was on his way up.

The man finally turned his eyes to me. "You really ought to mind your manners around me, Florrie Fox, because I will be the next owner of this store. You see, I am John Maxwell's sole heir."

Chapter 3

He turned his attention back to the map.

"Delbert?" I blurted. "You're Delbert?"

He looked up at me. "I am. And your job is toast."

At that exact moment, Professor Maxwell spoke from behind me. "Delbert, your mother has been looking for you."

Delbert leaped from the chair. "Uncle John! I have always admired this office. It's so"—he gazed around at the bookshelves crammed full of books, tribal masks, primitive hatchets, spears, and unusual artifacts from the professor's adventures—"interesting."

In a dry voice, Professor Maxwell said, "Your mother is waiting."

Delbert hurried from the room, a completely different person from the one who had been so smug only moments before.

As he clattered down the stairs in a rush, Professor Maxwell said to me, "I'm sorry, Florrie. Whatever he said or did, I'm very sorry. Are you okay?"

"I'm fine." I watched the professor walk down the stairs, so elegant and refined. Professor Maxwell, for all his intelligence, breeding, and money, had two flaws that I could see. He loathed confrontation and avoided it at every opportunity.

Being passive was a wonderful trait in a human being. It meant congeniality and pleasant times. It made him a lovely boss, and a terrible manager.

He also had no internal clock or sense of time. For someone like me, who was unfailingly punctual and couldn't imagine being otherwise, it was impossible to grasp that anyone could lose himself in thought to such an extent that he didn't notice whether it was day or night. But that was Professor Maxwell.

What Delbert had said was probably true. As far as I knew, Professor Maxwell didn't have any children, except for the one that went missing and was likely deceased. Delbert probably would inherit the entire Maxwell estate eventually.

The rest of the evening was a lot of fun. Bob was always amusing, and the browsers bought a good amount of books. At ten o'clock, I flipped the OPEN sign to CLOSED on the front door and while Bob shooed out the downstairs shoppers, I checked the second and third floors for lingering patrons.

The door to Professor Maxwell's office was open. He sat in his desk chair, his elbows on his desk and his head in his hands. "Professor Maxwell? Is everything all right?" I asked.

He raised his head and sucked in a deep breath. "For generations, the Maxwell family has been a Washington institution. Oh, we've had our oddballs, no doubt about that. One of my relatives was caught stealing pigs, and another had a bad habit of painting other men's wives in the nude. He was ultimately shot by an angry husband. They say he survived to continue that ill-chosen hobby. I suppose that illustrates either stubbornness or idiocy. Perhaps it's *his* blood that has resurfaced in Delbert. In any event, I am troubled that the Maxwell family treasures and heirlooms will eventually land in Delbert's possession." He paused. "It's Saturday night. I'll have this little matter taken care of by Monday morning. Good night, Florrie."

I bid him a good night and checked the other rooms to be sure everyone was gone. He was still sitting there, deep in thought, when I passed him again. Bob and I locked the front door and headed to our favorite pizza place. We waited for our orders together, extra cheese and pepperoni for Bob, mushrooms and black olives for me, before splitting up and heading to our respective homes.

For the first time since I had worked at Color Me Read, I didn't have to drive home. I walked leisurely, enjoying the air of the warm summer night. Georgetown always bustled, but on Saturday nights it was especially vibrant and seemed to hum with intensity as couples and groups sought out the nightlife.

Part of me felt I ought to enjoy it, but the other part wanted nothing more than to curl up in my jammies, draw, eat pizza, and sleep. I walked on the sidewalk across from Color Me Read. It was a prime location. If I counted the attic with dormer windows, the yellow brick Federalist-style building was three stories tall. Four if I included the basement. So far the basement was only in use for off season items and extra display racks. On the street level, a graceful awning sprawled across the front. Stained glass windows added to the charm in transoms over the front door and the windows on the second floor. The professor's office was on the third floor, along with the rare books. A light still blazed in the dormer windows of his office.

I walked on and was home in minutes. When I unlocked my door, Peaches waited as though she had known I was on my way.

Peaches had been rescued from a stable when she was only two weeks old. She refused a bottle and by six months refused kitten food. Now that she was eight months old, she clearly wasn't going to be a petite cat. Voracious and spunky, she sampled everything she could. I had even caught her chowing down on a roasted sweet potato.

Her tail had always seemed just a little bit too long for her body. She had mostly grown into it, but she had a habit of marching around with it held high, the top part curled like a question mark.

There was no way I could eat my pizza in peace unless I fed her first. I spooned chicken dinner for cats into a bowl and set it on the floor next to her water. She settled in and ate, a sign that all was well in my new abode. If anyone had been there, she would have let me know.

I walked upstairs and changed into an oversized T-shirt made to look like a green crayon. I grabbed a pillow, a blanket, and jeans because I planned to sleep downstairs. If Delbert lurked around during the night, I would know about it sooner. I didn't want to wake up and find him in my bedroom.

I stared out at the dark garden as I ate pizza. It would be so pretty at night if I hung some fairy lights. I hoped Delbert had found a new place to live that he loved as much as I adored the carriage house. That would put an end to his interest in it.

Still wide-eyed, I sketched the face of the person who haunted me. Delbert, of the strangely square chin and somewhat Neanderthal brow. When it took shape, I found I had captured his cunning expression.

I hadn't expected to get much sleep but it had been a full day and exhaustion finally overcame me. At seven minutes to three in the morning, Peaches yowled, and I jerked up. A dark, hunched shadow was trying the handles of the French doors!

Chapter 4

I sprang to my feet. My cell phone and sketch pad fell to the floor. A host of colored pencils rained down, clattering as they hit the wood floor.

The person outside must have heard the commotion because he ran past three French doors and around the right side of the carriage house.

My heart beat like crazy. I was afraid to turn on the lights. On my knees, I scrounged for the telephone. In my panic, I hit the autodial for Professor Maxwell. After all, he could be here in seconds.

And he was. Outdoor spotlights caught me off guard. The garden in back of my house lit up nicely. The professor and Mr. DuBois, carrying a baseball bat, were at my front door before I had zipped my jeans. I let them in.

Professor Maxwell switched on the indoor lights. "Are you sure it was Delbert?"

"No. It was just a dark shadow."

"Maxwell," said Mr. DuBois, "you must be realistic. Of course it was Delbert."

"Did you see this person at the front door?" asked the professor.

Now that I was safe, I took a deep breath and explained precisely. "I was asleep. Peaches yowled, and I guess the sound woke me. Someone was trying to get in through the French doors. When I jumped up, I must have scared the person, and he ran to the right of the house."

Professor Maxwell strode to the French doors, unlocked one, and stepped outside.

"Maxwell! You're not armed. Have you lost your mind?"

The professor ignored DuBois, who lingered safely inside the door. The old fellow wore an elegant black silk bathrobe.

Seconds ticked by. DuBois hoisted the baseball bat as if he were preparing to clobber someone.

"Do you hear anything?" I whispered.

"Only you." He sounded annoyed.

"It's been thirty seconds," I said. "Should we call the police?"

DuBois stiffened. "I think not. The professor would be appalled to see the Maxwell name in local reports of the police log. Besides, this is a family matter."

DuBois turned to look at me. His gaze drifted to my collection of clocks on the bookshelf. "Good grief. How did I miss that earlier? How many clocks do you have?"

"I like to be punctual."

"One clock would suffice."

Professor Maxwell returned in under two minutes. "Whoever it was is long gone. Florrie, I cannot apologize enough. I honestly didn't think Delbert would do anything of this sort. I would like to think he just meant to frighten you, but even that kind of behavior is disturbing. How would you feel if I slept down here the rest of the night?"

"You would leave me alone?" DuBois's eyes widened.

A faint smile danced across the professor's lips. "*You* have a baseball bat."

DuBois made no attempt to hide his displeasure when he

choked, "Which I will need to protect you down here. I shall return with linens."

I was too agitated to sleep, of course, but I scooped Peaches into my arms and went up to bed anyway. Still unnerved, I sat up against my pillows and drew a sketch of what I had seen. Without exception it was the darkest thing I had ever drawn.

The reason was obvious and it wasn't because it had been sinister. It had been nothing more than a dark shape. And a hunched shape at that. Had it not moved and tried the door handles, I might have thought it an illusion or an odd reflection.

Peaches rubbed her head against my hand and tried to push away my sketch pad. I flipped it closed and set it aside. Satisfied, she climbed onto my chest and purred. I fell asleep to the soothing sound.

When I woke in the morning, Professor Maxwell snored on my sofa. But Mr. DuBois and any linens he may have brought for himself were gone.

I was tiptoeing into the kitchen to make my tea when a phone played the Indiana Jones theme music. Professor Maxwell jerked to an upright position, blew air out of his mouth, and said, "Maxwell."

I didn't mean to eavesdrop but I couldn't avoid it. I ran water into the kettle to make my tea and let him know I was present.

"I can't say I'm surprised. He tried to break into the carriage house last night."

There was a pause. "I'm sure I don't know why he would do that. No one chased him. I'd have liked to, though."

Another pause.

"He's a grown man, Liddy. Okay, okay. Please don't cry. I'm sure he's fine. Give me enough time for a shower, and I'll drive over."

Maxwell shook his head, slid his phone into a pocket, and muttered, "He'll turn up before I get there." He rose and stretched. "Good morning, Florrie."

He picked up Peaches and stroked her while walking over to me. "I must apologize for Delbert's behavior last night. I promise it won't happen again."

"Tea?" I asked.

"No, thanks. DuBois probably has breakfast waiting for me."

I summoned courage to say what I was thinking. "Look, Professor Maxwell, I love this place. The light coming through the French doors this morning makes me want to stay. But after last night, I think this was a mistake and that I should move back to my old place."

"Florrie, if I thought for even a nanosecond that Delbert would hurt you, I would never have suggested you move in here. The Delbert I know is a con artist, a trickster who manipulates people and takes advantage of them. But he has never been violent. My best guess was that he meant to do exactly what he did"—Maxwell pointed his forefinger at me—"frighten you out of the carriage house!"

"Well, it worked. I'm scheduled to be at the store today, but I think Peaches and I will sleep at my parents' house tonight. I'll move my belongings back as soon as I can."

Professor Maxwell's shoulders sagged. "I suppose I can't blame you. But my darling Florrie, even those of us who are timid face times in our lives when we must brace our shoulders and stand our ground. The fates like to test us. Instead of running, we must use our little gray cells to outwit those who are in the wrong."

"Was that him you were talking about on the phone?"

He nodded. "Delbert has been staying with his parents in Maryland since his roommates booted him out, but he didn't come home last night. Not terribly surprising given his misbehavior. He's ashamed to show his face. It's typical of Delbert to avoid taking responsibility for his cunning ways. He'll turn up soon. The way Delbert burns bridges, I doubt he has anywhere to go but back to the parents who indulge his errant behaviors."

Professor Maxwell walked to the door. "Again, I'm so sorry this happened. I wish you would reconsider."

He let himself out.

When the door shut, I turned to Peaches but she had already scampered across the room and was watching birds through the glass. I supposed I should start packing, but after the rush the day before, that held no appeal whatsoever.

Sipping my tea, I mixed a quick batter for blackberry muffins and slid the pan into the gorgeous oven that sparkled as though it had never been used. I set a timer, made a second mug of tea, and ambled over to the French doors. Leaving Peaches inside, I stepped out to see if it would be safe for her. To the right of the carriage house, a high wall offered privacy from the mansion on the other side. Some kind of odd rim ran across the top of the fence, but I couldn't quite make out what it was supposed to be.

On the left side of the carriage house, the fence was interrupted by a wooden door with a round top. It latched securely. Delbert must have sneaked in that way last night. Maybe if Professor Maxwell installed a lock?

I opened a French door to let Peaches into our garden. She explored it with caution. I kept a very close eye on her lest she decide to scale the wall. Happily, the goldfish captured her attention. She prowled the edge of the sizable pond like a tiger.

Meanwhile, I strolled the little paths, admiring coral trumpet vines and pink climbing roses. Several plants had been trimmed in formal fashion, leading me to believe this was the work of an avid gardener. I fetched a sketch pad and a pencil and drew Peaches at the pond with the flowering vines in the background until the oven timer went off.

I carried our breakfasts outside on a tray and settled at a small table in the sun. While I enjoyed blackberry muffins, Peaches ate mackerel.

And suddenly, I was very angry with Delbert. My apartment in Reston didn't have French doors or even a tiny balcony. There were no goldfish, no pond, and no fireplace. I longed to stay in this tiny corner of paradise. Maybe I just had to do what my sister Veronica would do, tell him off to his face!

Like that was going to happen.

I took the tray inside and returned to pick up Peaches, who mewed in protest. "Sorry, sweetie, I have to go to work." I checked all the doors to be sure they were locked and dashed upstairs to shower and change.

Dressed in a boatneck navy blue-and-white–striped top and a bright lemon-yellow skirt, I filled Peaches's bowl with food to munch on while I was gone, packed two muffins, and ambled to Color Me Read.

Close to a show window was a bench and an oversized terra-cotta pot of vibrant red geraniums. Jim was already there.

When I approached the bookstore, he said, "I hate Sundays. Have to wait half the day for my coffee."

I grinned at the grumbler and handed him the muffins. "Good morning, Jim."

He peeked inside the package. "These smell great!" He bit into one immediately.

Jim, who had never shared his last name, sat on the bench outside the store every morning with all his worldly possessions packed in plastic bags and attached to a rusted dolly. Professor Maxwell had told me that Jim moseyed toward the canal as the day went on because a restaurant gave him their leftovers for dinner every night.

"I'll bring your coffee in a few minutes."

"Thanks, Florrie."

I loved Sundays at the bookstore. Aside from the luxury of sleeping late, it was Helen's day off. I unlocked the door and keyed in the password *sleepy conscience* for the alarm system. Maxwell, Bob, and I had argued over a memorable password and finally settled on something we saw every day. On the wall behind the cash register counter was a sign that said GOOD FRIENDS, GOOD BOOKS, AND A SLEEPY CONSCIENCE: THIS IS THE IDEAL LIFE. —MARK TWAIN.

Flicking on lights as I went, my first stop was the coffee machine. I measured coffee, added fresh water, and in seconds the heavenly scent drifted up to me. Next stop—music. Professor Maxwell insisted that classical music play softly in the background. He thought it made people linger longer and enjoy the bookstore even more.

I flipped the CLOSED sign to OPEN and took a quick walk through the rooms on the main floor, straightening up and making sure it was tidy. The cleaning man did a great job, but people were prone to picking up books in one area, changing their minds or forgetting about them, and leaving them in the wrong section of the store. I walked up to the second floor and did a quick check, but I could hear customers murmuring downstairs and rushed back.

Bob arrived just as I was taking a cup of coffee out to Jim. A couple of our regulars entered the store followed by two well-dressed ladies who had probably enjoyed brunch with champagne because they acted just a wee bit too giddy.

We were busy for the next hour. Professor Simone, a friend of Professor Maxwell, phoned to ask if we had a copy of *All the World's Birds* by Buffon. The computer showed that we had two but they carried vastly different prices, and I couldn't tell what the difference was. Promising I would call her back, I walked up the stairs. The rare book room was on the third floor, but when I reached the landing where the stairs to the third floor turned ninety degrees, my sandal caught the carpet and I pitched forward.

I stood up and brushed off my legs. A lovely bruise would undoubtedly appear in a few hours. Otherwise, no harm done.

But there appeared to be a wrinkle in the carpeting on the landing. I bent to straighten it but something small and hard prevented me from pulling the carpet flat. We certainly didn't need anyone tripping and falling down the stairs. I tried to wiggle the hard bit toward the edge. After a couple of minutes of determined prodding, the small item rolled out of a loose corner of carpeting.

A pearl! It was drilled through as though it had come from a necklace. That was odd. I hadn't noticed the wrinkle or the loose corner before.

I tugged at the carpet to straighten it but it moved far too readily. It was a hazard and someone else would surely fall. I would have to close off the third floor and get a carpet layer in to repair it on Monday.

I studied it for a moment. Something wasn't right. Surely one of us would have noticed the problem before this. How could a carpet come loose like that? I lifted the corner to peer underneath. Could mice be nibbling at it?

The overhead light shone brightly on the oak floor. As I rolled the carpet back, I could make out the very fine perimeter of a trapdoor and a hole for lifting it.

Did Professor Maxwell know about this? He would think it incredible. I plunged a finger into the hole and lifted. The door was hinged on the other side and opened with a loud screech.

Chapter 5

Someone was inside! I screamed and dropped the door. It slammed shut with a bang that reverberated in the stairwell. I shook my head. Had I really seen someone lying in there with a spear jutting out of his back? That couldn't be.

Bob ran up the stairs, breathless. "Was that you? What happened?" He stopped talking as he took in the misplaced carpet and the trapdoor. "What's going on?"

A small crowd climbed the stairs behind us.

I could hear someone asking, "Florrie? Are you okay?"

"There's someone in there," I whispered to Bob.

"That's very funny. Is today trick-your-coworker day?"

I shuddered.

"You're serious? Why would anyone be in there? Should I get a weapon?"

"He's lying on his stomach. I'm not sure you'll need a weapon."

Bob leaned forward. His forefinger hovered over the hole briefly. He yanked his hand back and straightened up. "Stand on it."

"What?"

"Stand on the hatch to make it more difficult to open. Just

do it. I'll be right back." He ran up to the third floor and in the direction of Professor Maxwell's office.

I stepped onto the door timidly, as though I thought I might plummet into the well beneath, which made no sense at all because I had unknowingly walked across it hundreds of times. There was no reason it should give way under me. Still, now that I knew of its existence, I couldn't help feeling like it might break, plunging me down a frightening rabbit hole.

Besides, even if there wasn't an Alice in Wonderland–type slide inside, I certainly didn't want to fall on someone who lay in a position all too reminiscent of a crime scene body outline. I had only seen it for a moment. Maybe it wasn't really that scary?

I tried to be reasonable. But there wasn't a good reason for a person to be inside. Just because he was on his stomach didn't mean he was dead. But I really ought to call 911. If he was alive, he might need help.

Mr. DuBois's words from the night before ran through my head. The Maxwells didn't like publicity about trouble. It couldn't be helped this time. But what if it was a gag? A manikin or something?

I pulled my cell phone out of my pocket and dialed Professor Maxwell's cell number. He was probably at his sister's house dealing with devilish Delbert.

When he answered my call, I asked, "Do you know about the trapdoor in the stairs?"

"In the store?" he asked.

"Yes."

There was a long moment of silence before the professor said, "Yes, I do."

"You might want to come over here. There's someone inside it."

I heard a quick intake of breath. "What? Who is it?"

If it was a manikin, he had no knowledge of it. "I don't

know yet. I'm standing on the door so he can't open it, but," I said, lowering my voice to a whisper, "Professor Maxwell, I'm afraid he might be dead."

"Thank you, Florrie. I am on my way. Don't take any chances." He sounded completely calm, as though I had told him the mail had arrived. His phone clicked off.

Bob returned wielding an intimidating primitive hatchet-type battle-ax from one of the professor's adventures. He stood beside me and whispered, "Okay, you open it, and I'll be ready." He lifted the hatchet in preparation.

"Maybe we should wait for Professor Maxwell."

"You think I'm not macho enough to clobber whoever is in there?"

"This isn't about being macho." I didn't know what it was about. I gazed at the collection of people on the stairs below us and back at the trapdoor again.

It gradually dawned on me that we had a bigger problem. "Bob," I whispered, "he could have closed the cover on himself, but he couldn't have pulled the carpet over the closed trapdoor."

"What are you saying?" asked Bob, following my example and speaking softly. "That he had an accomplice?"

I hadn't thought of that. But why would he hide in there? Was he waiting for us to close the shop and leave? That didn't make sense. "No. What I'm saying is that someone must have left him in there." I lowered my voice to the barest whisper. "I'm thinking he could be . . . dead."

Bob blanched. "I am *not* jumping in there with him to find out."

I took a deep breath and squared my shoulders. I raised the door again and let it lean against the wall. The person inside didn't move. He lay on the floor about four or five feet below the opening.

"The jig is up! Come out of there!" Bob did his best to

sound tough, but he wouldn't have scared anyone older than eight. He was just a big softie.

A couple of Professor Maxwell's friends had made their way past the others and stood one step down from Bob, looking on. One of them yelled, "Hey! You!"

I pulled out my phone again. "I'm calling an ambulance."

Bob looked queasy.

I reported that we had found someone who might be injured and was in a difficult location. They promised to send someone right away.

A couple of Professor Maxwell's friends squished between us and looked down at him.

Professor Goldblum, a tiny man with small eyes and a pudgy figure, had boundless curiosity. "Fascinating! A hiding place for liquor during Prohibition. I have heard about them but never had the good luck to see one."

Really? That's what interested him? He couldn't see the man lying at the bottom with a spear jutting out of his back?

"It's not holding liquor now," observed Professor Bankhouse.

"Indeed. Most curious. I'm too short. You jump in, Bankhouse."

Edgar Bankhouse blanched. "Where's Maxwell? He's the intrepid adventurer."

What was wrong with these men? I was a little scared myself, but I hoped someone would have the courage to jump in if I were the one lying inside. Someone had to help him! I sat on the edge of the hole, wishing I had chosen to wear trousers. It wasn't that big of a jump. I took a deep breath and leaped, doing exactly what I had wanted to avoid—I landed directly on top of the man, narrowly avoiding the spear.

"Florrie!" yelled Bob. "Are you okay?"

"Yeah, I'm fine." I would be bruised all over later on but for the moment I was okay.

The guy on the floor hadn't grunted or moved. That couldn't be a good sign. I scrambled to my knees and crawled toward his head. A shock went through me when I recognized the slightly Neanderthal brow and the features I had sketched just the night before. I dared to touch his neck in search of a pulse. His skin was cold and stiff. Delbert was dead.

Chapter 6

So many thoughts ran through my head that I felt my life swirling like a kaleidoscope.

The head of the spear wasn't visible. The wooden shaft protruded from Delbert's back. His shirt was stained with a large area of blood. Even his trousers showed blotches of blood.

I glanced around. The space wasn't very large. There wasn't much to see except quite a bit of dust. Most of the dust on the floor had been kicked up, but in the corner, I spied the very clear treads of a shoe.

I pondered it briefly. I hadn't been over that way. Just to be doubly sure, I looked at the bottom of my sandal. It was smooth, without treads.

About a foot away from the shoe print in the dust, there was a gouge in the floor. Relatively thin, maybe two inches long. I suspected it was new or at least recent because the damaged part of the wood was closer to raw oak in color, while the rest of the wood surrounding it was darker, like wood that had been stained.

Too many questions were dancing through my mind when I heard a commotion above me.

Bankhouse and Goldblum moved aside as two cops peered down at me.

One of them raised his eyebrows in surprise. With the ease of an athlete, he leaped down into the hole with me, landing on his feet. I looked up into delphinium-blue eyes that took my breath away. The name engraved in a shiny bar just over the right pocket of his police-blue shirt said SERGEANT JON-QUILLE. He was out of my league with loose chestnut curls that seemed to have minds of their own and a tan that suggested he liked the outdoors. I flushed just to look at him.

"I think he's dead," I choked.

Jonquille searched for a pulse much like I had. "I believe you're right. Who is he?"

"Delbert Woodley, the nephew of the owner of the store."

"Are you the one who found him?"

"Yes. It was completely by accident." I explained about the carpet and the pearl. "If it hadn't been for the pearl, we would have walked over him for days. Or until he smelled bad. And then we wouldn't have known where the odor was coming from."

"You're the manager?"

I nodded. "Florrie. Florrie Fox."

Unfamiliar voices above us prompted me to look up. An emergency medical technician jumped into the pit with us. "What have we got here?"

Sergeant Jonquille very politely said, "Let me give you a boost out, Florrie."

He formed a bridge with his hands for me to step on. I couldn't believe I had worn a short skirt. But who planned for this kind of thing? He boosted me up. His partner who was standing on the floor above us grabbed my hands and hoisted me to the stair landing like I weighed nothing.

From below, Sergeant Jonquille called, "Florrie! Can you

go downstairs and put up a *closed* sign so more people won't enter the store?"

"Yes, of course." I started down the stairs, saying *excuse me* repeatedly to get past everyone.

Bob followed me. When we reached the main floor, he seized my arm. "Did I hear you say that it's Delbert?"

"I'm afraid so."

"Oh man! Maxwell is in big trouble."

It wasn't as though that hadn't occurred to me. I had visions of being called as a witness at his trial. *Ms. Fox, what exactly did Professor Maxwell say to you about Delbert the night before his murder?*

He said he would have the Delbert problem taken care of by Monday morning.

In my heart, I knew Professor Maxwell couldn't have had anything to do with Delbert's demise. I was certain of it. A distinguished man with such enthusiasm for the mysteries of life would never kill anyone, except possibly in self-defense.

As I flipped the sign on the door, my stomach did a little flip, too. At that exact moment, Professor Maxwell jogged up to the store. We saw each other through the glass briefly before I opened it for him.

"I see there's an ambulance outside," said the professor. "Was someone injured?"

How to answer that? *Not exactly?*

Fortunately, he babbled on, "What a day. First Delbert disappears and now this."

He hurried toward the stairs. I debated telling him. Was it better to hear it from me or from the cops? What if he heard it as he walked up the stairs? I didn't have much time to think about it. "Professor?"

He turned to look at me.

"It's Delbert."

Professor Maxwell was many things, but I seriously doubted that he was enough of an actor to pull off the shocked look on his face.

He rushed to the stairs and tried to take them two at a time, but too many people were in the way, hampering his progress.

"Bob," I said, "stand by the door and don't let anyone leave. I'm going to get them off the stairs. Make sure the passage to the door is clear, okay?"

"What if they want to leave?" His sweet round face was fearful.

I took a wild stab from reading too many mysteries. "Tell them the police want to talk with everyone."

For the next fifteen minutes, I herded people into the various rooms of the bookstore, imploring them to clear the stairway for the emergency medical technicians who would be carrying a stretcher.

As it turned out, I was dead wrong. The EMTs walked down the stairs all right, but they departed without Delbert. More police arrived, carrying cameras and other equipment. The crowd inside grew restless and a new group formed on the sidewalk outside of the store.

Sergeant Jonquille found me. "Thanks for keeping everyone here. How did you know to do that?"

"Just a guess. I read a lot of mysteries. I thought you might need to verify what Bob and I tell you."

"We'll start collecting names and addresses and let them go one by one."

When he asked my address, I paused before giving him an address, which prompted him to shoot me a quizzical look.

"I moved yesterday."

"Somewhere around here?"

"The carriage house behind Professor Maxwell's estate."

He stared at me for a long moment.

I wished I knew what was going through his head.

"Phone number?" he asked.

I gave him my cell number and email address.

"When did you last see Delbert Woodley?"

"I never met him until yesterday. The last time I saw him was here at the bookstore." The image of him seated at Maxwell's desk and acting so brazen haunted me. I didn't mention that he had told me I was toast and that he had left like a frightened child when Maxwell caught him. Maybe I should have. Everything was happening so fast. I felt the need to be honest, yet cautious.

Particularly as it concerned Maxwell. He had made no secret of his antipathy toward Delbert. Bob was right. Maxwell was in serious trouble. I didn't need to add to it. I told myself to keep it simple. The wrathful relationship between Delbert and the professor would come out soon enough. I chose my words carefully. "He was leaving, I think."

"Time?"

"Dinnertime. Around six thirty or seven."

"How did Professor Maxwell and Delbert get along?"

And there it was. It hadn't taken him long. My gaze met those clear blue eyes.

"Loyalty is a great trait, Florrie, except where murder is involved. The truth always floats to the top."

"Delbert was a worm. He told me that he would inherit Maxwell's estate and that I was toast. It's not surprising that Maxwell, a man of great integrity, would be disappointed in his nephew."

"Did they have an argument yesterday?"

They might have when Delbert and his mother found the guesthouse occupied. But I didn't really know. "Not that I saw or heard." I let out a relieved breath. That was the truth.

"Thank you, Florrie. I may need to contact you with more questions."

"Sure. Anytime."

"Florrie!" called Bob.

Sergeant Jonquille nodded. "Go on. If you have trouble with anyone who wants to leave, just let me know. We'll be processing them fairly fast now."

I made my way to Bob at the front door and immediately saw the problem. My mother and father stood outside peering through the glass.

I knew I would upset the people who were itching to leave, but I unlocked the door and slipped out anyway. Mom and Dad embraced me so tightly I could hardly breathe.

"Thank heaven you're okay." Mom held me at arm's length and looked me over. "You are okay, aren't you?"

"I'm fine. How did you hear about this?"

"It's all over Twitter. Norman's mom, Irma, called to tell us because she knows you work here."

"What happened?" asked Dad.

In a whisper, I said, "Delbert is dead."

Mom shrieked. Her hand flew up to cover her mouth.

Dad stared at me in shock. He leaned toward me and whispered in my ear, "Do you need a lawyer?"

"No! His body . . . well, it's kind of a long story. Why don't you grab a bite, and I'll come join you when I can?"

My mom seized my hand and held it tight. "I was so scared. I thought we had lost you."

"Linda, honey, let's get you a bracing cup of tea . . . or bourbon." Dad took her arm and gently steered her away. But he looked back at me and there was no doubt in my mind that my mom wasn't the only one who had been terrified.

Ignoring the reporters who tried to thrust microphones in my face, I turned my back and knocked on the door. Bob let me in.

The police were processing everyone in an orderly fashion, and Bob was releasing them. With that part of the chaos under control, I went in search of the professor.

I found him on the second floor, seated in a floral armchair in the mysteries and classics room. The summer sun shone brightly through the colors in the stained glass that ran across the tops of windows that opened like French doors to the balcony that overlooked the street. A bust of Shakespeare and a faux raven that perched on a rolling library ladder appeared to fixate on the professor. His cell phone lay on a nearby table where books were displayed.

I quietly slid onto a chair across from him. "Are you all right?"

"Liddy, my sister—I don't think she'll ever get over this."

"You spoke with her?"

"I didn't want her to hear it on the news. Telling her was one of the worst things I have ever had to do in my life."

"Is she on her way?"

"Of course. I hope they'll have removed him by the time she and her husband arrive. I don't want Liddy to see him like that. No one should have to see a loved one splayed . . ." He closed his eyes tight as if he wished he hadn't seen Delbert's corpse.

He tented his fingers and pressed them over his nose and mouth. "Who could have done this, Florrie?"

I didn't have an answer.

Chapter 7

Maxwell rubbed the back of his third finger against his upper lip, deep in thought. He rose and closed the door before returning to his seat.

Speaking softly, he said, "Florrie, I am very sorry to say there is a good likelihood that I will be arrested."

I sucked in a deep breath of air. "Surely not," I said, knowing full well that he was probably right.

"In that event, you will be solely in charge of Color Me Read. I have asked my attorney to draft the appropriate documentation so that you can step into my shoes, so to speak, and handle any matters that should arise. I have total confidence and trust in your judgment."

"But . . . even if they arrest you, won't you be out on bail?"

"Possibly. But my attorney informs me that bail may be denied because of my *escapades,* as she calls them, around the world. They may fear that I could disappear into the wilds of Borneo or the Amazon River Basin, never to be seen again."

I gazed into his eyes, as sincere and kind as ever. "I promise to take good care of the bookstore. Don't worry about that."

"I know you will, Florrie. You are a rock in my turbulent world."

Professor Maxwell winced and massaged his mustache. "You can imagine that I feel enormous guilt."

What? Was he about to confess? *No!*

"Don't look so horrified, Florrie. I didn't murder Delbert or anyone else." He leaned forward and patted my shoulder in a gesture meant to be reassuring. "Delbert was born with every advantage in life. He never missed a meal, never wanted for anything, attended the best schools. Yet he turned out to be an immoral, unprincipled degenerate. Clearly, his parents and I failed him somewhere along the way. Delbert had the intellectual capacity to be anything he liked. But he had the character to be devious and manipulative. He used his brain, not for good, but to prey on others to his own advantage. My guilt arises from the conflict of relief that I no longer have to worry about his next scam, and the intensely deep sorrow I feel at the loss of my nephew." He looked straight at me. "Because I do feel a loss. I'm not sure how to reconcile those two emotions."

I didn't know, either. I searched for something sage, or at least comforting, to say. "Isn't that how love of family is supposed to work? We care about them, no matter what they do."

Maxwell smiled at me. "When you entered this room, I was contemplating the great thinkers and their philosophies, but you, my little artiste, put it all in simple perspective. You're quite right, Florrie. We have to take them as they are, don't we?"

Sergeant Jonquille knocked on the door as he swung it open. "Florrie, may I have a word?"

I jumped to my feet and joined him in the hallway.

"Who has a key to the bookstore?" asked Jonquille.

"The professor, Bob, Helen, and I. There are a couple of other people who work here but they don't have keys."

"Thank you, Florrie. You're free to go."

"Sergeant? I have worked for the professor for five years. He's a very fine man. He couldn't have murdered Delbert."

Jonquille smiled. "I've heard that about a lot of convicted murderers."

Oh! How annoying of him. "I'm sure you have," I said sweetly, "but I don't think you understand. Professor Maxwell uses his brain. He's all about the power of the mind. If he were going to kill someone, it would be better thought out. It would be sneaky and look like an accident. He would never be so crass as to stab someone, nor so stupid as to do it in his own store with an implement that belonged to him."

Sergeant Jonquille stared at me for a long moment. "I go by facts, Florrie. Facts are undeniable."

I hated that he made sense. I would have said the same sort of thing if I didn't know the professor so well. I walked down the stairs, noting that Delbert's body had finally been removed.

Because of the long days of summer, it was still light outside when I left the building and heard a cop lock the door behind me. I texted my parents, who texted back that they were having dinner with my sister in a nearby restaurant.

I sucked in a deep breath and took a few minutes to call Helen and the other employees to let them know Color Me Read would be closed on Monday. Every single one of them asked how long it would stay closed. I had no idea.

Fifteen minutes later, I joined my family in a world that seemed far removed from the reality of my day. Mom and Dad made such a fuss that I could feel my face flaming red. I thought they were going overboard, but Veronica actually called them on it, announcing that I would forevermore be the favorite child simply because they thought I might be dead. Our parents were not amused but they must have gotten the message because they toned it down after that. Over tender crab cakes, my family pumped me for information.

Dad stabbed a French fry with his fork. "Was there any sign that someone broke in?"

His question surprised me. I hadn't given it much thought. "Not that I know of. I didn't notice broken windows or anything like that."

"Did you open the store?" asked Mom.

"Yes. Nothing appeared out of the ordinary." I told them who else had keys.

Dad stopped eating, sat back, and mused, "It seems to me that the list of potential suspects is severely limited to those who have the key to the building. We can eliminate you, which means only three suspects."

I hated to admit that he was right. "Bob wouldn't have done it and had no reason to. I don't know if Helen even knew Delbert."

"It's all going to fall on the shoulders of the professor, then." Veronica finished the last drop of her wine.

Mom leaned toward us and whispered, "What about Mr. DuBois? He's the one who feared being murdered in his bed, and I bet he has easy access to the professor's keys."

It was an interesting observation and a definite possibility. Mr. DuBois had certainly appeared to be more dramatic and emotional than the professor.

Dad waived his hand. "In any event, I'll be glad when you're out of that carriage house. I resent Maxwell involving you in this."

"But," I sputtered, "now that Delbert is dead, I have nothing to fear there."

"Only Maxwell," said Mom.

"Why would he harm *me*? I had nothing to do with this. It's not like he's a deranged killer running around randomly hacking people up. Besides, he needs me to take care of the bookstore."

"Honey!" Mom was aghast. "You can't stay there."

"Once he's in jail, he'll lose the bookstore and the house. His sister will kick you out on the street." Veronica spoke without emotion, as though she were stating fact.

I did not like where this was going. "You've all convicted him! Granted, you don't know him as well as I do, but there's no way he killed Delbert. It's simply impossible."

"I believe you mean *inconceivable,* not *impossible,*" Dad said dryly. "Not only was it possible, it happened."

"There has to be some other explanation," I insisted.

Mom's hand crept over mine. She gave it a squeeze. "Florrie, you have always been the champion of lost causes. I love that about you. But this is *murder,* not a sick kitten or a wilted, leafless plant."

"And everything points to the professor." Veronica poured part of Dad's bourbon into her empty glass.

"Listen to your sister, Florrie. What kind of evil person would use a spear to kill someone?" Mom shuddered.

"Exactly," I said with satisfaction. "*Not* the professor."

When Dad paid the check, Mom started a campaign for me to sleep at their house. I declined as kindly as I could, and after a round of hugs, I walked home.

It was the kind of peaceful Sunday evening when families were out for a walk. Children licked ice cream cones and adults window-shopped.

I rounded the corner and everything changed. Ahead of me, three police cars were parked on the left side of the street. A lump formed in my throat, and I started an anxious jog. As I feared, they were in front of the Maxwell mansion.

Just as I reached the house, the front door opened and a uniformed officer escorted a handcuffed Professor Maxwell down the front steps.

Chapter 8

Reporters ran toward him. Cameras were pointed at him.

Professor Maxwell held his head high. He turned and spotted me. "Florrie!"

I ran to him.

"The little gray cells, Florrie. Use the little gray cells and the eye of the artiste."

He bent to slide into the police car, and a moment later, it pulled away.

I lingered on the sidewalk, watching the car.

A male reporter thrust a microphone in my face. "Was that a code? What are the little gray cells?"

"Seriously?" Clearly not a fan of Agatha Christie. Her sleuth, Inspector Poirot, was always talking about the little gray cells—by which he meant his brain. It was classic Professor Maxwell to plead that I use my brain to figure this out. It was exactly what I fully intended to do. I pushed the mike away and looked back at the Maxwell mansion.

Mr. DuBois rushed down the stairs and grabbed me by the arm. "What's wrong with you people?" He escorted me into the house, closed the door behind us, and locked it.

The strain of Maxwell's arrest showed in his weary eyes.

"Vile police!" he sneered. "They treated Maxwell like a common criminal. I always knew that Delbert would be the death of us. Look what he has done now, that miscreant!"

Given Delbert's behavior, it stood to reason that he may have done something that brought on his own death, but blaming the dead guy made me a little uncomfortable.

He led the way into the kitchen, still muttering about Delbert. Two empty martini glasses stood by the sink. Mr. DuBois proceeded to wash one with a vengeance, scrubbing the delicate crystal with such force that I feared it would explode in his hands from the pressure.

He rinsed it, and while drying it with a kitchen towel, he turned to me, lifted it up to the light to be sure he had buffed out any potential water spots, and demanded, "So what do you plan to do?"

I blinked at him for a moment.

He stashed the gleaming crystal in a cabinet with a glass door. "He's depending on you."

I fully intended to do what I could. Nevertheless, I asked, "Won't he hire a private investigator or some other professional to find out who murdered Delbert?"

Mr. DuBois's lips tightened. "His overpriced attorneys are putting some wet behind the ears lawyer on it. They're most competent at managing estates and drafting business contracts, but I have little hope that they are crafty enough to uncover the truth about devious Delbert."

"But I am?" I seriously doubted that.

"The professor has great confidence in you."

As lovely as that was to hear, I didn't even know where to begin. I tried to sound casual when I asked, "What did the professor tell you?"

Mr. DuBois's eyes widened in surprise. "I have never revealed the confidences of my employer, and I don't intend to now."

Was he kidding? "Mr. DuBois," I said gently but firmly, "if

you want Professor Maxwell to be exonerated, then I need to know everything that pertains to that night and his relationship with Delbert. I don't care who he might be sleeping with or the details of his private life."

DuBois polished the second martini glass, held it to the light, and put it away. "Understood."

I tried to get him talking. "The last time I saw the professor, he was in his office at the bookstore. I presume he took his sister and Delbert out to dinner before that?"

Mr. DuBois appeared to think before responding. He sat down in a kitchen chair. While his back was perfectly straight, his face revealed exhaustion. "That is my understanding. I had the evening to myself. In fact, I did not see him until you phoned about Delbert trying to enter the carriage house."

That was a pretty good-sized gap of time. The light in his office was still on when I walked home with my pizza, though in retrospect, that probably didn't mean anything. He could have been battling Delbert at that very moment. Something had transpired in the hours between the time I left the bookstore and noon the following day. I didn't know the professor's whereabouts from approximately ten o'clock on Saturday night until three o'clock in the morning on Sunday. Five hours was plenty of time to kill Delbert, open the trapdoor, dump his body inside, and cover it up again. "Too bad he doesn't have an alibi for that night."

"Perhaps he does. . . ." Mr. DuBois mused. "After all, I was here."

"You're planning to lie for him?"

"Don't be ridiculous. His bed was slept in. I put the clothes he wore yesterday in the laundry hamper." He gasped. "Aha! Had the professor killed Delbert, surely there would have been blood on his clothes."

Mr. DuBois jumped to his feet and hurried out of the room. He returned momentarily carrying an olive-green shirt and a pair of khakis. He held them up and turned them around, examining them. "There, you see? No blood."

"I'm surprised that the police didn't take those clothes. Do you have a paper bag?"

"I beg your pardon?"

"I believe that's the best way to preserve evidence. At least, that's what I've read. We should turn them over to his lawyers."

Mr. DuBois fetched a paper bag, folded the clothes precisely, and inserted them. "I don't plan to let these out of my possession unless I am forced to do so. I've heard about evidence getting lost. I'll not have some imbecile tossing Maxwell's clothes with the trash." He closed his eyes briefly. "There. We have exonerated him."

I didn't think the professor's clothes would get him off the hook, but if Mr. DuBois was happy to think that, who was I to disabuse him of that notion?

I suspected he knew a good bit more, and I wanted to pull it out of him. "So who *did* kill Delbert?"

"Ordinarily, I would not speak of these things. However, considering that the professor is counting on you to help him, perhaps he would be understanding of my indiscretion this once. Delbert's favorite method of making money is to, hmm, piggyback, perhaps that's the best way to describe it, on the hard work of others. For instance, online he booked tours led by the professor and kept the money."

"He cheated the professor?" That was very bad news. No wonder Maxwell didn't like him. The prosecutor would surely bring that up against him.

"He defrauded Maxwell and the people who signed up for the fake tours. Maxwell had no idea that the worm was using his name to sell nonexistent tours. It tarnished his reputation, of course. Quite the scandal. Maxwell tried to keep it quiet. He refunded the money to those who signed up and forced Delbert to shut down his website. All quite audacious. Delbert had used photos from Maxwell's trips. It looked completely authentic."

"But that was behind them, right? Did Maxwell harbor a grudge?"

"No time for that. Delbert moved on to his next scam. He stole the contents of books and self-published them as his own."

"What?" I'd never heard of such a thing.

"Indeed. An odious act. As I said, he piggybacks on the success of others. In this case, it came to light because he stupidly stole the books of Maxwell's second wife, Jacquie Liebhaber."

"The women's fiction author?"

"The very same."

"I didn't know she had been married to the professor."

"It was quite the love affair. Such a pity that they divorced. Apparently, one of her devoted fans bought Delbert's book and recognized it as Jacquie's. The reader immediately notified Jacquie. It was verbatim. Delbert didn't even take the time to modify the books. They weren't similar, they were exact copies. Of course, it was a huge brouhaha. Once again, Delbert was bailed out. This time his parents paid restitution to the authors affected. He was banned from the self-publishing site that he used and more money exchanged hands to keep them from prosecuting."

"So you're suggesting that a whole lot of angry authors might have reason to kill him? You said restitution was made."

"What I'm saying is that a lot of people could have had it in for him. After all, those are the scams we know about. Heaven only knows what else he might have done."

Mr. DuBois had a point. An excellent one, in fact. A crumb like Delbert may have cheated, lied, and pilfered his way through life. There was no telling who might be angry enough to kill him.

With that in mind, I bade Mr. DuBois a good night. I left

the mansion through the kitchen door in the back and, passing the garage, crossed the broad driveway to my carriage house. As far as I could tell, not having actually explored the mansion, a sizable garden existed on the east side of the property, blocked from view at the driveway by the two-story garage.

Peaches must have already acclimated to her new surroundings because she wasn't waiting at the door like she had in our old home. I found her snoozing, almost upside down in her melon-colored bed.

I made myself a mug of hibiscus tea and took it out to the garden with a pad and a collection of pencils. I fully intended to draw Professor Maxwell's face, but once again the roadmap of lines failed me. It wasn't a bad likeness. I imagined it was how he had looked a decade or so ago. Maybe when he was married to Jacquie. I flipped the page on the pad, and found myself drawing the trapdoor in the stairs. Had they really hidden booze there during Prohibition? I drew the hatch in the open position and the sad figure of Delbert's corpse lying below on the ground, the spear jutting into the air.

As I sketched, two things became obvious to me. The killer knew about the trapdoor, and he did not come prepared to kill Delbert. He had taken the spear off the wall.

Both of those notions posed more questions in my mind. Who knew about the trapdoor? Was it common knowledge? I doubted that. If it were, the professor's friends would have known about it. Someone would surely have mentioned it during the time that I had worked there.

But Washington, DC, was packed with historians and history buffs. I could run a quick computer search to find out if it was the kind of thing they would know about. And, of course, anyone whom the professor had told about it could have located it easily.

Somehow, someone had entered the building. Maybe even Delbert. I didn't know how he could have gotten the keys, but it wasn't outside of the realm of possibilities. Had he invited someone to join him?

The spear posed a different set of problems. Was Delbert engaged in some kind of new scam? Had he sat in the professor's chair and tried to convince someone that it was his bookstore or his inheritance in order to con someone out of money? Had one of them grabbed the spear in self-defense or to threaten the other person?

Ugh. I flipped the page. My new sketch took a darker turn. The spear had hung on the wall of the office, so whatever happened that night either happened in the office or close-by. Someone had seen the spear. There might have been an argument in the office and one of them pulled the spear off the wall. Or the killer retrieved the spear and chased Delbert to his death. Had he dragged Delbert into the hatch, or had Delbert already been inside of it?

No wonder police used fingerprints and DNA to solve crimes. It wasn't easy to reconstruct what might have happened.

Two things were certain. Someone, maybe Delbert himself, had keys, and the killer, whoever he was, had not come prepared to murder Delbert.

Although I had left the door open, Peaches hadn't bothered to join me. I went inside and found her snoozing again. I stroked her. She didn't seem sick.

I walked upstairs, changed into my Crayon nightshirt, and crawled into bed. But unlike Peaches, I just wasn't ready to sleep. By all rights I should be exhausted, but no matter how I twisted or turned, my mind returned to the professor in jail and Delbert dead on the floor.

I went downstairs and hit the computer for information on Delbert. They say money talks, and as far as I could tell, it had done a great job of keeping Delbert's shenanigans quiet. Not a word about the authors he defrauded or about the fake tours he promoted. If that information had ever been on the web, someone had cleaned it up pretty well.

There was quite a bit about the Maxwell family and their wealth. I was happy to see enthusiastic reviews of Color Me Read, but found no mention of the trapdoor in the building, even on historic building sites.

I finally dragged up to bed, anticipating a restless night. Peaches woke long enough to race up the stairs after me.

Sad as it was, I fell asleep thinking I no longer had to fear Delbert.

In the morning, a brilliant goldenrod sun shone in a sky as clear and blue as Sergeant Jonquille's eyes. A beautiful day that neither the professor nor Delbert would see.

Delbert's poor mother would probably spend the day picking out a casket and making arrangements for his funeral. I couldn't imagine how torn she must feel that her own brother had been arrested for the murder of her only child. How could anyone cope with that scenario?

I probably could have slept in since the store would be closed. It was because of the yellow police tape, but it seemed fitting out of respect for Delbert.

I had no idea what the day might hold, but I had a sneaking suspicion I would be seeing Sergeant Jonquille again. I dressed in a simple white blouse with black trousers and a silver cuff bracelet. I didn't want to look flashy or too bright when Delbert had just been murdered. The blouse could be fairly sexy, but I pinned it so no cleavage showed.

I lazily walked downstairs, fed Peaches, made coffee, and called my landlord to officially give up my old apartment in Reston.

I drifted out to the garden to enjoy the morning air. I had been wanting to sketch a coloring book featuring plants and gardens. It seemed like every corner of my little paradise could be a page all its own.

But my phone rang inside, and I had a bad feeling I wouldn't get much drawing done, even if the store was closed. I fetched my cell phone and answered it.

Sergeant Jonquille asked if I could stop by the bookstore. Naturally I agreed, but I'll admit the thought ran through my mind that I didn't really want to help him collect information against Professor Maxwell. On the other hand, maybe I could pick up some information from him. . . .

I took the time to pop frozen muffins in the oven for Jim. He deserved them even if everything at the bookstore had been turned topsy-turvy.

With a package of two muffins in hand, I left Peaches inside watching birds through the French doors. The Maxwell property appeared calm and serene until I walked out to the sidewalk. Local TV station vans lined the street. A couple of reporters ran up to me.

Ignoring their questions, I held up my empty palm and said, "I don't know anything." I kept walking and they lost interest.

I stopped by a local coffee shop to buy a cup of java for Jim. I doubted the cops would let me make coffee in the bookstore this morning. While I waited for my order, I heard patrons speculating about Maxwell. It took every ounce of strength I had to not defend him.

When I left, I stopped by the newspaper vending box outside. Naturally, **Maxwell Heir Murdered** was on the front page along with a picture of Delbert. But it was the sidebar headline that nearly caused me to drop the coffee. *Maxwell Family Curse.*

Chapter 9

My mouth went dry. I reminded myself that there were no such things as curses. I knew that. Everyone knew that. And yet, I quivered a little bit at the thought.

I fumbled in my purse for change and plunked coins into the machine.

Juggling the coffee and muffins, I folded the newspaper so I could glance at the story while I walked.

It led with a carefully phrased allegation that Professor Maxwell had murdered Delbert. From there, it recited unfortunate deaths of their ancestors from a drowning in the Potomac River to a couple struck by lightning on their wedding night. It made mention of the pig thief and the man who photographed other men's wives in the buff, and concluded with the mention of the professor's daughter being kidnapped and most likely murdered.

Granted, the Maxwells had a good number of strange events in their lineage, but the article went back generations. If I, or anyone else for that matter, went back a couple hundred years, wouldn't we have some relatives who disappeared or died under odd circumstances? Probably. I chalked the article up as one intended to sell newspapers.

I tucked the paper under my arm and hurried to Color Me Read. As I had anticipated, yellow police tape hung across the front door.

Jim sat in his usual spot on the bench, a blissfully normal sight on a stressful day.

"Good morning, Jim." I forced a smile as I handed him the coffee and muffins.

"Didn't know if I'd see you this morning."

"You heard about it, huh?"

"Everybody's talking about it. That Delbert was trouble. Sunday wasn't the first time I'd seen him lurking around."

I didn't recall him coming into the store. "Did you see him here often?"

Jim took a big swig of coffee. "Good stuff. He came around now and then. Often enough that I recognized his picture in the paper this morning."

"How did you know he was trouble?"

"When you live on the street, you spend a lot of time people watching. Partly out of boredom, partly out of self-preservation. Gotta keep an eye on who's around. I like this part of town. Not as stressful. Most folks are decent. You get to recognize traits in people. Kind of like tells in poker. I always thought that Delbert was up to something. Just a hunch, you might say. He didn't seem to have any business here. Wasn't meeting a girl or waiting for a bus. Looked to me like he mighta been scouting for something. Planning to break into a business maybe."

"Thanks, Jim. Let me know if you hear any scuttlebutt on the street, okay?"

"Sure thing. We know the professor didn't do it."

Hope welled in me for a second. "How do you know that?"

"Maxwell is a decent fellow. He could have run me off a long time ago. But he takes an interest in everyone. He's the kind of man who would have been smarter about getting rid of a goon like Delbert."

"I couldn't agree more." I waved and headed to the bookstore, feeling odd about having to knock on the door of the shop that I ran.

A man wearing a white button-down shirt, navy blazer, and jeans opened the door. "Florrie Fox?"

"Yes."

He waved me in. "I'm Detective-Sergeant Guy Zielony." He flipped his badge at me. "Sorry to bring you down here. I'd like to ask you some questions."

"Of course."

"How did you come to find the victim?"

I didn't want to be rude, but I had already told Sergeant Jonquille. "What happened to Sergeant Jonquille? I told him everything yesterday."

"He's your beat cop. I'm investigating the homicide."

Happily, he didn't sound miffed by my question. I told him how I discovered the trapdoor.

"When and where did you last see Delbert?"

"Around dinnertime. I found him seated at Professor Maxwell's desk. He acted somewhat pompous and told me he would inherit the Maxwell estate and that my job would be toast. The professor came along and told Delbert that his mother was looking for him."

Zielony's eyebrow twitched. He was a large man with a bulky torso and thinning hair. No wedding band graced his pudgy fingers. Most of the time, his expression remained doubtful, as if he didn't trust anyone.

"So you saw Delbert and the professor arguing." He stated it like a fact.

"No. It wasn't like that. It wasn't an argument at all. Maxwell told Delbert that his mother was waiting for him. I think the three of them were going out to dinner."

"Were you aware of the professor's animosity toward his nephew?"

There it was, the question I had been dreading. I told him about moving into the guesthouse so Delbert wouldn't take up residence there.

Detective-Sergeant Zielony stared at me dead on. "You're saying the professor was afraid of Delbert?"

"His butler seemed to be afraid of Delbert. I think the professor was more ashamed of him than afraid of him. In case you don't know it yet, Delbert was something of a con artist. Professor Maxwell took great pride in the family name, and Delbert was an embarrassment."

"Did you hear the professor say he would take care of Delbert before the weekend was over?"

My sharp intake of breath gave me away. Bob must have overheard the professor. How else could he know that? "I did not take it to mean that he was going to murder Delbert. I guess it could have been misunderstood that way out of context." I held my breath. Would Zielony buy that?

"Then what did you think he meant?"

"That he would do something legally. Put the family fortune in a trust or disinherit Delbert. Really, Detective-Sergeant Zielony, if you knew the professor, you would realize that he's not an idiot. Had he meant to murder Delbert, he would not have announced it to anyone, he certainly wouldn't have done it in his own bookstore, and it would have been much more civilized and hard to detect. Nothing so brazen as stabbing him with a spear that he owned."

Zielony's mouth twisted to the side. "Come with me, please."

I followed him upstairs to the professor's office.

He walked close to the wall. "Please avoid the flagged marks so they won't be disturbed."

Small white pieces of paper lay on the maroon carpeting of

the hallway. I paused and peered at them. They were numbered. "What is this?"

"Markers of bloodstains. They're hard to see on the red carpeting. We sprayed luminol last night. It picks up even minute amounts."

"So there was a little blood here?" I asked.

He looked at me. "No. There was actually quite a bit." He continued to the professor's office.

"Florrie," said Zielony, "I would like you to take a look around the office and think back to last night. Is anything different?"

"That chair wasn't knocked over." I studied the top of the desk. "I couldn't say exactly what papers might have been on the desk, but I recall seeing a map when Delbert was seated there." And then my gaze drifted to the blank space on the wall. I sucked in a sharp breath of air. It didn't really come as a surprise, but was shocking nonetheless. "The spear, of course. The spear was hanging on that wall."

"Where the empty hooks are?"

"Correct."

"Was Professor Maxwell in the habit of taking it down to show to people?"

"Not that I'm aware of."

"You never saw him hold it?"

"No. All the exotic objects in this room are mementoes. The professor might have shown them to interested parties. I don't know about that, but most of the time he focused on research."

Zielony nodded as though he had heard that before. "Anything else out of place?"

"The hatchet that Bob removed. But everything else seems in order."

"Is there anything else you would like to tell me?"

"Delbert tried to break into the professor's carriage house at seven minutes to three in the morning on Sunday."

Now I had Detective-Sergeant Zielony's interest. "You saw him?"

"I saw someone. It was still dark outside, so I didn't see his face—just a dark figure really, but it must have been him."

"Why would he want access to the carriage house?"

"To scare me? Maybe he thought I would move out and he could live there?"

"Did you call 911?"

"No. I called Professor Maxwell. He came over and looked around."

"So there's no record of this?"

He didn't believe me! "The professor's butler, Mr. DuBois, was with him. He can confirm what I told you."

He appeared dubious. "That's all for now. I'll be in touch."

"Do you have any idea when we might be able to open the store again?"

He leveled a slightly amused gaze at me. "Probably by the end of the week."

"Today is Monday!" It came out as a screech.

"What a conscientious employee you are to be so very eager to get back to work." He tilted his head a touch. "A murder was committed here. It's my job to preserve the evidence."

I could hear the bookstore phone ringing. "May I answer the phone at least?"

He shook his head in the negative. "Probably just reporters anyway."

I left by the front door, imagining that I felt his eyes burning my back as he watched me leave. I liked Jonquille much better. Why did Zielony have to be so dour?

I stood on the stair stoop and looked out at the busy street and other shops. People passed just below me, gawking and pointing at the bookstore. I needed to make a little sign to post so our customers would know what was going on and that we would reopen as soon as possible.

I turned around and knocked on the door again.

A cop opened it. Inside, Zielony gazed in my direction.

"Books that were special-ordered for customers will be arriving. Obviously, they were not here when the incident occurred. Would it be possible for you to leave the boxes just inside the back door so I can retrieve them and make sure the customers get them?"

"No." Zielony turned his back, effectively dismissing me.

I looked at the cop who had opened the door.

He made a face of incredulity to let me know what he thought of Zielony. I bit my upper lip to hide my smirk.

"Come back in a couple of hours," he hissed.

"Thanks," I whispered. I walked down the stairs thinking I could tap into the bookstore computer to get the names of people who had placed orders. And maybe I could notify the delivery companies to bring packages to the carriage house instead of the bookstore for the rest of the week. Wondering what other details I had forgotten, I crossed the street to my favorite coffee shop, Café Du Conté.

It reminded me of a Parisian café with bistro-style tables on the sidewalk and a bright awning. But it was definitely self-serve. Everything seemed so normal there. People lounged at the tables, chatting or reading. I pushed open the door and heard my name.

My eyes took a minute to recover from the bright sun. The professor's usual cadre of intellectual friends were seated at a table by the window.

Professor Zsazsa Rosca motioned to me. "Florrie! Come!"

Born in Eastern Europe, Zsazsa had been named after the famous actress from Hungary. She lived up to her legacy by being a bit dramatic. She had just retired from teaching art history at a local university. Vivid fiery-colored hair fluffed around her remarkably unwrinkled pale face. She wore dark eyeliner and fake eyelashes that curved nearly up to her eyebrows. She had confided to me once that her Spanx were so tight she thought she might not ever get them off. Even though she leaned to the plump side, she always looked voluptuous and didn't hesitate to show off her ample bosom.

It had bothered me that I thought of her as Zsazsa, while I thought of the men by their titles or their last names. After all, they had the same credentials. She was entitled to equal respect. But when I mentioned my discomfort to my mom and Veronica, they pointed out that I felt closer to Zsazsa. I had delivered books to her apartment many times. On most of those occasions, she had tea and some kind of pastries ready. She had introduced me to fabulously sinful Danish *kringles*. So while I recognized her as an authority in her field, she treated me as a friend, and I embraced that.

Zsazsa held out her hand and squeezed mine when I neared. In her charming accent, she asked, "Dahlink, how is Maxwell? Have you heard from him?"

"No news yet. I hope they'll let him out on bail."

Professor Bankhouse, who had the lean, lanky physique of a runner, stood up and pulled a chair out for me. "I'm just going for a refill. May I get you a coffee? My treat."

"That's very nice of you. A latte, please?"

I tried to smile at Professor Goldblum, who sat across from me. He looked so hopeless.

Zsazsa leaned toward me. "You must tell us everything you know. I cannot believe I wasn't in the bookshop yesterday. I missed it all."

Bankhouse returned and set a latte in front of me.

I thanked him and told them what little I knew.

Professor Bankhouse eyed me. "Can you sketch how Delbert lay?"

"Sure." Bankhouse handed me a sheet of paper. I rummaged in my purse for a pencil but found only a plum purple crayon. It would have to do. I quickly drew the image of Delbert that burned in my brain. He lay on his abdomen with his face turned to the left and his right hand extended. His left knee had been bent, and the staff of the spear jutted out of his back. I added the footprint about two feet to the left of his shoulder and the nick in the floor near his head.

Zsazsa gasped. "Horrible," she murmured. "Our Maxwell would never have done such a thing to anyone. Not even to the terrible nephew."

Goldblum peered at it. "Most intriguing. Maxwell would have been intelligent enough to know the body would begin to deteriorate rather quickly. Another point in his favor. He would never have hidden a body there."

Bankhouse slid on frameless reading glasses and looked at my drawing closely. "Unless he intended to return last night to remove the body. Most people would have planned to come back the following night to remove the body under cover of darkness. Though it would have been difficult for one person. Easy enough to throw the body into the pit but getting a lifeless body out of there by oneself would have posed a problem for anyone."

"I think the use of the spear indicated that it wasn't planned," I said. "Maybe the killer panicked and didn't think it through when he disposed of the body there."

"An excellent point, Florrie. Were you able to go up to the third floor?" asked Goldblum.

I nodded. "This morning." I told them about the bloodstains.

"Aha!" cried Goldblum. "I suspected that some sort of fight ensued."

"One wonders," said Bankhouse, "if it ended in the pit or

whether Delbert was dragged there. From the angle of the spear, I'm betting it was mano-a-mano combat. I can imagine our friend Maxwell doing such a thing, but not against an inferior opponent like Delbert."

"Then who would?" I asked.

"That, my dahlink," said Zsazsa, "is what we must deduce. The only way to save our Maxwell is to identify the real killer."

Chapter 10

"It seems most likely that one of the employees would be the perpetrator because they had easy access to the building," Zsazsa mused. "Anyone else would have had to break in and turn off the alarm."

Goldblum snorted. "*Sleepy conscience.* How many times have I seen one of you punch in the password to turn off the alarm? Half the regulars probably know it."

"That's true." Zsazsa shot me an apologetic look. "I knew it, too."

I gazed around the table. Didn't they realize they had just enlarged the pool of suspects and included themselves?

"What about Bob?" Bankhouse stirred his coffee, clinking the spoon against the mug. "Helen tells me he reads a lot of thrillers."

"Bob Turpin?" I couldn't believe anyone would imagine he could murder, much less with a spear.

"Sure, you saw him wielding that ax when you opened the hatch." Bankhouse sipped his coffee, looking at us over the rim of the mug.

"Bob?" Goldblum sounded incredulous. "He hasn't got the grit to stab someone. I'd put my money on Helen. Did you know that she has never read *To Kill a Mockingbird*? What's someone like that doing working in a bookstore anyway?"

Bankhouse's coffee mug clunked to the table so hard that a bit of milky brown liquid spewed out and onto the wood tabletop. "I beg your pardon. Helen is my stepdaughter!"

Goldblum, Zsazsa, and I stared at him in a long awkward pause.

Goldblum stammered, "Sorry about that. I had no idea. You don't have the same name. Isn't she Helen Osgood?"

Bankhouse tilted his head. "She uses her birth father's surname. Helen didn't want anyone to know that Maxwell hired her as a favor to me. She was embarrassed about the circumstances that resulted in the termination of her last job. Frankly, Helen has never been the student I'd hoped she might be. She has the brains but was never interested in school. I tried steering her to social media, but from what I gather, those positions are extremely popular. Nevertheless, in spite of Helen's general disinterest in books, I can assure you that she had no reason to murder Delbert. I doubt she even knew him."

"She must be thirty," Zsazsa said. "You look far too young to have a stepdaughter that age. Do you have grandchildren?"

That drew a smile from Bankhouse. "I try to stay in shape. Helen had one disastrous marriage straight out of college. Thankfully no children arose from that ill-fated union. Since then she has dated quite a few fellows, most of whom are equally unprepared to make a living. Her mother indulges her every whim, but I insisted she absolutely had to have a job, even if it wasn't her dream position."

Goldblum sighed. "That's about it for the employees, except for you, Florrie."

I chuckled. "I minored in spear throwing in college."

Fortunately, they all smiled. While I had no doubt that battling with a spear was something that could be done equally well by any size or gender person, it was preposterous to imagine that I, notoriously unathletic and exceedingly incompetent at activities involving such things as balls and other items that had to be thrown, could possibly have seized a spear as my weapon of choice.

"Please," begged Bankhouse, "not a word about this to Helen. She would be furious if she knew I had told you the sordid details about her."

Zsazsa pretended to close a zipper on her lips. "Your secrets are safe with us."

I bid them farewell and headed home, wondering if there was a reason Bankhouse had wanted Helen to work at Color Me Read. I had no reason to think he had a motive to hurt Delbert, but still, it would have been easy for him to gain access to the building with Helen's keys.

When I entered the carriage house, Peaches lifted her head briefly, but didn't budge from her spot in the sun. That was the second time she hadn't come running like she used to. I wasn't sure I liked this development. On the other hand, maybe it simply reflected her comfort level at living in our new digs. With all the French doors that overlooked the garden, there was a lot more for her to do than in our old apartment.

I spent the next couple of hours having the Color Me Read phone forwarded to my cell phone and making calls to the various delivery companies so they would reroute all parcels to the carriage house.

I had just hung up the phone when there was a knock on my door. I approached it cautiously and saw Detective-Sergeant Zielony outside.

Ugh. Not him again. I opened the door.

"Hello, Florrie. May I come in?"

I realized that I had read far too many mysteries when I wondered if I was giving him permission to snoop if I let him inside. What could he want in my quarters, anyway? Did he hope to see shoes that would match the print I had seen on the floor?

But what could I do? Would he get a search warrant if I said no?

Reluctantly, I stepped aside.

Detective-Sergeant Zielony entered and gazed around.

I felt like he was taking in every tiny detail. It was rude of me not to invite him to sit down or to offer him a beverage, but I didn't want him to stay long. "How may I help you?"

"Nice place."

"Thank you."

"No wonder Delbert wanted to live here."

I didn't respond.

"Wouldn't you rather live in the mansion?" he asked.

What an odd question. "No."

"Is there a bedroom?"

"Yes."

"May I see it?" He started for the stairs.

"No, you may not."

He turned around, his eyes reflecting his shock at my response.

"What do you want, Detective-Sergeant Zielony?" The question slipped out of my mouth, startling me. I wasn't usually so brave.

His chin raised slightly as he regarded me. "Who will inherit the Maxwell estate now that Delbert is dead?"

He caught me by surprise. "I have no idea."

"Are you sure about that?"

"Quite sure. Detective-Sergeant Zielony, I work for Professor Maxwell. We talk of many things, like Mark Twain's humor, and whether there is a treasure at Oak Island. We speak of Tolstoy and Harry Potter, of bookstore business and curious world events. Until two days ago, I didn't know of Delbert's existence. I have no idea what comprises the Maxwell estate or who might be in line to inherit it. Nor do I care."

"One of his friends called you his *right-hand woman*."

"That's very flattering. I suppose I am when it comes to Color Me Read."

"Then surely he has discussed his personal life with you?"

"Only to the extent of his adventures around the world. You know the kind of thing. Tales of his travels."

"You are aware that I can get a search warrant to see what you're hiding upstairs."

In truth, every nerve in my body tingled with fear. I tried to hide my anxiety. Didn't they say animals sensed fear? Did cops have ways of knowing that, too? I lifted my chin, much as he had, and said, "Then by all means go right ahead."

I trembled a bit and tried to hide it from him. Where was this bold Florrie coming from? Too much Nancy Drew and Monsieur Poirot?

He strode toward the door. As he passed by me, he whispered, "You're more of a spitfire than I had thought."

I had to restrain myself not to slam the door behind him. It would only feed his ego. But I quivered and leaned against the closed door, trying to reason with myself. I had nothing to fear. I had done nothing wrong. Then why did he make me so nervous? And why had he come to scope out the carriage house? What had he expected to find?

I finally walked away from the door and made myself a mug of black tea with milk and sugar to help me get myself together.

Maybe instead of fearing awful Detective-Sergeant Zielony, I should consider what he knew that prompted him to come to the carriage house. What could he have been looking for? They had the weapon.

Clothes! Of course. How stupid could I be? They had found blood on the carpet of the third floor. Chances were good that the killer had blood on his clothes, or that he was bleeding, too. Had Delbert managed to inflict an injury on his killer?

I hadn't given much thought to the killer walking out of Color Me Read. He or she likely had to go home wearing bloodstained clothes. We knew it was definitely after ten at night, so it would have been dark, but the streetlights and lights from stores and restaurants would have been sufficient for people to notice if someone bloody was walking along the streets. How did the killer get away without anyone noticing him? Had he parked close to the store?

I cupped the warm mug in both my hands, thinking with great relief that there was no blood upstairs. I seriously suspected that the search warrant had been an idle threat intended to scare me, but even if Zielony managed to get one, he wouldn't find anything of interest among my belongings.

After finishing my tea, I walked over to the mansion and knocked on the back door. Mr. DuBois answered, tidy and official in his butler's uniform, but showing signs of fatigue.

"Miss Florrie!" He glanced around before seizing my hand and pulling me inside. "These are dark days for the Maxwells."

"Have you heard from the professor?"

"Indeed. His lawyers tell me he's doing fine, but they are no closer to finding the real murderer." He peered at me. "Are you afraid you shall be killed, too?"

Chapter 11

I hadn't been up to that moment! "Why would you ask such a thing? Why would anyone want to kill me?"

"Because you know too much."

"Then I have nothing to fear because it's all a mystery to me. Mr. DuBois, when they arrested the professor yesterday, they searched the mansion, didn't they?"

"Indeed. Left a mess behind. No courtesy whatsoever."

"Do you know what they were looking for?"

At that moment, the doorbell tinkled a tune. DuBois's eyes opened wide. He seemed paralyzed.

"Perhaps they'll go away," he whispered.

"You think it's the press?" Maybe they had been annoying him.

A woman yelled something.

I couldn't make out what she was saying, but there was no doubt that she was angry.

Mr. DuBois sagged. "Ugh. The professor's sister, Liddy."

He didn't budge.

"You're not going to answer the door?"

"I am debating that action. It would be rude not to do so, and it is my job to take care of such matters. On the other hand, Maxwell is not home, and I trust she is fully aware of his current incarceration. Nothing good can come of her visit."

He had a point.

"Ugh," he uttered. "I suppose there's no benefit in putting it off. She would surely return later."

"I'll go with you."

We walked through the elegant house to the foyer. The floor was a checkerboard of black-and-white marble. The walls were covered with an elegant soft gold paper with just a hint of an Asian feel. A large round mahogany table sat in the middle of the room holding a tall vase of vibrant gladiolus.

Mr. DuBois opened the front door. "Good day, Miss Liddy."

She barged inside. Plump, with thin brown hair, her eyes were red-rimmed, probably from crying. She passed DuBois without any acknowledgement. "Who are you?"

I held out my hand. "I'm so sorry for your loss, Mrs. Woodley. I'm Florrie Fox. I manage Color Me Read."

She shrieked as though I had told her I was the devil himself.

Mr. DuBois hastened to close the door. "Miss Liddy! Please."

She eyed me through mere slits. "You have your nerve being here. This is all your fault. If you think you're moving into the mansion, you're quite wrong." She pointed her forefinger toward the door. "Out! You're through, you little harlot!"

"Now just a moment, Miss Liddy."

I was surprised to see DuBois intervene.

"Ms. Fox is a legitimate tenant on a month to month basis, and I believe she is entitled, *by law,* to one month's notice. Not to mention the fact that Mr. Maxwell's current situation does not change his possession of this house."

She burst into tears.

DuBois and I looked at each other like we were wondering what to do. I guessed he was as unenthusiastic about comforting her as I was.

After what seemed an uncomfortable eternity but was probably only a minute or two, Mrs. Woodley regained her composure. "One would think a mother who had lost her only child at the hands of her own brother might elicit more sympathy. And you, DuBois, should be ashamed of yourself for treating me like a stranger. I can see that my lawyers will have to undertake the eviction of both of you from the property." She turned on her heel but made a slow exit. Just outside, she looked at us again and said, "Maxwell will rot in prison for what he did to my little boy, and the two of you will join him for your actions as his accomplices. Make no—"

With one swift motion of his right hand, DuBois effectively slammed the door in her face.

He looked at me with a mischievous grin. "Oooh. That felt good!" He rubbed his hands together with satisfaction. "I shall hold down the fort from the invading relatives. Now, how do we find the real culprit who dispatched Delbert?"

It spoke well of Maxwell that all of the people who knew and loved him didn't question his innocence. If only the police could come to that realization.

"Can you obtain information from Maxwell's attorneys or the police?" I asked.

DuBois's eyes reflected his excitement. "I shall make it my quest. What do you wish to know?"

"I imagine they're going to do an autopsy on Delbert—"

"Undoubtedly!"

"Don't you think it would be helpful to know the time of death? The three of us were together at three in the morning. After that, the professor was with you or me until morning. So we could provide him with an alibi for those times. Right?"

DuBois nodded. "Indeed. And what about fingerprints on the spear? Maxwell's will be there, of course, because it belonged to him. But the killer's fingerprints will be on it, as well."

DuBois bustled into a library, and I followed him. Fine paneling and woodwork lined the walls. The fireplace was so large I could almost walk into it. A massive desk with claw feet and four-inch-wide lions' heads on the corners took center stage. I didn't know what kinds of woods comprised the inlay, but I knew without any doubt that it was an antique and may have been in the Maxwell family for generations. I couldn't imagine living in a house like this. Had members of the Maxwell clan curled up in the cushy chairs by a blazing fire to read one of the thousands of books on the shelves?

DuBois sat at the desk like he owned the place.

"How long have you worked for the professor?" I asked.

"Maxwell was a mere boy when I came to work for the family. I knew his parents well. Such dignified and proper people."

After working for the Maxwell family so many years, he probably did feel that it was his home, as well.

"So you have known Liddy a long time, too. She must have been a small child when you started working here."

He jotted notes with a pen that I recognized as Swiss and pricey. "Indeed she was. Fortunately, a nanny looked after her. To be correct, a series of nannies watched over her. Miss Liddy always was a demanding and imperious sort. You can tell a lot about people by the way they treat the help. Is there anything else I should inquire about?"

"I imagine it would behoove us to know the status of the house and the store." I hated to even think it, but if the professor was held for a longer period of time, they might become issues.

DuBois made a note. "I happen to know that Maxwell has the right to use of this property until his death or such time as he no longer desires to reside here. The family assets, like this house, a beach residence, a horse farm, some paintings of significance, and the jewelry, especially the famous Maxwell emerald and diamond necklace, are the subject of a rather complicated family trust, intended to ensure that everything remain in the family. Small wonder that Maxwell was concerned about Delbert inheriting everything."

"A necklace?" I gazed around the room. "Is there an alarm system?"

"It was installed forty years ago. We are the proverbial sitting duck, ripe to have our feathers plucked by a half-witted burglar. I have begged Maxwell to update it. Times have changed so much. But that sort of thing bores him. He always says, *DuBois, you are a far better alarm system than any mechanical one.*"

"So you don't think his sister could make a demand for the house and throw us out?"

"I doubt it. But I will express our concern to his solicitors."

I let him know that packages intended for the bookstore would be arriving. He was most agreeable about it.

"Mr. DuBois, either you or Maxwell made reference to Delbert's roommates kicking him out. I doubt that Liddy would tell us who they were. I'd like to know what happened there. Do you have any idea how to contact them?"

DuBois's head gave a little jerk. He sat with a straight back and stared at me without a word.

I wasn't sure what was going on, but had found that often when I was quiet or didn't respond immediately, the other person in the conversation felt it necessary to fill the silence, so I simply waited for him to respond.

"Under the circumstances, I expect it would be acceptable

to break protocol and snoop. After all, the professor needs our assistance." He pushed something on the desk, and retrieved an iPad.

"The police didn't collect the computers?"

DuBois smiled. "Perhaps they weren't aware of the secret compartments in this house. Pity, eh?"

He spoke as he typed. "2450 Langsworth Place." He peered at the iPad and in only a few seconds, a brilliant smile lighted his face. "Scott Southworth and Lance Devereoux. I do love modern technology."

That was far too easy. "The professor had their names and the address?"

Mr. DuBois didn't look up at me. "There was a bit of a kerfuffle when Delbert's father cut him off and Delbert couldn't pay the rent. Intended as tough love, I believe. Apparently he wanted to force Delbert to stand on his own two feet and stop playing the role of rich kid. Delbert went to his mommy, who would do anything for him. Liddy didn't want her husband to know that she was paying Delbert's rent, so she came to Maxwell, who wrote the check for the rent and smoothed things over with the roommates. I must say, though, that he was in full agreement, as was I, with Delbert's father. It's ridiculous to have that young man cruising around spending money like water and getting into trouble at every turn."

"Delbert didn't have a job?"

"Hah! Delbert has had many jobs, most often acquired through his parents, though I must say he is well educated. Assuming, of course, that he didn't lie, cheat, and steal his way through college. He has been fired from almost every position he has ever held."

He jotted their names and address on a sheet of paper and handed it to me. "I would come with you, but I feel the need to protect the mansion. I don't dare leave it."

I was beginning to wonder if the old fellow had developed a bit of agoraphobia. "Can I pick up some groceries for you? Or takeout, perhaps?"

He appeared to be touched by my question. "Thank you for your consideration, Miss Florrie. I have a standing order with the greengrocer, the florist, the organic food store, and my favorite Japanese restaurant. Home delivery is a marvel."

I checked the time when I left the house. Did I dare go back to the bookstore as the other police officer had suggested? I squared my shoulders. Why not? The worst-case scenario was Zielony being angry with me. I was pretty sure I had already accomplished that.

I strolled over to the bookstore and ducked into the alley behind it where the deliveries were made. I had to build up a little courage to knock on the door. I sucked in a deep breath and hit the door with my knuckles.

Sounds of shuffling and footsteps came from inside the store. The door swung open. The friendly cop who had suggested I return smiled at me. He picked up four small boxes and a large envelope. "Need help carrying them home?"

"No, I'm fine. I am so grateful to you. Thank you."

He shrugged. "Zielony can be a jerk. Let me know if you need anything else."

"Thanks." I walked away and went straight back to the carriage house, where I made arrangements to deliver the books to the buyers. I phoned Bob, who agreed to deliver half of them and then accompany me on a little visit to Delbert's roommates.

At six in the evening, it was still light outside with a couple more hours of daylight left when Bob and I set off to meet the roommates. I wasn't particularly fearful, but if they were anything like Delbert, I thought it best to bring a friend along. Not that Bob would be much help in a crisis, but I felt better anyway.

They lived across the Potomac in Arlington, Virginia. I drove and Bob checked house numbers. The tiny redbrick Cape Cod had seen better days. The yard was void of plants other than grass, but had been freshly mowed. Near the sidewalk, a sign declared FORECLOSURE SALE and stated a date the following week.

We walked up to the house, and I rang the bell.

A friendly-looking fellow opened the door. He wore jeans and a Washington Redskins T-shirt. His hair was tidy and cut short. He stood only five inches or so taller than me.

I introduced myself and Bob. "I'm so sorry to disturb you, but I believe you were roommates with Delbert Woodley?"

He groaned. "I'm not talking to the press."

"We're not reporters."

He tilted his head. "You're with the police?"

"No. We're looking into the circumstances of Delbert's death," I said carefully. That was true.

He looked from me to Bob and back again. "I don't understand. Insurance investigators?"

Bob blurted, "We work at the bookstore where Delbert was . . . found."

The guy seemed to sag with relief. "Come on in."

"Are you Scott or Lance?" I asked as we entered.

"Lance Devereoux." He showed us to the living room.

"This is Scott." Addressing his roommate, he added, "They work at the bookstore where Delbert was killed."

His roommate stood up and shook our hands. Only slightly taller than Bob, he wore his hair in the modern style that Bob disliked. It was short on the sides and stood up on top probably thanks to some gel. He wore the scruffy one-day beard growth, too. "I know that bookstore. I've shopped there a couple of times. Cool place."

Bob nodded. "I think I've seen you there."

It was a tiny house furnished in modern man cave style. A billiard table occupied what would normally be the dining room. The living room featured a fireplace that was dwarfed by a giant TV set. I didn't see any packing boxes, but if that sign out front was correct, Lance and Scott would probably be moving soon.

A comfy U-shaped modular sofa barely fit in the living room. There was plenty of room for the four of us to perch on it. An empty blue cupcake box from my favorite cupcake bakery perched on the sofa with us.

I pointed at it. "Great cupcakes! Sugar Dreams are my favorite."

"Ours, too," said Lance. "We were in line to get one of the last boxes before they move."

"Where are they going?"

"I'm not really sure. They're staying in Georgetown, but I used to pass by regularly for work, so we got a little spoiled."

"Did you know Delbert long?" I asked.

"I knew of him in college but we weren't close," said Lance. "I hadn't seen him in years. When I posted for a roommate on the college online site, Delbert responded."

How did investigators do this? There must be a trick to asking questions so people would relax and talk. "When did he move out?"

Lance glanced at Scott, then rested his elbows on his knees and bowed his head as though he was in pain. "Last week. My friends keep trying to tell me this would have happened to him sooner or later, but I can't help feeling like he might be alive if I hadn't given him the boot."

Scott winced. "You can't blame yourself. Where he lived had nothing to do with his death. It's not like he was homeless and wandering around." To us he said, "His parents live an hour from here. He could have stayed with them." He looked at his roommate again. "You're not responsible for his death."

"I've had some lousy roommates," said Bob. "What did he do?"

Lance looked up at him as though they had made a connection.

Chapter 12

"I have a great job selling pharmaceuticals," said Lance. "I was on my way up. I worked my tail off on that job, and Delbert knew it. He swiped my company credit card number and went wild ordering stuff online. One of the company auditors caught on fast and called me in, thinking I had done it."

"How did you find out it was Delbert?" I asked.

He leaned back. "They showed me a list of the charges. That idiot didn't think it through. They suspended me from work pending an investigation, so I was home when some of the packages were delivered. I saw the logo for a fancy store that I can't afford, and became suspicious. Delbert comes from money, so I didn't want to jump to conclusions. When he went out, Scott and I ransacked his room. We found pricey shoes and Bluetooth speakers that corresponded to some of the purchases made on the card. When he came home, we confronted him. He denied it and said I couldn't prove anything." Lance shook his head. "He left me no choice. It was him or us, and our names are on the lease, so he had to go. Who steals a roommate's credit card? Even worse, one issued by his employer?"

"How are things with your job? Did you tell them what Delbert did?" Bob looked so comfortable I thought he was ready to move in and take Delbert's room.

I, meanwhile, kept an eye on the bottom of Lance and Scott's shoes. The print I had seen in the dust was so distinctive. They probably had other shoes, as well, but when they sat with their legs positioned so I could see the soles, I couldn't help getting a good look at the treads. They didn't match.

"Of course I told them! I don't think they believed that anyone would do something like that. What an idiot. He didn't just jeopardize my job but my career! There's a big meeting coming up next week that will decide my future. If they can me, I probably won't be able to get another job in pharmaceuticals. I don't know what I'll do."

"But you knew him in college. Didn't you hear stories about him back then?" I asked.

"We were a couple of years apart and hung with different people. All I knew was that he was loaded and would be able to afford the rent. I figured he was an okay guy. You don't expect something like this, you know? Now I feel incredibly guilty. I hated Delbert. Probably always will. I was shocked when I heard he was dead, but Scott and I realized that it was just a matter of time before he crossed the wrong person. I . . . just never thought it would be so soon."

"Did he pull any stunts like that on you, Scott?" I asked.

Scott shook his head. "I work for my dad. I've got the best job security ever. I know my dad would believe me over anybody else if something like this happened."

"Do you know anyone else who would have wanted to kill Delbert?" I asked.

Bob elbowed me, and I realized I had phrased my question poorly since it sounded like I thought they were suspects.

"That's what the cops wanted to know," said Scott. "For a

long time I assumed he was a trust baby who didn't have to work. It was weird. Either he had a lot of money and spent it lavishly, or he was too broke to pay the rent."

Lance's jaw tightened. "It makes me mad. I was easy pickings for him. I never imagined I had to hide my stuff from a roommate."

"You didn't hear from other irritated people?" I asked.

Lance reflected for a moment. "When I think back, I'm wondering about little things. Now I'm seeing them in a different light. There were some restaurants that he refused to go to. It wasn't as though he didn't like a particular kind of food, but he flat-out refused to grab a bite at some places. He brought home a 2,500-dollar tuxedo once for a black tie wedding we all attended. I was so impressed. It was really nice. Initially, I thought he bought it. Then he returned it, and I assumed it had been rented. But now I wonder if he returned it to the store after wearing it. I'm sure the store owner wouldn't murder him for something like that, but I can't help wondering if there were a lot of people who despised him."

"Man, what a bummer." Bob winced. "And now you have to move, too?"

Bob was so smooth. He sounded like he was their buddy. I had to learn from him!

"You mean the foreclosure? Scott's dad is going to work something out. I'm not too worried about it. He has a lot of clout in real estate."

I stood up. "Thanks for talking with us."

Lance shrugged. "It's not like I have anything else to do right now. And, much as I hated Delbert, I didn't want him dead. I'm glad someone is asking questions and looking for his killer."

"You don't think Professor Maxwell murdered him?" I asked.

"Delbert talked a lot about inheriting the Maxwell mansion and the bookstore. He always said he would throw lavish parties and marry Sonja. If one of them was going to kill the other one, I would have expected it to be the other way around. Is it wrong of me to be glad that Professor Maxwell, a man I have never met, is the one that survived?"

I wasn't paying attention. I had picked up on something else. "Who is Sonja?"

"The most gorgeous bartender in Washington. You'll find her at Club Neon."

We thanked him profusely and stepped outside. We had made it as far as the sidewalk when Bob said, "Guess who Scott is?"

"Scott Southworth."

"That's not what I mean. He's the customer Helen has a crush on."

"Are you sure?"

"Pretty sure."

On the drive back to Georgetown, Bob said, "I've never been to Club Neon. Should we pay them a visit?"

We agreed to meet at Club Neon at nine o'clock.

When I dropped him off, he said, "Florrie, dress like an artist."

"What?"

"I think it's kind of a cool place. You know, people with purple hair and outrageous clothes."

Oh swell. I'd be right in my element.

When I returned to the carriage house, I called Veronica, certain she had been to Club Neon. I was right.

"Don't freak out," she told me. "Wear torn jeans with high heels and a bright top. Add lots of silver bracelets and you'll be set. Let your artistic side speak through your clothes."

I preferred to let my artistic side speak through my coloring books. An hour later, I waited outside the Georgetown club wearing old jeans that weren't actually torn, dressy sandals with bling on them, and a peasant-style blouse. Probably not exactly what Veronica had in mind.

Bob arrived looking surprisingly chic. I had to laugh about his sunglasses at night.

"You won't be able to see a thing."

"We have to look cool."

We ventured inside. Raucous music blasted. The walls must have been painted black because they seemed to vanish, the only clue to their whereabouts were the huge neon signs that glowed in the low light. The place was packed with people.

Bob removed his sunglasses immediately. I shouted into his ear, "Do you see the bar?"

A guy wearing a beat-up fedora-style straw hat watched us, giving me the willies.

Bob led the way to the bar. I was on the lookout for a drop-dead gorgeous woman. I spotted Sonja in a heartbeat.

Tall and willowy, she laughed along with customers as she made her way down the long bar. Under the neon lights, it appeared that her hair was raven. She wore it pulled up in a messy chignon. A plush plume attached to the right side of her head glowed fuchsia under the lights. As she neared, it was obvious that she could beat any Miss Universe. Dimples appeared when she smiled, which was often.

Bob leaned over and spoke in my ear, "Follow my lead, okay?"

He'd done so well with Lance that I was more than willing to try whatever he had in mind.

We ordered a glass of wine for Bob and a sparkling water for me.

Speaking louder than normal to be overheard, Bob said, "I can't imagine who would have done that to Delbert. The poor guy. What a way to go."

"And what could Delbert have been doing in a closed bookstore in the middle of the night?" I asked.

Sonja's dimples disappeared. She studied us. "Do you speak of Delbert Woodley?"

"Yes," said Bob. "Did you know him?"

In an accent very much like Zsazsa's, she said, "He was one of our regular customers. I was very sad to learn of his death. He was much too young to die."

"And such an awful death," I shouted over the music.

She nodded somberly. "But they have arrested his killer, no?"

Bob spoke up. "We think they have the wrong guy."

Fear flashed in her eyes.

"Do you know of anyone who was angry with him?" I asked, paying her a super hefty tip.

Sonja glanced around nervously. She grabbed a napkin, wrote on it, and shoved it to me.

Heinrich's Bakery. Two p.m. tomorrow.

She moseyed away from us, as though she didn't want to be seen with us. Bob and I exchanged a look. Maybe we had happened upon someone with valuable information.

We didn't linger long. Over our drinks, we people watched. I felt twice my age. I just didn't see the attraction of squeezing into a place too noisy to talk. No one danced, no one ate as far as I could tell. I didn't see the beauty of it. I would have to ask Veronica.

Truth be told, when we left, I was very relieved to be outside in the cool night air. I guessed I just wasn't the nightclub type. I took deep breaths, enjoying the peace and quiet.

Bob and I walked up Wisconsin Avenue. He offered to see me home, but I wasn't afraid to walk the few blocks to the mansion by myself.

The streets were still busy in Georgetown, but calmed considerably as I strolled into the residential neighborhood. The reporters' cars had vanished, and peace had returned to the street.

I turned into the driveway and walked past the mansion. Only steps away from my door, I heard a whimper.

Chapter 13

I paused to listen. Crickets chirped in the night. I didn't hear any more whimpers. I slid my key into the lock and heard a moan.

Where was it coming from? Lights over the three-car garage illuminated the driveway. Opposite the garage was a high fence, hidden by tall bushes.

"Hello?" I called timidly.

"Gah."

Okay, someone was out here. But where? "Hello? Keep talking. Where are you?"

"Gah."

Well, that didn't help at all. I peered at the dark bases of the bushes but didn't see anyone. Maybe I would see better if more lights were turned on. I walked to the back door of the mansion and had raised my hand to knock when I realized the door hung slightly ajar.

I pushed it open. The lights were off inside. Something wasn't right. I pulled out my phone and was pushing the numbers 9-1-1 when the lights of a car entering the driveway brightened the area considerably. The blue light on top flashed. I put my phone away.

Sergeant Jonquille stepped out. "Hi, Florrie. Having a problem?"

I explained what I had heard.

"Stay here," he said. "I'll have a look around."

He walked inside. In two seconds, I followed him.

He proceeded cautiously, flicking on lights as he went.

I stopped in the kitchen and looked around. Everything appeared to be in order. But where was Mr. DuBois?

I flicked on more lights and accidentally hit the switch for floodlights to the pool area. I had never been out there before. It was located on the back side of the garage.

And there, on the concrete pool surround, lay a body.

"Sergeant Jonquille! Over here!"

The door leading to the pool area hung wide open. I dashed outside and kneeled by the limp form of Mr. DuBois.

"Are you okay?" I asked, which was stupid because I could see that he wasn't.

He lay on his side, wincing. There wasn't much I could do except place a hand on his shoulder and try to say something soothing. "We're here now. Everything will be fine."

Jonquille radioed for an ambulance.

I patted Mr. DuBois's shoulder, which he probably resented, but what else could I do? I didn't see any blood, so maybe that was a good sign.

"Do you know him?" asked Jonquille.

"Maxwell's butler."

Jonquille bent over him. "Are you in pain?"

DuBois moaned.

"What happened?"

DuBois could hardly speak. "Chased . . ."

"Someone chased you out here?" I suggested.

"Gah."

The ambulance arrived quickly. One of the emergency medical technicians pulled me aside to get basic information. I didn't know his age or whether he had any allergies. I didn't even know his first name. I wasn't any help at all.

Meanwhile, a backup policeman arrived and searched the mansion with Jonquille.

I waited outside, keeping an eye on Mr. DuBois. It appeared he had broken his wrist and possibly a leg. At least he hadn't been stabbed by a spear.

It wasn't until the ambulance whisked him away that I entered the house. I found Sergeant Jonquille and the other officer upstairs in Maxwell's bedroom.

What appeared to be a Warhol of Maxwell dominated the bedroom. The pop art version of a younger Maxwell in four different colors hung on a wall the color of heavy cream with a dose of nutmeg. I had never seen a leather bed before. Blocks of rich tan leather covered the headboard of the platform bed and more matching leather lined the edge of the platform. The bed was made perfectly. In contrast, clothes had been thrown out of the drawers of an antique dresser. On the opposite side of the room, stunning windows overlooked the street. Leather wingback chairs and a small table nestled in front of built-in bookshelves that stretched to the ceiling next to a fireplace. The perfect corner to curl up and read.

"Florrie!" said Jonquille. "Great timing. Can you tell us if anything is missing?"

"This is the first time I have ever been in this room. But I would hazard a guess that the drawers don't usually look like they've been ransacked."

Jonquille tilted his head and peered at me. "Really?"

I pointed at the bed. "Clearly Mr. DuBois made the bed. I hardly think he would have left the drawers in such a mess."

Jonquille suppressed a smile. "I meant that I was surprised you have never been in this room before."

"This is the first time I have ever been upstairs."

He raised his eyebrows and shook his head. "Okaaaay. So

as far as we can tell then, this was most likely an ordinary burglary. Some enterprising thief probably read about Maxwell's incarceration and thought it would be a fine time to burglarize the house."

"But he didn't expect to encounter Mr. DuBois?" I asked.

"Evidently not."

I guessed that made sense. Still . . . "How do we know this isn't related to Delbert's murder?"

Jonquille nodded. "It could be, but we often see this kind of thing when a house is empty and there's a lot of publicity. It's like a written invitation to burglarize the house."

"So what now?" I asked.

"We'll take fingerprints, but it's unlikely we'll catch the perpetrator."

I didn't like the sound of that. "In other words, you have bigger crimes to worry about." I clapped a hand over my mouth in regret as soon as the words slipped out.

Jonquille didn't appear to be offended. "More or less."

It was a long night. While I waited for the fingerprinting to be done, I tried out keys from a key rack until I located one that worked on the back door. I locked up after the police left, and drove to the hospital.

Mr. DuBois was still in the emergency room when I arrived. They were reluctant to let me in until DuBois signed a document authorizing my presence.

He looked fine, but the nurse assured me that they had administered morphine, which was taking the edge off the pain. His fingers had been attached to something that looked like a medieval torture device. His hand hung in the air with a weight attached to his elbow. The nurse explained they were separating the bones so they could be positioned in place.

Unfortunately, he had also broken his tibia, a bone in his lower leg.

"Mr. DuBois?" I leaned over him and smiled.

"Miss Florrie." He reached for me with his free hand and clutched mine. "Thank heaven you found me. You must phone Strickland, Wheeler, and Erba immediately. The number is in the library desk. Call the private number to reach Ms. Strickland directly. She will make the necessary arrangements." He closed his eyes briefly as if gathering strength. "You will look after everything, won't you? Maxwell and I are counting on you . . ." His voice faded and he appeared to have drifted off.

The nurse assured me that was normal under the circumstances.

Dawn was breaking when I left the hospital. I stood at the entrance for a moment, watching Washington come to life. Had I really only moved a few days ago? It was Tuesday morning. I hadn't slept in twenty-four hours and all the strangest things that had ever happened in my life had occurred within the last three days.

I took a deep breath, found my car, paid for parking, and drove straight to my parents' house in Vienna, Virginia.

They were surprised to see me. I knew I was slowing Dad down, and he had to get to the office, so I talked fast while Mom cooked eggs sunny-side up. Explaining everything that had happened, I slid bread into the toaster, and concluded with, "So I'd like to take Frodo back with me if that's okay."

At the sound of his name, Frodo, a large golden retriever, ambled over to me, wagging his tail.

"Honey, I don't like the sound of this at all." Dad poured milk into his coffee. "Frodo is wonderful but he's not much of a guard dog. He would lick someone to death before he bit anyone."

"I know that. I just want him to be alert and let me know if he hears or smells anyone."

Mom sat down at the table. "It's such a lovely place. I understand why you want to live there. Now that Delbert is dead, I thought things would settle down. Are you sure you want to stay? You could come bunk with your dad and me while you look for a new place."

I sat back in my chair and considered. "I totally understand what you're saying. But I feel like I would be deserting the professor and Mr. DuBois in their time of need."

My parents exchanged a look.

"That's what we get for raising her right," said Dad. "This is all your fault. She gets that from you."

I only half listened to my parents argue about which one had instilled values in Veronica and me. I wasn't about to let the professor down. "The doctor said Mr. DuBois would probably be released from the hospital today. DuBois told me to call Maxwell's attorneys. My best guess is that they'll arrange for a nurse around the clock because he won't be able to take care of himself."

Mom reached over and clutched my hand. "They're lucky to have you looking out for them. And I feel better knowing that a nursing staff will be right next door."

I finished my eggs, kissed each of them on the cheek, and left with Frodo, his food, his bed, and his favorite toy, a stuffed butterfly.

When I got home, I checked on Peaches first. She and Frodo had met before. I was pleased to see that Peaches showed no fear and even touched noses with him.

I fed her on the counter because Frodo would have finished her food with two quick licks of the tongue. Satisfied that all was well in the carriage house, I latched Frodo's leash onto his halter, locked my door, and crossed the driveway to the Maxwell mansion.

I was glad I had brought Frodo. The house was silent and a little eerie. I had no reason to think anyone could be hiding in the house, but Frodo would have let me know, which dispelled some of the spookiness. I unlatched his leash inside so he could follow his nose. We went straight to the library. I found the personal number for Ms. Strickland and called her.

She was horrified by the events of the previous night. I took a little satisfaction in the fact that, like me, she thought there must be a connection to Delbert's murder.

"How's the professor doing?" I asked.

"As well as can be expected under the circumstances. I think he regards it as one of his adventures. I must tell you that Maxwell holds you in the highest regard, and it has been a big comfort to him that you're keeping an eye on everything. The news about DuBois will make him flip, though. The old fellow has been with him so long that he's like a beloved cranky uncle. I'll arrange for around the clock nursing care for DuBois. And I think we should hire a guard to keep an eye on the property. Is that okay with you?"

It was perfect. "I appreciate that. Have the police given you any indication when we might open Color Me Read again?"

"They're not being as cooperative as I would have liked."

"You mean Detective-Sergeant Zielony?"

She groaned a little, which made me much more comfortable with her.

"He's a gem, isn't he?" Her voice was ripe with sarcasm. "If he gives you any grief, you just refer him to me, okay?"

I felt much better after speaking with her. Finally, I had an ally. Someone I could go to if necessary. And a guard on the property would go a long way in alleviating any residual fears about living there. I sat back in the desk chair and gazed around the library. Who would have ever thought all these strange things would happen? Had they all been triggered by my moving in? Or by keeping Delbert out? Or had Delbert and his mother wanted him in the carriage house for a reason? But why? Was it part of Liddy's quest to regain possession of the mansion?

Mom was right. I had probably landed in some kind of bitter family feud. Except for one thing. What was Delbert doing in the bookstore in the middle of the night? And who could have been there with him?

I checked the time. Jim would be wondering where I was. I locked the back door and left, stopping by a coffee shop takeout window where I bought coffee and four bear claws, two for Jim and two for me.

When I approached the bench near Color Me Read, Jim ignored me entirely. He held out both arms to Frodo, who went straight into them as though Jim were an old friend.

Chapter 14

Jim ruffled Frodo's fur, petting and hugging him. Frodo's tail showed his joy.

"Good morning." I couldn't help smiling at the two of them. "I guess you've had dogs."

"Lots of 'em. No better creatures on the face of the earth. They always love you. What's his name?"

"Frodo."

"Folks that walk by either avert their eyes or stare at me like I'm some kind of oddity. But Frodo here didn't judge me. He knew right away that I was a good person. Dogs are much smarter than people in that respect. He doesn't care that I'm not dressed in a suit or wearing a Rolex. That wouldn't mean a thing to him. Dogs go straight to what's important—a person's character."

Jim was correct, of course. But it made me wonder about him. How had he landed on the street? Had he had a job? He wasn't young. What had he done in his life? Didn't he have any family who had a warm bed he could use until he was back on his feet? He seemed like an agreeable guy.

I handed him the coffee and bear claws. He broke off a

corner of a bear claw and fed it to Frodo, who appeared to like him more every moment.

There was no place to sit on the bench thanks to his possessions. I stood, holding Frodo's leash. "Someone broke into Maxwell's home last night."

"Word on the street is that the butler had a heart attack."

"Someone got that wrong. He broke his wrist and a bone in his leg." That had been incorrect, but maybe one of his street friends had seen something? "Do you know why someone would have entered the mansion?"

Jim looked up at me briefly before focusing on Frodo again. "There are bad people in this world who think they can take what belongs to other people. Even folks like me get robbed. Can you believe it? Rich folks are big targets."

"Let me know if you hear anything, okay?"

He winked at me. "You bet. I like the professor. Hate to see him in trouble."

I waved and walked up the stairs to the bookstore entrance. I still hadn't posted a sign! How could I have forgotten about that? I rapped on the door. No one answered. Cupping my hands around my eyes, I looked inside, but didn't see anyone.

"Nobody there this morning," called Jim.

Frodo and I walked back to him. He had finished one bear claw.

"How long have you been out here?"

"I come up this way around six in the morning. I know because I always look at the big clock on the corner of M and Wisconsin. Nobody has gone in or out of the bookstore today. Of course somebody could have entered through the back door, but the cops probably don't have the key to that door."

"Thanks for keeping an eye on the store, Jim." I started to walk away.

"Hey, Florrie!"

I stopped and turned around. "Tell Maxwell that I miss the old coot. I'm keeping an ear to the ground for him."

I couldn't help grinning. It spoke to his innate goodness. How many people with Maxwell's money had bag people on the street looking out for them? Maxwell had friends everywhere. Just maybe not in his own family. My cell phone rang. It was the nursing company, letting me know that Mr. DuBois was on his way home.

Frodo and I hurried back just in time to find two aides helping Mr. DuBois out of a van. The poor guy looked exhausted.

"Are you Florrie?" asked one of the assistants.

After introducing myself, I unlocked the back door for them. I had no idea where Mr. DuBois's room was, which necessitated a quick search through the mansion. I found it on the main floor on the far east side of the house. Giant windows and French doors looked out over a small private garden.

Frodo and I returned to Mr. DuBois, whom the assistants brought inside in a wheelchair.

They settled him in his bed. He grasped my hand. "Tell Maxwell I'll be fine."

"I will. You just rest. They're sending a guard to watch over the property."

He closed his eyes. "Thank . . ."

One of the assistants smiled at me. "It's the morphine. He'll sleep most of the day." She crooked a finger at me.

I followed her into the kitchen.

"I'm Doris. I'll be doing twelve-hour shifts, and Fred will be taking the other twelve. Is there anything I should know?"

"I suppose you're aware of the general situation with Mr. Maxwell?"

"I read about it in the paper."

I wasn't sure how much to tell her. Maybe the newspaper

coverage was all she needed to know? "I live in the carriage house out back. Please call me if you need anything. I'm told a guard will be coming to keep an eye on the property."

Doris grew pale.

Uh-oh. More information was necessary after all. I explained what had happened the night before. She deserved to know that much if she was going to be staying here.

"Well!" She braced her shoulders and lifted her chin. "Nothing of that sort will happen on my watch!"

Glad about her presence, I headed home.

I was eager to shower and change into fresh clothes but thought I'd better put a sign up on the bookstore pronto. It was easy enough to make on my computer.

Temporarily closed.
Please call regarding books on order
as we are receiving deliveries.
Watch for our reopening very soon.

As it printed, it dawned on me that we should probably have some kind of reopening party or festivity, maybe a book signing. My next thought shocked me to the core. Apparently, I was more devious than I had realized. I could invite Jacquie Liebhaber to sign books. What better opportunity to ask her questions about Delbert stealing her books!

Now if I only knew when the store would reopen. I couldn't exactly invite her if I didn't have a date.

I rushed to the copy shop to have the sign laminated to protect it against the weather. I bought a couple of hooks to hang it with and asked them to punch holes.

Frodo and I returned to the bookstore and hung the sign. Jim had left his position on the bench. I guessed he had moved on someplace else for lunch.

I knocked on the door again and looked inside the store. I

couldn't see a soul. Hmmpf. If they were through, they should give us access again.

There was one more errand before I could go home. Possibly the most important of all. Frodo and I walked to the chic shop that masqueraded as a home and hardware store. I found what I wanted in a matter of minutes—door bolts. I hated to deface the professor's property without asking him first, but under the circumstances, I thought my personal safety and sanity were far more important. Happily, the store offered trendy hardware, albeit at astronomical prices. I wasn't paying rent, so the least I could do was buy stylish bolts. I purchased two, along with a screwdriver, and we finally headed home.

The sofa beckoned after my night without sleep. But first, those bolts had to be installed. I wasn't particularly adept at home maintenance, but this didn't seem too difficult.

I worked on the gate first. The wood was harder than I had expected. I used a rock to hammer a starter hole, which worked fairly well. Installing the screws by hand was exhausting but I was determined to do it. In the end, I slid the bolt into place and decided I was entitled to an entire pint of mint chocolate chip ice cream as a reward.

The interior bolt was easier to install. I slid it in place, pleased by my independence. At least no one would be getting inside while I was home. I relaxed just knowing that.

Next I placed a call to Sergeant Jonquille. I got his answering machine and left a message asking when we might be able to reopen the store since no one appeared to be collecting evidence anymore.

As much as I needed to shower, I collapsed on the sofa, closed my eyes for a few minutes, and drifted off.

At one o'clock I woke with a jerk and remembered that I was supposed to meet Sonja. I hurried through a shower, and dressed in a pale lime sheath and white sandals. "Sorry, Frodo, but you'll have to stay home with Peaches."

He opened his eyes but didn't bother to lift his head. I took that as an indication that he was pleased to stay and nap.

Peaches slept a foot away from him. They would be fine.

I walked up Wisconsin Avenue fast, the sun beating down on me mercilessly. A full five minutes early, I walked into the cool bakery, grateful for air-conditioning. It was a modern place, with a minimalist decor. The focus was on the huge cases of baked goods. My eyes went straight to the chocolate eclairs, cupcakes, and beautiful tortes.

Sonja wore a traditional soft pink waitress uniform. She wasn't wearing a stitch of makeup but still looked gorgeous.

"You came! I wasn't sure you would." She gestured toward a simple round table with two metal folding chairs. "It's always slow this time of day. After lunch but too early to pick up something to take home for dessert. I hope you won't mind if a customer comes in, and I have to serve him."

"Of course not."

We sat down, and she wasted no time. "Delbert had a little crush on me."

I smiled. I was fairly certain he was in good company. Sonja must be used to men chasing her.

"He told me that he is very wealthy and will inherit a mansion from his uncle. Many men say things like that, so I didn't pay much attention." She kneaded her fingers and shot me a weak smile. "When men are drunk, most of them say they are wealthy, successful, and incredible athletes. I was surprised to learn that in the case of Delbert, he actually did come from a wealthy family."

She paused and stared out the plate glass window, but I didn't think she was seeing anything. She could have told us that last night. It was hardly worth a special meeting. She had to know something more.

Sonja swallowed hard. "It was strange because from what I

could see, Delbert did not have a pleasing personality, yet he was always the center of attention. Women flirted with him and men wanted to be his friend, even buying him drinks."

"I guess money attracts some people."

"Exactly. But there was one woman who watched him with anger in her eyes."

Chapter 15

Now we were getting somewhere! "Do you know her name?"

Sonja shook her head. "She isn't a regular. I serve hundreds of people every night. Most I know only by sight. She's very attractive. A tall blonde with good taste in clothes."

That could be nearly half the women in Georgetown. It didn't fit anyone who worked at the bookstore, but Helen fell into three of the categories. "You're sure she's a blonde? Not a redhead?"

Sonja took a big breath. "The neon lights sometimes cast misleading tints, but I remember her as a blonde."

My excitement fizzled. There had to be more to this. Why would she bother telling me? "This woman just watched him?"

"It was the way she did it. Almost from the shadows, like she was spying on him. And there was no mistaking her anger. Later on, when a few drinks had loosened her up, she talked silliness of revenge on Delbert because she hates her new job."

"Did you tell the police?"

She mashed her eyes closed briefly. "No. They haven't talked to me. I didn't report it that night because I would have to call the police all the time. Drunk people say a lot of things they don't mean."

"Did Delbert notice her?" I asked.

"I was working, so I couldn't watch them continuously. I saw him look at her once. His glance remained on her. I remember wondering if he found her attractive, or if she was a previous girlfriend whom he had discarded in a cruel manner."

That was no help at all. Jacquie Liebhaber was a blonde. I couldn't imagine her hanging at Club Neon, though, unless she was trying to torment Delbert. "Age?"

"Late twenties? The typical Club Neon age group."

That eliminated Jacquie.

I took a slip of paper out of my pocket and wrote my cell phone number on it with a blue-tipped colored pencil. "Would you call me if she comes in again?"

Sonja looked at the paper like she feared it might bite her.

"Sonja, I appreciate this information very much. But I can't help feeling like there must be something more. You could have told me this at Club Neon last night."

Her gaze flew past me. She appeared to scan the street outside. We were alone, yet she spoke in a hushed voice. "A man came into the club asking questions—"

I interrupted her. "When?"

"Last night. Before you arrived. He was very large." She balled her hands into fists and held up her elbows. "Strong like a fighter. On his left arm, just above his elbow, was a tattoo of a butterfly. He was bald, but I remember thinking perhaps he shaves his head because he had a bushy black mustache. Florrie, he scared me. He was like a character from a movie. The big bad dude who comes in to break the knees of the quivering scrawny guy."

"And he made inquiries about Delbert?"

"Oh yes. He asked for me by name, which made me very nervous. How would he possibly know my name?"

Maybe he had paid a visit to Delbert's roommates like I

had. I turned to look out the window. "You thought he was watching you?"

"He *was* watching me! He was still there when you came in. You weren't the first person to be talking about Delbert. A lot of people knew him. His death was a hot topic. But"—she smiled—"you and your friend didn't look like Club Neon types. I felt more comfortable with you." She leaned across the table. "I'm not afraid that you're going to punch me or haul me off to a dark warehouse to grill me."

I wondered if she had seen too many thriller movies. Then again, maybe she was right to be wary of the man with the butterfly tattoo. Scott and Lance thought Delbert had finally crossed the wrong person. It could be someone with unsavory connections. But if Butterfly Man or a pal of his had murdered Delbert, why would he be asking about him?

I bought several slices of raspberry cream torte from her as thanks, and because they looked delicious.

I walked home wondering if there were no end to the people Delbert had hurt. He was like a human wrecking ball. The professor knew that. Surely Delbert's parents must have realized it. They had paid to clean up his messes.

In spite of myself, I kept an eye out for a big bald guy with a large mustache. Not one person matched that description. I felt sort of silly about it as moms with darling children in strollers passed me. The men in ties and business suits, or golf shirts with shorts, didn't seem very threatening, either. It was a nice neighborhood. Bullies like Butterfly Man were few and far between.

I walked along the driveway to the carriage house. In front of the garage, Sergeant Jonquille chatted with a guy in a uniform different from Jonquille's.

"Florrie!" Jonquille sounded pleased to see me.

My heart skipped a beat when my eyes met his.

"I was just filling Felipe in on the details."

I shook Felipe's hand. His name tag read FELIPE NUNEZ, MONTOYA SECURITY. He was shorter than Jonquille, but on the pudgy side. I guessed him to be close to fifty. "We're all very glad to have you here."

"You're in good hands with Felipe. He used to be on the police force with me, but he got smart and retired. Now he snags all the cushy jobs," said Jonquille. "I stopped by to let you know that you can go back into the bookstore if you stay off the third floor. We blocked it with crime scene tape. You can reopen to the general public on Thursday morning."

Day after tomorrow. Thank goodness. "That's fabulous! Thank you so much. Any leads yet?"

Jonquille cocked his head. "Leads?"

"To the killer."

He blew a breath out of his mouth. "I understand how you feel about Maxwell. He's lucky to have someone as loyal as you. But I'm afraid you're going to have to get used to the idea that he knocked off his nephew."

"You're not even considering that someone else might have murdered Delbert?"

Jonquille looked away for a few seconds. "It's not up to me, Florrie. I'm not in homicide. But it doesn't look good for the professor. I'll tell you what. If you come up with a legitimate suspect, or concrete evidence, I'll take it to homicide."

"Who's on the case?" asked Felipe.

"Zielony."

Felipe groaned. "The man's like a terrier after a squirrel. He won't give up even if the squirrel jumps to another tree. Good luck changing his mind."

"But what about justice?" I was horrified. "I understand doing your job, but what if I'm right and the professor isn't guilty? It would be unfair to incarcerate him while the real perpetrator gets off scot free. Or worse—kills someone else!"

"Florrie," said Jonquille, "we're all about justice. But *you're* one of our witnesses. You told us that Maxwell was planning to do something to take care of Delbert. Deep in your heart, you probably know the truth. You're just not ready to accept it."

I tried not to scowl at him. Something had happened at the mansion the night before that put Mr. DuBois in the hospital. He knew that, but would poo-poo it by saying there was no connection.

There was nothing to do but thank them both and go home. It had been a very stressful twenty-four hours, and I longed to pull out my sketch pad and relax. Besides, if we were going to reopen, I needed to invite Jacquie Liebhaber to a grand reopening party. If Jacquie came to sign books, it would be a huge success. I'd have to order extra books right away and get on the ball. I hoped I could get them fast enough.

I unlocked the door to the carriage house. Peaches and Frodo waited for me, purring and wagging. There was no warmer welcome home.

After the requisite petting, I fed both of them. "What do you think of the carriage house, Frodo? Are you okay being here?"

He was too busy snacking on dog cookies to respond. I logged into the bookstore computer and searched for contact information for Jacquie Liebhaber. Her agent's number came up, and I called it.

When the agent answered, I explained that I wanted to invite Jacquie to a signing on rather short notice.

I heard a sharp intake of breath on the other end.

"Who is this again?" she asked.

"Florrie Fox of Color Me Read, in Washington, DC. I believe Ms. Liebhaber was once married to the owner, John Maxwell?"

There was silence on the other end. Finally, the agent said, "I'm terribly sorry, but I don't believe she'll be available on such short notice."

Chapter 16

That was disappointing. I would have to find someone else.

I went through our list of local authors. Aha! Emily Branscom had a new nonfiction book out on little-known historic oddities of Georgetown. That was just the ticket. She was always popular. I phoned her agent and left a message asking if Emily would be interested in doing a signing.

That pending, I took my sketch pad out to the garden and doodled. I found myself drawing a cupcake. I really ought to bake some cupcakes. Would people buy a coloring book of desserts and pastries?

Inspired by a butterfly in the garden, I sketched a butterfly landing on a cupcake. And then just a butterfly. The thought that a butterfly would fit beautifully in a new garden coloring book flitted through my mind before I returned to the important thing—who was Butterfly Man and what did he want?

What had Jonquille said he needed? *A legitimate suspect. Or concrete evidence.*

I flipped the page to make a list of suspects. An ivy-colored crayon poised over the paper, I hardly knew where to begin but wrote Lance Devereoux's name, the roommate whose career Delbert ruined. I sketched his face from memory but wasn't pleased with the likeness. Had his pal Scott Southworth helped him? What about Jacquie Liebhaber, the author whose books Delbert published as his own? I added their names.

Reluctantly, I wrote Helen's name next and drew a sketch of her face with her gorgeous copper hair tumbling over her shoulders. It was ridiculous, of course. She had no motive. At least not one that I knew about. She did have access to the bookstore, though. So did Bob. I kept coming back to that. Along those lines, I had been a little bit disturbed to learn that Zsazsa, Bankhouse, and Goldblum all knew the alarm code. Bankhouse had access to the keys through Helen, but any one of them might have finagled the key situation. Could one of them have left the back door unlocked? Again, though, I knew of no motive that they might have.

My only remaining suspect thus far was Mr. DuBois. He would do anything for Maxwell. And he certainly had access to keys. But the fact that someone had chased him almost prevented me from adding his name. I needed to get over there to talk with him and find out exactly what had happened last night.

I looked over my list with disgust. Only Jacquie and Lance were plausible suspects.

There was a knock at my door. I hurried inside and peeked through the window. To my relief I saw Felipe, the guard. When I opened the door, he handed me a business card. "There's a Mr. Hambrick here to see you. Do you want to talk to him?" He lowered his voice. "You don't have to. I can send him away."

I had no idea who he was. I looked at the card in my hand. IAN HAMBRICK, PRIVATE INVESTIGATOR. Could this be Butterfly Man? "Maybe Maxwell's lawyer hired a PI. I'd better talk to him. Can you stay with me?"

"Sure. It would be my pleasure." Felipe signaled him to approach.

It was kind of cool to have my own private guard. Was this how the wealthy lived?

Ian introduced himself. About six feet tall, he spoke with a slight British lilt. In spite of the heat, he wore a driver's cap of beige linen. His face, while not unattractive, was very narrow. His chin and nose were somewhat pointy. His beard was short and well trimmed.

Although he didn't fit Sonja's description of Butterfly Man, I looked at his arms anyway in search of the tattoo. Unfortunately, he wore a long-sleeved shirt that covered his arms.

"I'm looking for Jacquie Liebhaber. The nurse at the main house referred me to you. Have you heard from her in the last week?"

I was taken aback. "Looking for her? Jacquie Liebhaber, the women's fiction author? She's missing?"

"I'm afraid so. No one has seen or heard from her since Saturday."

My knees went weak. How many things could go wrong? "Oh my gosh! What happened?"

"We don't really know. It's like she disappeared into thin air."

"Sorry, but I don't know Jacquie. She was once married to John Maxwell, who owns this property, but I'm sure you have read in the papers that he is currently incarcerated."

"So she hasn't been here?"

"Not that I know of. I assume the only reason she would come would be to see Maxwell, and he hasn't been here since Sunday."

He nodded. "Thanks anyway. If she shows up looking for him, please give me a call. Everyone is very worried about her."

"I can understand that. I hope they find her soon. If there's anything I can do, please let me know. I have always enjoyed her books."

"Thank you." He strode away.

I was reeling. There was no reason to imagine a connection between Delbert's death and Jacquie's disappearance. But the timing was certainly coincidental.

"Everything okay?" asked Felipe.

"I don't know. Must be boring out here," I said.

He smiled and shrugged. "I've worked in worse situations." He looked at the sky. "Rain, snow, sleet. Yecch. Those are the days I wonder why I don't get a nice cushy security job at some office building. Today, the weather's good, the house and grounds are beautiful, and I seriously doubt that the scumbag who broke into the mansion last night will be back."

"Could I offer you a cold drink?"

He motioned over his shoulder with his thumb. "Thanks, but I came prepared with a cooler."

I stepped inside and closed the door. Could Jacquie have murdered Delbert? It seemed unlikely. Would she have a key to the bookstore? Only if she had been having midnight rendezvous there with Maxwell. That thought shocked me for a moment. After all, it wasn't outside the realm of realistic possibilities. He went to the bookstore a lot at weird hours. They truly could have been meeting there secretly.

That changed everything. Maxwell might have entrusted her with a key and the password to the alarm system. But would Delbert have been there? Could she have arranged to meet him there out of anger because he stole her books? It might not have been difficult to lure him with the promise of money or even some scam.

Or had she gone to see Maxwell and discovered Delbert there instead? Had she been waiting for Maxwell when Delbert arrived? She could have murdered him and then taken off. Was she in hiding because she had killed Delbert? Would she let Maxwell suffer in prison for her crime?

I wished I knew more about her. She had divorced Maxwell.

Were there hard feelings after all these years? Had she plotted this to land Maxwell in prison for something that had happened in their marriage so long ago?

I hadn't considered his ex-wives. There had been three I believed. But what about girlfriends? Had he been dating someone and dumped her? Oh no! That opened a whole new group of people to consider.

The only person who would know who might have it in for Maxwell was DuBois. He could fill me in on Jacquie.

I found it curious that the private investigator bothered to come to the mansion. Did that suggest that she and Maxwell were still in touch? Why hadn't any private investigators come around looking into Delbert's death for Maxwell's benefit?

What a dolt I was. Of course! I bet that was Butterfly Man. A quick phone call to the lawyers and I would know.

I brought Peaches and Frodo inside and secured the doors. I didn't see Felipe when I crossed the driveway to the main house.

I knocked on the back door, but when no one answered, I used the key I had found earlier in the day. It had been so early in the day that it felt like several days had gone by.

Felipe and the nurse chatted in the library. I stopped to say hi and headed for Mr. DuBois's room.

The curtains had all been drawn. He lay in bed, a tiny motionless figure. His mouth hung open in the throes of deep sleep.

When he gasped and snapped his mouth shut, I jumped in alarm. But he didn't wake.

I gazed around the darkened room. A large TV hung on the wall, the screen black. His bookshelves overflowed with mysteries and true crime stories. I couldn't help noticing that he had a full set of Jacquie Liebhaber's books.

A collection of photos were mostly of DuBois with members of the Maxwell family. I wondered if he had any living family of his own. The pictures led me to believe the Maxwells were his adopted family.

I ambled out to the library. "How is Mr. DuBois doing?"

"He's as fine as can be given his injuries. He'll sleep most of the day today. Don't you worry about him, honey. Sleep is always the best thing for recuperation."

I suspected she was right.

"I can give you a call if he wakes. Would you like that?" the nurse asked.

Shaking my head, I said, "No, thanks. I'll stop by a little later to check on him. I did want to call his attorneys, though." Feeling a little guilty for acting like I owned the place, I stepped behind the desk, located the phone number, and dialed.

The two of them quickly excused themselves.

I pawed through the top drawer of the desk for a piece of paper. The only tablet for notes was embossed with an elegant crest and the name MAXWELL. I tore off a sheet and jotted down the number, in case I needed to phone Ms. Strickland from home.

She came on the line. "How's Mr. DuBois?"

I filled her in on his condition and thanked her for arranging the nursing staff and security. "Is there anything I can do for the professor? Call him, perhaps?"

"He has limited access to the phone. But he takes great comfort in knowing that you're taking care of business matters for him."

Fudging a little bit, I said, "I hear there's a fellow around asking questions. A big guy with a tattoo of a butterfly on his arm?"

Chapter 17

"Interesting. Do you know his name?" asked Ms. Strickland.

"You didn't hire him?" My comfort in thinking he was working for her fizzled.

"No. We use Simon Baker."

I didn't want to be pushy but the professor was in jail. Time was of the essence here! "He hasn't been around to talk with me yet."

"He's probably working his police contacts first," she said. "Keep me posted if anything else happens."

I assured her that I would, and hung up. I couldn't help grinning a little bit. Just as Mr. DuBois watched too many true crime shows, I read too many mysteries. It made perfect sense that a private investigator would first tap his police contacts for information. They knew far more than I did. After all, they had collected fingerprints and DNA. They would get the autopsy results, too. The police were a far bigger font of information than DuBois or me. If only Zielony hadn't made up his mind that Maxwell was guilty, the police would be out searching for the killer, too.

I returned to the hot pavement between the two houses.

No sign of the private investigator hired by Jacquie's family. I wondered if her family would speak to me. But what would I ask? I couldn't exactly inquire whether she was having midnight rendezvous with Maxwell or if she had killed Delbert. Then again, that private investigator did drop by. That had to mean something.

At that very moment, I wanted nothing more than to curl up and sleep. But the sight of Felipe standing in the middle of a pile of parcels reminded me that I had to take care of the store.

"Need a hand with these?" he asked, looking up at the sky. "They're calling for a thunderstorm tonight. We need it. It's been so dry that my wife's vegetable garden is withering."

I unlocked the door. He petted a very enthusiastic Frodo, then helped me carry packages inside.

"Felipe, is it possible to unlock a door without the key?"

"You don't have to worry, Florrie. I'm watching out for you. Someone will be here around the clock."

"Thanks. But I was thinking about the bookstore. There wasn't any sign of a break-in. Not many people have the key, so I was wondering if it's possible to get in without"—I exaggerated to make my point—"blowing the lock off the door with a gun."

He smiled at me. "It's way too easy. Look up *how to bump a lock* on your computer."

I froze. "I hope you're joking?"

"Sorry. I wish I were. Of course, there are ways to pick a lock, too, but bumping is easy."

I thanked him for his help. If what he said were true, the field of suspects wasn't as narrow as I originally thought.

As soon as he left, I reached for my iPad and typed in *How to bump a lock*. Uh-oh. Turned out it was actually fairly easy to *bump* a lock. Who knew? It was probably common knowledge among the unsavory. With the help of a key that had been filed down, a quick bump on it followed by a swift turn could open almost any lock.

There was still the matter of the alarm password, though. Assuming Maxwell hadn't forgotten to turn the alarm on when he left that night.

Taking a deep breath, I phoned Bob and Helen to let them know that the store would be reopening. Bob was delighted. Helen took it more calmly. I wondered if she were sorry her brief vacation would come to an end. She didn't even ask about Maxwell.

That done, I unpacked the books that had arrived and phoned the people for whom we had special-ordered them.

It was past the dinner hour when I finished. And I still needed to come up with a clever reopening idea. I glanced at my sketch pad, longing for the days when I had had time to doodle.

Eureka! A coloring extravaganza. Why not? We could give away adult and children's coloring books, colored pencils, and crayons as prizes. I phoned Helen again and asked if she would like to do a special Saturday morning book reading for children. When she agreed, I sent out colorful emails to the people who had signed up for our mailing list about children's events.

Now for the adults. We could do the same sort of thing, but we needed something to pull in the more intellectually inclined. I checked my email. Emily Branscom's agent had sent me her phone number, saying Emily would be delighted to sign at Color Me Read and that I should contact her to make arrangements.

I phoned Emily, who was thrilled to come to the store on Saturday afternoon, in spite of the short notice.

A crack of thunder sent Frodo running to my side. The garden had grown dark and a little spooky. Rain pelted the leaves.

Unlike Frodo, Peaches didn't care. She looked out at the storm, her eyes darting to the drops that hit the glass.

I rubbed Frodo's ears and murmured comforting words, but I was thinking that the grand reopening was coming together nicely. If only Delbert's murder could be solved so easily.

The thunderstorm continued. I hoped it would abate soon for Frodo's sake. He became a Velcro dog when I went to the kitchen to make dinner. The fridge was beginning to look sparse. I noted that I really needed to stop by the farmers' market for some goodies.

But for tonight, I had some chicken tenders to sauté. Frodo remained with me through the entire cooking process, occasionally sticking his nose between my knees in desperation.

I made a salad for myself, and added some chopped chicken tenders to Frodo and Peaches's dinners. Not surprisingly, the storm didn't dampen Frodo's appetite.

At nine o'clock, the storm still raged. I longed to go to bed, but felt obligated to check on Mr. DuBois first. I didn't dare leave Frodo alone in his hysteria. I latched a leash on his collar and dashed across the driveway through driving rain.

I had my key at the ready. We were inside the mansion in a matter of minutes, albeit damp on arrival.

The light was on in the kitchen but no one was there. I found the nurse in Mr. DuBois's room, changing a bandage on his leg.

"He must have scraped his leg when he fell," she said. "It's a fairly nasty wound."

The bandage she removed was hideous. The injury had to ache unbearably.

She placed a fresh bandage over the wound. Mr. DuBois didn't flinch. In fact, his eyes were closed.

"Has he wakened at all?" I asked.

"Oh yes. He had a lovely bowl of soup for dinner." She

walked past me and whispered, "Don't let him tell you he didn't like it. He ate every bite."

She left the shadowy room. It was lighted by a single lamp in a corner, which made it possible to see, but the room remained dim. I presumed that was to encourage sleep and calm. The drapes on the French doors had been opened. Rain pitter-pattered outside. It was a soothing sound that made me want to curl up in a chair and read.

I walked closer to Mr. DuBois. "Are you awake?" I whispered. Frodo neared the bed, wagging his tail and sniffing curiously.

At the precise moment that a bolt of lightning filled the air with light, Mr. DuBois seized my hand and sat bolt upright. "The ghost!" he wheezed.

Chapter 18

I screamed.

Frodo stuck his nose between my legs and whined.

Mr. DuBois's fingers grasped my hand like talons. "The ghost," he repeated.

Collecting myself, I spoke as soothingly as I could. "There's no ghost. It's just a thunderstorm. Look, Frodo came to visit you."

Frodo was in no mood to be friendly. He was intent on crawling under the bed.

I patted Mr. DuBois's hand, which felt like a vise. "How are you feeling?"

"There's someone in the house."

"That's your nurse. She's taking care of you." I smiled at him in what I hoped was a reassuring manner.

"You don't understand. I saw it. I saw the ghost."

He spoke with such conviction that I wondered if there was a story about a ghost in the mansion. The building *was* a couple hundred years old. Someone had probably died there along the way.

"What ghost?"

He sagged back against the pillows, as if he had spent all the energy he had. "Here. In . . . house . . ."

DuBois's grip on my hand relaxed, and his eyes closed. His breathing became regular. He was asleep again.

I felt certain he was confusing the nurse with a ghost. Sort of certain. Maybe he was hallucinating?

I tugged on Frodo, who had managed to wedge his head and shoulders under the bed. We were in the hall outside the door, when I heard, "Help! Help me!"

I turned around. Mr. DuBois twisted in his bed, flailing the arm that was bound in a cast.

I rushed back to his side. "I'm here. It's Florrie. You're going to be fine."

He relaxed a little but gazed at me with wild eyes. "Beware of the ghost."

His eyes closed, and he fell asleep again.

Wow. I had never seen anyone act like that. I was glad I wasn't the nurse who would be dealing with his hysteria all night long.

Frodo and I slipped out of the room. The nurse was making tea in the kitchen.

"Are you sure Mr. DuBois is all right?" I asked. "He seems a little confused."

"He still has morphine in his system, and he's on some powerful drugs to stave off the pain."

I lowered my voice in case he could hear. "That scrape on his leg looked awful!"

She nodded. "Elderly people often have very thin skin that tears easily. Imagine how that would hurt."

"So it's okay for him to be delusional?"

"I wouldn't say it's all right, but it's to be expected. Have you ever had morphine?"

"No."

"They gave it to me once in the hospital. It was the strangest feeling. I would mean to say one thing and something else entirely would come out. My husband nearly divorced me when I said I was waiting for the pilot to come. I had dated a pilot before him, and he thought that I was waiting for my old boyfriend to come to visit me! What I was trying to say was *I'm waiting for the doctor to come.*" She laughed aloud, her double chin wiggling. "That was the angriest my husband has ever been with me. It took a lot of smoothing over to convince him that it was the morphine that was talking."

She eyed me. "Did Mr. DuBois mention a ghost?"

"Yes."

She gazed around the kitchen. "These old houses often have them. But don't worry, sweetheart, I haven't seen it. I think it's just the drugs in his system. Give him a day or two to come around. A break is a very big deal for the elderly. It takes a toll on them initially. But he'll get better in time."

That was a relief. I wished her a good night and rushed across the driveway with Frodo before another clap of thunder or lightning strike could freak him out.

It was a little bit early for bedtime, but I was bushed. I made sure all the doors were locked, and now that I knew about bumping a lock, I wedged a chair under the handle of the front door in addition to throwing the bolt. That left all the French doors, but I didn't have enough chairs to do that to all of them. And we had security looking out for us anyway.

I trudged up the stairs thinking about the trapdoor in the bookstore stairs. There wasn't room for one here. The stairs were broad and not quite circular, though they curved as they went up. In a way, it was surprising that the stairwell was so large. But there were no landings for trapdoors.

I fell into bed with Peaches and Frodo and didn't wake until the sun shone again.

In the morning, I baked a quick bread with fresh raspberries. When it came out of the oven, I let it cool while I made a reopening sign for Color Me Read.

My hot coffee in hand, I sent out press releases to the local newspapers about the reopening, and updated the store website. I placed a few orders for the giveaway items we would need on Saturday and for extra copies of Emily's book. Everything should arrive by Friday.

That done, I drizzled a white vanilla glaze over the quick bread. I cut a slice for my breakfast and fed Frodo and Peaches.

Dressed in denim shorts and a salmon-colored sleeveless top, I set off with Frodo to run errands. I carried the sign carefully in my hand, and took along a couple of expandable shopping bags, as well as some of the quick bread for Jim.

We headed for the print shop first to have the sign laminated. Once it was sturdier, I picked up coffee for Jim on the way to the bookstore.

Once again, Frodo acted like Jim was an old pal. Jim looked so scruffy to me, but Frodo was convinced there was a great guy underneath that rough exterior.

I handed Jim his coffee and quick bread. He ignored them and concentrated on Frodo.

While they exchanged affection, I swapped the new sign for the old one. I peered into the store. No sign of any activity.

I returned to Jim. "Where did you weather the storm last night?"

"Under the overpass. Need to find a new place. It gets too crowded these days. All sorts of doubtful characters show up to take refuge. Thanks for the coffee and breakfast. And for bringing Frodo by."

I didn't want to be rude, but maybe he knew about these things. "Jim, have you ever heard of *bumping a lock?*"

He gave me a surprised look. "You think that's how somebody got inside the bookstore?"

"Is it a possibility?" I asked. "Is it common knowledge?"

He resumed stroking Frodo's neck. "Most street people respect doors and boundaries. But, yeah, folks know about it. You want me to try it on the bookstore?"

"You have a filed down key?"

"Not right now." With a twinkle in his eye, he added, "I've used 'em before. They're easy to make."

"Thanks for offering to test the locks, but I don't think that's necessary. I had never heard of *bumping* and wondered if everyone knew about it."

"It's known among certain people. Probably not *your* friends, though."

"The bookstore is opening again tomorrow."

"'Bout time. The cops haven't been in there for two days. It will feel better when things get back to normal around here."

It would feel better for all of us. I waved and strolled leisurely toward the farmers' market. It was a feast for the eyes. Would a farmers' market sketch be appropriate in a garden book?

Frodo and I paused as we entered. The colors and scents awed me. Red, yellow, and green peppers. The rich purples of eggplant. All the shades of green in string beans and various types of lettuce. Strawberries, raspberries, blueberries, blackberries. I gathered them up as though I was ravenous for color.

"Florrie! Florrie!" Zsazsa waved at me and beckoned me to her.

She petted Frodo immediately. "Hello, sweet darlink. What a good boy you are! Florrie, did you see these tomatoes? The golden ones with red running through them are always the best. I'll make you a tomato tart."

"You don't have to do that."

"It would be my pleasure. I'm so happy that the bookstore will be open again. I've been off my stride since it closed. I was very pleased to see that Emily Branscom will be the featured speaker on Saturday. I love hearing her talk about the little secrets of Washington." Zsazsa winked at me. "She's pretty good at keeping secrets."

"I'm not following you."

"Emily's husband has been quite public about her affair. Didn't you know? They're separated. But no one knows the identity of her lover." Zsazsa picked up a cucumber. "These are so refreshing on hot summer days. Have you tried the farm-fresh eggs? You must!" She slid a dozen into my bag, and I paid for them.

"Then how do you know she's having an affair?"

"Her husband has blabbed about it to everyone. Maybe he hopes someone will reveal the identity of the other man?" She picked up a bundle of fresh parsley. "Anything new on Delbert's murder?"

I told her what had happened to Mr. DuBois.

She forgot all about the herbs. "No! The poor man. I shall bring him some of my homemade chicken soup." Zsazsa reached for an onion and a bunch of carrots with the greens still on them. "So unfortunate. I am meeting with Bankhouse and Goldblum later today. We must consider the implications of this new development. Would you like to come?"

I told her I would try, but made no promises. We both bought some cheeses. By that time, my bags bulged with as much as I could carry, and I was eager to head home.

Felipe sat outside in the driveway on a lawn chair with a cooler beside him talking with Sergeant Jonquille, who said, "Hi, Florrie. I hear you had an uneventful night."

"Pretty much. Could I ask you a question?"

"Sure." His brow creased and his concern was endearing.

I wanted to like him. Why couldn't he understand that Maxwell hadn't murdered Delbert? "Maxwell's second wife is missing. Her name is Jacquie Liebhaber. Do you know anything about that? She lives somewhere in Washington."

He nodded. "Yeah, I heard about it. Never came home on Saturday. No one has any idea where she went."

I gasped as I made a connection. "Like Agatha Christie!"

Jonquille tilted his head.

"She disappeared. I think she turned up in a hotel in London. I'm not sure. But she was fine. She just took off without telling anyone. Do you think that's what Jacquie did?"

"I didn't know that about Agatha Christie. You think Jacquie could be doing the same thing as a publicity stunt?"

"I hope not. But I don't know her personally. I don't know if that's the kind of crazy thing she might do. There are no leads? No signs of abduction?"

"Not that I've heard. I'm sure they're looking at her current husband carefully, though. They always do."

"Is he the last person who saw her?" I asked.

"I don't know. I'm not involved in the case. I think she lives up in the fourth district." His eyes narrowed. "How did you find out?"

I told him about the visit from the private investigator and what happened when I called Jacquie's agent.

"Florrie," he said with a hint of polite warning in his tone, "just because she was married to Maxwell does not mean there's a connection to Delbert's murder."

"It doesn't mean there isn't a connection, either."

"Most of the time when a woman takes off like that it's related to a domestic crisis of some kind. Her husband might have a mistress or maybe they had a big fight over money. A lot of things happen in marriages that cause separations. You should hear some of the calls we get when spouses argue. I'm betting she'll turn up somewhere."

Like Agatha did. I hoped so. "Thanks. Keep me posted?"

Jonquille smiled. "Of course."

After unloading the groceries, I took my frustrations out on a yeast dough, kneading it and rolling it out into a rectangle. I sprinkled it with cinnamon sugar and tiny wild blueberries from the Georgetown Farmers' Market. Starting at the short end, I rolled it up and cut it into twelve slices, which I fit into a round baking pan, covered, and refrigerated. They would rise slowly overnight.

I called all the delivery companies to change the delivery address back to the store, and stopped the call forwarding of the store telephone number.

In the afternoon, I delivered the special-order books that had arrived. Color Me Read offered home delivery to customers who lived in the Georgetown area. Just a little perk to keep them coming to the bookstore. Of course, most of them asked about Maxwell or petted Frodo, so the trip around the neighborhood took longer than usual.

It was good for me to get out, though Maxwell and the murder were on my mind the whole time.

Chapter 19

The sun streamed through my windows on Thursday morning. I could hear Peaches playing with something on the floor. Probably a hapless stinky bug. I stumbled out of bed and peered at her toy. Poor little bug. I scooped him up, flicked Peaches a crinkle toy to bat around, and tossed the bug out the window. Happily, he did not release his stink on my hand.

Frodo and I trotted downstairs. I preheated the oven and removed the buns from the fridge. I put on coffee and drank my first cup while I let Frodo out in the garden to do his business.

With the buns baking, I showered and dressed, and stepped into a dress the bluish-green color of sea glass. I slid my feet into sandals that glittered with bling. There was something so acceptable about bling on shoes. It was never too eye-catching or tacky. And it was appropriate at any time of day. Even on Keds. I eyed a boring pair in my closet and thought I really should dress them up.

I could hear the timer on the oven downstairs. Peaches watched me, then sped ahead to the bottom of the stairs as if she thought something important would happen. Frodo ambled along with less interest.

I took the buns out of the oven. The entire carriage house smelled heavenly of pastry.

But I understood Peaches's enthusiasm and didn't forget her and Frodo. I spooned mackerel and chicken into Peaches's bowl. She settled down to consume it. Frodo would have to wait a bit for his breakfast.

I made a quick sugar glaze of powdered sugar and orange juice and drizzled it over the buns before I ate one. After all, I couldn't give them away to other people if I didn't try one and know they were edible. I pulled out three aluminum foil tins with lids and packed buns in them.

Saddled with my purse and a bag with the food, I said, "Back soon for you" to Peaches, and locked the door behind me.

There was no sign of a guard yet.

I stopped at the mansion and rapped on the back door, which was unlocked. I stepped inside and found Felipe and Doris having coffee in the kitchen. I handed them buns I had packed for them.

"There are some for Mr. DuBois, too. Do you think he can eat solid foods yet?"

Doris laughed at me. "Sugar, he didn't break any bones in his mouth. I'm sure he'll love them."

I left them unwrapping the goodies and went to see Mr. DuBois. He was sitting up in a chair.

"You're looking much better! How do you feel?"

"Groggy," he mumbled. "Like I can't quite get a grip on my thoughts."

"Maybe that's the medicine? That feeling will probably clear up."

"I hope so. I don't like having all these people lurking around. Can you make them go away?"

"Mr. DuBois, I don't think you're ready to get up and walk around by yourself yet. And isn't it a treat to have someone serving you for a change?"

"Bah! They're sneaking through the house. I hear them at night, you know. They think I'm asleep, but I hear their footsteps and voices. They have no business nosing around."

"I don't think that's the case. They're usually in the kitchen when I arrive. Besides, they were hired by Ms. Strickland. She would have employed only the best people. I thought you would be happy to have a security guard on the premises."

He held out the hand that wasn't in a cast. "Come closer, Florrie."

I crouched by him. Frodo wagged his tail and placed his head in Mr. DuBois's lap.

"The man who broke into the house was the one who killed Delbert. He would have murdered me, too, if we hadn't heard the siren of the police car."

"What happened that night?"

"I was asleep but not in deep slumber yet. I woke when someone opened the door to my room. I tell you, it's a good thing I have a strong heart. I thought I might perish on the spot from fear. Luckily, the door closed. I don't know if he saw me or not. I slid out of bed and tiptoed to the bust of Shakespeare on my shelf."

"Like the one in the bookstore? They're very heavy."

"Indeed! That was what I wanted. I carried it with me and heard him walking up the stairs."

"You saw him? What did he look like?"

"The lights were off, of course. What I saw was a mere shadow, dressed in dark clothing and wearing a hood."

"Could it have been a woman?" I asked.

"It impressed me as a man, but perhaps it could have been a woman. The person walked into Maxwell's room and ransacked the drawers like a savage. He was just grasping the Warhol, his back to me, when I rushed him and slammed Shakespeare into him. Alas, I didn't lift it as high as I'd have liked. I missed his head and hit his shoulder. He turned on me and tried to grab my neck. I knew it would be curtains for me if he got a good hold. I scrambled away as fast as possible, fell down the stairs, and ran outside, intending to hide, but I tripped by the pool."

"It's a good thing you called 911. Sergeant Jonquille arrived before I completed my call."

"I didn't call 911. I never had a chance."

Clearly he was still confused. "Mr. DuBois, you shouldn't have attacked him," I chided.

Mr. DuBois glared at me. "It's my job."

He probably thought it was. "You're a man of great honor and very brave. But I don't think the professor would want you risking your life for anything."

"I would do it again!" he declared, raising his chin.

I stood up. "You'd better not. What would Maxwell do without you?" I changed the subject, hoping to get some information. "Tell me about Maxwell's wives."

"You promised you wouldn't ask about personal matters regarding the Maxwells."

"I need to know if they could be suspects in Delbert's murder."

His head snapped up, and he looked at me with wide eyes. "Unlikely, but I see your point. He married his first wife far too young. His parents were distraught because she wasn't exactly the fine young lady of which they had dreamed. The marriage lasted an entire year. She had the depraved disposition to commit murder, but she died many years ago."

"I'm sorry about that."

"The second, of course, was the delightful Jacquie Liebhaber. They should have stayed married. If their daughter hadn't been abducted, I suspect they would still be married today."

"They divorced because of their missing daughter?"

"Essentially. Neither of them knew how to cope with that tragedy and they took it out on each other. In the end, they parted ways. Maxwell went on reckless and danger-fraught adventures, and Jacquie poured her anger and grief into her books."

"And the third?"

"It's highly unlikely that she would have murdered Delbert. She never cared for him, but the last I heard she had married a count from some tiny European nation and was living abroad. I never was certain that the new husband was actually nobility, but he pretended to be. Real counts don't wear medals on their blazers."

So the only possible suspect out of the three was Jacquie. "Mr. DuBois, it pains me to ask this, but I must. Is the professor involved with anyone now?"

He shot me a stern look. "Maxwell enjoys the company of ladies, but I'm sure I am not aware of the status of his relations with any of them."

Doris bustled in with a tray. "Would you like to sit out in the sun a bit, Mr. DuBois? Or perhaps you would like to join me in the kitchen?"

I waved at him and called Frodo. He hadn't mentioned the ghost, so maybe it had been a result of the drugs in his system, just as Doris had suggested.

Frodo and I walked to the coffee shop to pick up coffee for Jim.

When we approached Jim's bench, he frowned at me. "You're early this morning."

"I have a lot to do."

Nevertheless, I exchanged pleasantries with him for a few minutes, while he indulged in some dog love from Frodo.

I couldn't stay long, though. When we left, we rounded the corner at the end of the block and strolled along the alley in back of the bookstore. I unlocked the door, punched the code which everyone knew into the alarm, and wondered how to change it. I studied the alarm pad. I had never realized how unhelpful it was. It had buttons with the alphabet and buttons with 1, 2, 3, and 4. Hoping for the best, I pressed each of the letters sequentially. Nothing happened. Thankfully, there was a phone number on the pad. I called it from my cell phone.

The man at the alarm company was able to walk me through changing the password to *freeMaxwell*. Feeling better about the safety of the store, I retrieved a good-sized metal dolly. Color Me Read was ominously quiet. I looked forward to bringing it back to life very shortly.

Frodo and I returned to the carriage house with the dolly. When we entered, there was no sign of Peaches.

"Peaches! Here, kitty, kitty."

I listened for the sound of her jumping off a chair. There was only silence.

"Cats can be so annoying, Frodo. They do what *they* want and have selective hearing. See if you can find her."

Frodo just wagged his tail.

I loaded boxes of books that had been ordered before the murder onto the dolly and fastened them with a bungee cord. "Peaches!"

I spied her sitting on the stairs, watching me. "You used to greet me at the door."

As if apologizing, she purred and slinked around my ankles.

I picked her up, placed her in her carrier, and set off for the store with Peaches, Frodo, and the dolly laden with books. It was slow going, but we made it there safely.

I pushed the dolly through the back door, locked it, and let Peaches out of her carrier to explore. Meanwhile, I turned on the coffee pot and the music. I walked through the store switching on lights, and it slowly came back to life like it had only been in a deep slumber.

As I was turning the CLOSED sign to OPEN, Bob and Helen

arrived, followed by the UPS deliveryman, who unloaded boxes of books for us.

Bob bubbled with enthusiasm. For a minute, I thought he might kiss the wall.

Helen scowled, clearly not as delighted but looking gorgeous, as always. I wouldn't have been caught dead in her tight pencil skirt the color of storm clouds. The fabric must have been part spandex because it hugged her like a plastic bag with the air sucked out of it. Her black tank top was surely cool for the hot summer day ahead but it wasn't my style.

She removed oversized Jackie O sunglasses and marched up to me.

"I wish you wouldn't feed that homeless fellow outside. Honestly, Florrie, you're only encouraging him to continue that lifestyle. He needs to go to a shelter where they can help him. Not to mention that he's hurting the store's image by hanging around here every morning."

I recoiled. "He's a nice man, Helen. Please don't make any trouble for him."

"Well, I don't like him being here. He gives me the creeps."

I set her to work organizing the books that had just arrived.

She heaved a huge sigh before she bent to open the boxes.

"I'll do that," Bob volunteered.

Helen wandered to the door and looked out.

"What's with her?" I hissed to Bob.

Helen must have heard me because she turned around. "I had the best time with my new honey, but now he hasn't called me. Not for two whole days. It was so nice to have a vacation from work. We could have spent more time together. We could have taken a drive out in the country or . . ."

Oh good grief. I tuned her out. A man was murdered in the bookstore. The owner was in jail, and she was moony over some guy she barely knew? "If you're going to stare out the window, why don't you change the display windows and freshen them up? Feature coloring books and colored pencils in one, and books by Emily Branscom in the other."

She groaned.

But at that moment, Zsazsa and Goldblum bounded in.

Zsazsa spread her arms wide and twirled like Julie Andrews had in the mountains in *The Sound of Music.* "The smell of books and coffee—I'm home!"

Goldblum grinned at her.

"And who's this? A cat! Every bookstore needs a cat." Zsazsa reached out to pet Peaches, who was sitting at attention next to the cash register as if she were an Egyptian cat statue.

Peaches purred so loud we could all hear her over the music.

"That's my kitty, Peaches. She's not a permanent employee, but I thought I'd bring her in and see how she does. She's acting a little different in our new quarters."

"That's nothing to worry about. We all need time to adjust to a new home. Especially cats. They're so sensitive." Zsazsa helped herself to coffee.

Peaches jumped down to the floor and followed Zsazsa as she ambled through the bookstore.

"Has my special order arrived?" asked Goldblum.

Bob pointed his forefinger in the air. "I was just unpacking it. *Murder in the Nineteenth Century?*"

"Precisely."

A woman walked in looking for books on seventeenth-century Paris. I led her to the section where she would find them. Just like that, we were up and running again.

The morning progressed smoothly until Sergeant Jonquille

stopped by. His presence shouldn't have made me nervous, but he looked so serious.

"I just came by to tell you that the fingerprints we took from the professor's house didn't turn up on any of the databases we checked. In fact, there was a surprising absence of fingerprints, which suggests that the burglar wore gloves. It was probably someone who has done that before."

"Oh please! Even I know to wear gloves," I cried.

He tried to hide a laugh. "So do you have any alternate suspects for me yet?"

I was ashamed to realize that I had concentrated on reopening the bookstore instead of the poor professor, who was rotting away in jail. I wasn't about to admit that I didn't have any super leads. "Delbert ruined his roommate's career. If anyone wanted to kill him, Lance Devereoux certainly had a good motive."

"Why murder him here in the bookstore?"

He had a point. "I don't know. It's bizarre that Delbert was here at all. It raises so many questions. Like whether he had a key and knew the alarm password. And whether he invited his killer to join him."

Jonquille shot me a coy look. "Or whether his uncle caught him in the bookstore."

I raised my chin in defiance. "Even if he had, Maxwell wouldn't have murdered him. Hey, do you know a big, burly guy with a butterfly tattoo just above his elbow?"

Jonquille raised his eyebrows. "I don't think so. Did something happen with a guy like that?"

"He was asking questions about Delbert."

Now I had Jonquille's interest. "He asked you questions?"

"No, he was asking around at Club Neon."

"Don't tell me *you* go to that place."

Every fiber of my being wanted to pretend to be cool. "I've been there."

"Well, stay away from big, burly guys with butterfly tattoos, okay?"

And then it happened. An event I had never considered. My mother and Norman's mom, Mrs. Spratt, walked into Color Me Read and marched right up to me.

"Florrie!" cried my mom. "Why didn't you tell me you were seeing someone?"

Chapter 20

I stared at my mother in shock. Norman must have told his mother, who blabbed to my mom. Unfortunately, Mrs. Spratt was now standing right beside my mother, her eyes trained on me, waiting to hear my answer. I couldn't tell my mother the truth in front of her friend without insulting Mrs. Spratt and creating havoc. Why wasn't I better at lying? I felt the moment of silence stretching out as I cast about for a response. "The relationship isn't that far along yet, Mom. We're not quite ready to meet families."

Mom looked at me with disbelief. "Still, you could have told me. What else don't I know?"

Why hadn't I prepared for this? Drat that Norman!

"Who is this lucky young man?" asked Norman's mom.

I scrambled for a plausible response. "Just someone I met in the bookstore."

They raised their eyebrows.

"I presume he has a name?"

Ouch! My mom was good at making a point through sarcasm.

Jonquille stepped up beside me. He held his hand out to

Mom and Mrs. Spratt. "Sergeant Eric Jonquille. Mrs. Fox, I see where Florrie gets her wit."

Mom actually blushed and giggled like a schoolgirl! "You're Florrie's mystery man?"

To my complete amazement, he nodded. I should have been grateful, but I was paralyzed with fear at what might happen next.

"A police officer," Mom gushed. "I'm so glad Florrie has someone in law enforcement looking out for her after Delbert's murder and all."

Jonquille wrapped an arm around my shoulders. "I'm keeping a close eye on her."

Norman's mom had blanched. I owed Jonquille big-time. He had saved my bacon.

Mom smiled. "Would it be too forward of me to invite you to a family cookout, Sergeant? Florrie's sister is bringing her new beau. We're eager to meet him. I know my husband would like to meet you, as well."

Jonquille didn't miss a beat. "That sounds great, Mrs. Fox. Thank you for including me."

I shot him a glance. "We'll talk about it, Mom. We don't want to rush anything."

When they left, my mother beamed. Mrs. Spratt, on the other hand, was clearly not thrilled by her son's competition.

The door shut behind them, and I realized I had been holding my breath. I released a mouthful of air. "Thanks for bailing me out. That was nice of you."

"My mom does the same thing. More to my sister than to me." He raised the pitch of his voice to mimic his mother. "Darcy, your cousin Loulabelle is younger than you, and she's getting married!"

I laughed at his portrayal. "Do you really have a cousin named Loulabelle?"

"Her real name is Louisa, but she's the cousin we all hate.

Do you have one of those? Always made straight As in school. Won the science contests. Was head cheerleader and homecoming queen. No matter what *we* did, we were always compared to her."

"Oh yuck. You'd *have* to resent someone who was perfect like that."

"Your mom seemed to like me, but that other lady was pretty upset."

"She has delusions that I will marry her son and live miserably ever after. The awful thing is that I lied to him. I made up a relationship just to get rid of him. Word obviously got back to my mom and that's why she now thinks I'm seeing someone."

"He can't be that bad. Is he a lech?"

"No. He's just . . ." I hated to say it, because people could say the same about me. "A bore."

Jonquille laughed. "Could be worse, I guess. So do you want me to attend this family gathering?"

"It's nice of you to offer, but you don't have to go through that charade. I'm actually very uncomfortable lying, which is probably why I'm not good at it. Especially to my parents. They're really wonderful people. There isn't anything I wouldn't do for them or my sister. What is it they say about lies? One begets another? Well, this lie stops here." I looked at my watch. "I'll give Mom enough time to have lunch, ditch Mrs. Spratt, and go home. Then I'll call and tell her the truth. How she and Dad handle it with the Spratts is up to them, but I'll be in the clear and won't have to worry about it anymore."

Jonquille looked at me with those delphinium-blue eyes, and I had the feeling that he approved. "I better get back out on the street. Call me if you need a pretend boyfriend."

I couldn't help laughing. "Thanks for coming by. And for saving me from myself."

He hadn't even reached the door when Helen sidled up to

me. "It didn't take you long to move on. Maxwell has only been in jail for a few days."

I shook my head like a wet dog. "What?"

"Florrie, you don't have to pretend with me. We girls have to stick together. Besides, everyone knew about you and Maxwell."

I turned to face her. "Knew what?"

"That you were living with him."

I froze. "People think I was having a romantic relationship with the professor?"

"You don't have to pretend anymore, Florrie. We all know about it."

"Eww. Eww, eww, eww. He's almost forty years older than me. Old enough to be my grandfather. Have you lost your mind?"

Helen brushed back a strand of her gleaming hair. "May-September romances are nothing new."

"Let's get this straight. I did *not* move in with Maxwell, nor was I involved in a romantic anything with him. Where on earth did you get a ridiculous idea like that?"

Helen cocked her head. "Are you denying that you live with Maxwell?"

"Yes, I am. I live in the carriage house on the rear of the property."

She had the nerve to wink at me. "How very convenient. Wish I had known he was open to younger women."

"Oh, that's just revolting. What is wrong with you? I work for the man. That's all."

"That's not what Detective-Sergeant Zielony thinks."

"Zielony?" I sputtered. I rubbed my temples as things became clear to me. His visit to me in the guesthouse. His desire to look at my bedroom. Jonquille's surprise that I had never been in Maxwell's bedroom. I gasped. "They all think that."

Helen clucked at me. "Did you really believe that you two could keep it a secret?"

"It's not a secret!" I blurted. "It's not true!"

"Don't get so upset. Your face is all red. Maybe you should have a cold drink to calm down."

I felt like I had been broadsided. But I could imagine how it had happened. Maxwell's sister, Liddy, probably planted the idea in the cops' heads.

"I'm sorry that he's locked up," said Helen, who obviously did not believe me. "I don't understand why it's so hard to find a nice guy."

Bob was talking with a customer, not too far from us. Poor guy, he wasn't flashy enough for Helen.

"Too bad that guy you like didn't call you. Maybe it's just as well and you should move on."

Helen fingered her pearls and spoke wistfully. "We went out twice, and he was so nice. Very attentive and humorous. And so cute! I thought he was attracted to me."

"Nice pearls, Helen." I couldn't help thinking of the pearl I had found on the landing.

"Do you like them?" She leaned over and whispered, "They're fake. I prefer to wear my real ones, but I couldn't resist these."

"They're lovely." I couldn't help wondering if something had happened to her real pearls. "I can't recall, Helen, did you know Delbert?"

"Only socially."

My radar went to alert status. "You dated him?"

"Nothing like that. I saw him around town. You know, where people hang out."

"Like Club Neon?"

"One of my girlfriends says DC is slim pickings for men our age. No wonder you went for someone older and more sophisticated."

I didn't bother denying it any longer. She clearly wasn't going to believe me no matter what I said. "Tell me about Delbert."

"I didn't find him that attractive in the beginning. But he was a smooth talker. He had a talent for engaging people and charming them. Before long, I was drawn to his charisma. He had a personal magnetism that was alluring."

How could that be? "He was dreadful to me!"

She shrugged. "He probably didn't like you getting cozy with his uncle. He had a lot to lose if Maxwell left everything to you."

Huh? Was that what people thought? Crazy! It was sheer nonsense. I shook off the insanity of that notion and focused. Delbert must have known how to turn on the charm. How could he have taken advantage of so many people otherwise?

Did Helen have a reason to murder Delbert? Could she have stabbed him with a spear? She didn't have a motive that I knew of. Had she wanted to impress Delbert by letting him into the bookstore after hours? It wasn't outside of the realm of possibilities.

The moment Helen left to help a customer, Zsazsa sidled up to me and whispered in my ear, "We have information."

Chapter 21

Zsazsa crooked her finger at me. I followed her upstairs to the very room on the second floor where I had spoken with the professor after Delbert's murder. Goldblum, Frodo, and Peaches waited for us.

Zsazsa closed the door and motioned me to chairs they had pulled up to a table. "We have been doing some investigating."

Goldblum leaned in and spoke in a hushed voice. "A bit of clever questioning of Bankhouse has revealed that Helen was fired from her last job because—"

Zsazsa interrupted him. "She flipped out!"

"What happened?" Helen might be grouchy at times, but I hadn't seen any signs of aberrant behavior.

Goldblum placed his elbow on the table and spoke confidentially. "She was a personal shopper at a very high-end clothing store, and it seems she was stalking one of their clients."

"The gentleman in question was flattered at first. But his mother found out and became afraid for him," said Zsazsa.

"Why would the professor have hired her?" I held up my palms. "Don't bother, I know exactly why. He believes in second chances. Did the guy bring charges against her?"

"No! That's the thing that's so intriguing," said Goldblum. "There's a very good chance that Maxwell knew nothing of this. Apparently, the guy was from a prominent family and they didn't want any publicity. Bankhouse and his wife did a little begging and promised to get help for Helen. So the police probably don't even know about it."

I sat back in my chair. "I never imagined anything like that. But it fits in a way. She seems obsessed with finding a boyfriend. She's interested in one of our customers. Maybe we should institute a rule about not dating customers."

Zsazsa snorted. "That would be impossible to enforce. How would you know if someone dated a customer? Would that include socializing in groups? Attending the same lecture?"

"Of course, this information doesn't tie her to Delbert's murder," I pointed out. "But it turns out she did know him."

"Really?" Goldblum's little round face looked mischievous. "What if the man she was stalking was Delbert Woodley?"

"That would change everything," hissed Zsazsa.

"But that's just speculation. And it would be a wild coincidence." I shook my head. "It would be highly unlikely. Though I could see her trying to impress Delbert by bringing him here."

Goldblum and Zsazsa exchanged a glance.

"We have an alternative theory," said Zsazsa. "The man who shops here and caught Helen's eye—what if it was Delbert?"

"That would explain why he didn't call her." I waved my hands like I was mentally erasing the thought. "That's impossible. She knows Delbert was murdered. She wouldn't still be talking about how he didn't call. No. No way."

"Not unless that was her devious way of deflecting suspicion. Did you notice that Bankhouse didn't show up today?" asked Goldblum.

I stood up. "I love both of you, and I'm all for thinking

outside of the box. But I fear you're grasping at anything. Bankhouse's absence thus far today doesn't mean a thing. Maybe he had a class."

"He's not teaching this summer," said Zsazsa.

"Then maybe he had a dental appointment. My point is that there are millions of plausible reasons for him not showing up today."

They looked so dejected. I had to say something to cheer them up. "But you did an amazing job of uncovering the story behind Helen's employment. It doesn't necessarily tie Helen to Delbert's murder, but it does show that she's capable of questionable and unsavory behavior. Do either of you know if she had a motive for the murder?"

Goldblum's mouth shifted to the side with dissatisfaction. "Mmmf. We're back to the drawing board."

I excused myself and went back to work. I now understood why Helen hadn't wanted anyone to know what had happened. I would never see her quite the same way again. And while it didn't tie her to Delbert's death in any credible way that I could think of, it did cast doubt on her judgment and temperament.

In the middle of the afternoon, I took a quick break to call my mom and confess that I had lied to Norman.

I winced at the sound of Mom's quick intake of breath when I told her the truth.

"Oh, Florrie! You should have warned me. What on earth are we going to tell the Spratts now?"

"You see my problem. I didn't want to hurt Norman's feelings. It seemed like an easy way to discourage him."

"So you're not dating that cute cop?"

"I'm afraid not. He was just being a good egg and trying to help me out of the muddle I had created."

"Darling, I'm glad you came clean and told me the truth, but now you've simply handed your problem to me."

I cringed. I guessed I had. "Maybe they won't bring it up again. Or you could tell them that you don't know because I'm very private about my relationships, which wouldn't be a lie."

"You *are* still coming to the cookout for Veronica and her new friend on Sunday, aren't you?"

"Will the Spratts be there?"

"Of course."

"With Norman?"

Mom giggled. "Maybe you'd better bring that nice cop to deflect Norman's interest. Sweetheart, would you mind baking one of your lovely desserts?"

"Of course not. Something fruity for summertime?"

"That sounds perfect."

I hung up thinking it was too bad Norman wasn't Helen's type and vice versa. That would solve both of their problems.

There was no sign of the guard when I went home that night. Maybe he was patrolling the other side of the mansion. I considered checking on Mr. DuBois, but it was after ten and I didn't want to wake him. Peaches was meowing so loud in her carrier that I had to let her out before I did anything else.

I turned the key and swung the door open in haste. Frodo ran inside and disappeared behind the kitchen island. I closed the door and opened the cat carrier. Peaches raced out and followed Frodo.

It only took seconds for me to see what had interested them.

A woman lay on the floor of the kitchen.

Chapter 22

I rushed toward her before I thought to check for a person who might be lurking in the house after hurting her. Hesitating for mere seconds, I scanned the rest of the room but didn't see anyone.

"Don't touch the fridge," she mumbled.

I dropped to my knees and looked closer. "Jacquie Lieb-haber?" What was the famous author doing on my floor?

"Don't touch the fridge," she repeated.

"Are you okay? Can I help you up?"

She nodded slowly. "Help me sit. But don't touch the fridge."

I reached under her arms and gently pulled her into a sitting position. "Don't let Kittikins touch the fridge, either. It will kill her."

"Kittikins? Do you mean Peaches?"

Peaches circled Jacquie, rubbing her head against her.

"Cute name."

"What's wrong with the fridge?"

"I don't know. It shocked me." Her eyes widened. "Did you arrange for it to do that?"

She wasn't making sense. "Did you collapse? Maybe I should call 911."

"*No!*" Jacquie leaned away from me. "Please don't do that, Florrie. I'll be fine."

"You know my name."

"Maxwell talks about you with such warmth. He has total faith in you."

That was lovely to hear, but I felt like I had let him down because I hadn't managed to find the real killer yet. "What happened?"

"I grabbed the door handle and a shock surged through me. It knocked me to the floor. I think I might have passed out."

"Let me see your hand."

She held her right palm up. Sure enough, it was blistered from the burn. I could see the line of the handle. "I don't want to scare you but that looks pretty ugly. I'll take you to the emergency room. My car is right outside."

"No," she breathed. "No, I'm much safer here."

There were so many thoughts running through my head that I barely knew where to start. The only thing I knew for sure was that she wasn't a threat to me.

"Are you strong enough to walk to the sofa?"

She nodded. "I think so." She grasped my arms while I tried to help her stand. She grunted in a most unladylike fashion that didn't seem like her at all. "Good heavens! It really knocked the stuffing out of me."

She leaned on me to walk to the sofa. "Better call a repairman before you accidentally touch the refrigerator door."

When she sat down, Peaches jumped into her lap and Frodo did his best to vie for her attention.

I retrieved hydrogen peroxide and nonstick gauze for her hand. While I gently cleaned it, I asked, "Is there someone I should call? Your husband, maybe?"

"*No!*" Her eyes widened. "No one can know."

I gazed up at her. There was no mistaking the terror she felt. "There's a private investigator looking for you."

"He came here?"

I nodded. "There must be someone you can trust. A sister? A best friend?"

"My best friend is in jail." She gripped my wrist. "All I have is you, Florrie. I realize that you don't know me, but I need your help. I never meant to involve you. If I hadn't been shocked by the refrigerator, I would have been gone by the time you got home. I'm so sorry, honey. But I beg of you—no one can know that you saw me. Okay? Please?"

Her desperation horrified me. What if I were in her shoes? What if I couldn't go to my sister or my parents? What would I do? But as I thought about it, I wondered what she had done that made it necessary for her to be in hiding. "What happened, Jacquie? What did you do?"

"Aside from marrying the wrong man, I didn't do anything. The law isn't after me if that's what you're worried about." Her grip tightened. "Swear to me that you won't tell anyone you saw me."

I hoped she wasn't lying about not breaking the law. "Tell me the truth," I said. "Were you involved in the murder of Delbert Woodley?"

"Ugh. I loathed that snake. I suppose you know he stole some of my books and passed them off as his own, otherwise you wouldn't be asking. He was a miserable louse, who will probably show up in one of my books one day under another name, but I didn't kill him. I wouldn't dream of doing time in prison for ridding the world of that vermin. He wasn't worth losing *my* life and freedom over."

I believed her.

"Please, Florrie. I have to figure out how to emerge from this mess unscathed. Promise me that you won't breathe a word to anyone."

I nodded. "I promise."

Her fingers relaxed, but her eyes were trained on mine like she was trying to tell if I was being honest.

"Are you okay here by yourself?" I asked. "I don't know which electrician the professor uses. I'll have to run over to the mansion to see if I can find a phone number."

"Used to be Alan Pettigrew. You'll find his number in the Rolodex on Maxwell's desk in the library."

Out of an abundance of caution, I fetched Peaches's carrier, lifted her off Jacquie's lap, and put her inside, apologizing for having to lock her up. "It's for your own safety."

Frodo still wore his leash. I picked the end up off the floor. "I'll be right back," I said to Jacquie.

She reached out and grasped my hand. "Florrie, I know this is all bizarre, but I'm not here. Do you understand? Please don't tell anyone. Not even the guard. I'm trusting you, sweetheart. If they find me, they'll kill me, and it will look like an accident."

It struck me that she wasn't being melodramatic. She meant what she had said.

Locking the door behind me, I hurried across the pavement to the mansion. The guard and a nurse I had never met before were eating pizza in the kitchen.

I greeted them briefly and made a beeline to the library. Amazingly, exactly as Jacquie predicted, I found Alan Pettigrew's number in Maxwell's Rolodex under *electrician*.

It was closing on eleven o'clock at night. I wondered if Alan took calls this late. Using the phone on the desk, I called him.

A man answered in a booming voice. "Maxwell! I thought you were in the slammer!"

He obviously had caller ID. "I'm afraid the professor is still in jail. This is Florrie Fox, his assistant."

"That's too bad. I wish they would let him go."

"I hope you don't mind me calling so late. It seems we have a dangerous situation."

"What's the problem?"

"I'm told the refrigerator is somehow electrified. It shocked a guest."

"Sounds like a short. I'll be there in half an hour."

"Thank you! That's wonderful."

Stopping by the kitchen on my way out, I informed the guard that we were expecting an Alan Pettigrew.

He nodded calmly and continued eating, which didn't do much to build my confidence in the fellow. But I thought I'd better get back to Jacquie. She was in no shape to be alone.

I unlocked the door and stepped inside. I took care to throw the bolt on the door, but when I turned around, there was no sign of Jacquie.

Chapter 23

Treading lightly, I approached the sofa. What if she had died? My heart pounded as I neared. But Jacquie wasn't on the sofa or the floor.

I let Frodo off his leash. Turning slowly in a complete circle, I scanned the room. There was no sign of her. None! The only key that she had been there was poor Peaches, crouched in her carrier.

I couldn't help wondering if the refrigerator really had a short. It was vaguely tempting to touch it to find out, but something had certainly knocked Jacquie for a loop. And Alan was on the way. I would know soon enough without taking the risk of touching it.

I opened a French door and ventured into the garden. It was dark as pitch in the corners. If Jacquie were out there, I couldn't tell. But she wasn't in any of the logical places, like at the dining table, or in a chaise lounge. I checked the gate, but the bolt held the door securely closed. She couldn't have left that way because the bolt could only be closed from the inside.

I returned to the carriage house, closed the door behind me, and made sure it was locked. I stood quietly and listened. I heard nothing but the ticking of my clocks.

With my cell phone securely in hand, I grabbed the heavy fireplace poker and tiptoed up the stairs slowly. Frodo didn't appreciate my caution and sprang ahead. The lights were off, so I flicked them on as I went.

When I reached the top, I felt an utter fool. There was no one in the bedroom, under the bed, in the closet, in the bathroom, or behind the shower curtain.

I perched on the side of the bed. It couldn't have been a dream. I was still dressed in the clothes I had worn to work. It was like a locked door mystery. Except it wasn't. Jacquie could easily have left by the front door of the carriage house. But I had unlocked it when I returned, hadn't I? Maybe I had thought it was locked, but it wasn't?

If she left by the front door, then she might not have made it very far in her weakened condition.

I scrambled down the stairs, still looking around in case she had collapsed somewhere. I grabbed my flashlight and was out the door with Frodo on his leash again. This time, I took great care to be sure the door was locked.

Flashlight on, I hurried out to the street. The streetlights were bright enough to see if a person were lying on the sidewalk. Still, I walked along, shining the beam in the bushes and gardens close to the sidewalk. After a couple of blocks, I crossed the street and repeated my search on the other side, going past the mansion in the other direction for another two blocks.

I was officially certifiable. I had lost my mind. Jacquie was missing, but there wasn't a reason in the world that she would have turned up in my kitchen. How could she have gotten in? Why would she have even tried?

The short. The short would be my test. If there were a short in the refrigerator, then I would know she had been there. That was logical. I wouldn't have known about it any other way. If the refrigerator had nothing wrong with it, then well, I was hallucinating or dreaming or something.

Feeling a hair apprehensive because either way something was very wrong, I strolled back to the carriage house just as a truck pulled into the driveway.

A tall, slender man stepped out. "Are you Florrie?"

I held out my hand and shook his. "Thank you so much for coming at this late hour."

"Not a problem. Technically I'm retired, but I have a few old clients who call me now and then. Gets me out of the house. Where's this refrigerator?"

I unlocked the door and showed him in.

"I always liked this place with the beams and all those French doors. Don't find gems like this in town too much anymore." He walked over to the tiny broom closet and opened an electrical box. "It didn't flip the circuit breaker like it should have if there was a short." He reached inside, and I heard a click, which I presumed was the breaker.

"You've been to the carriage house before?"

He smiled at me. "Honey, I wired this whole building back when it was built. There's not a thing I don't know about it."

As he pulled out the refrigerator to look at it, I realized that I wouldn't have known his name if Jacquie hadn't told me. I would have found it in the Rolodex, but I had known it before I went to the mansion. That was proof of her presence.

"So you knew Jacquie," I said.

"Lovely woman. My favorite of all Maxwell's wives." He looked over at me and winked. "I think she was Maxwell's favorite, too. It's a real shame that they parted. Didn't like the third wife one bit. For all his money and advantages in life, Maxwell was always very down to earth. Never has put on airs or acted superior like some wealthy people do. I sure hope somebody figures out who murdered his nephew. One thing's for sure—it wasn't Maxwell."

He grew quiet for a moment. "How's your friend?"

"I think she'll be okay." It wasn't a lie. I hoped she would be fine.

"She's very lucky. This could have killed her."

"How can something like that happen?"

"Looks like somebody crossed the wires. Either someone didn't have a clue what he was doing or"—his eyes met mine—"someone did it on purpose."

"I open that refrigerator all the time!"

He nodded. "It's perfectly safe now. You don't have to worry."

I hesitated to ask, but I had to know the truth. "Just to be clear, the crossed wires were probably like that for a long time? But the shock only kicked in now?"

Alan looked me straight in the eyes. "When is the last time you opened the refrigerator?"

"Early this morning."

"Have any workmen come in today?"

"No. This is beginning to sound like some kind of intentional hit."

His eyes flicked toward the fridge. "I'd guess that someone rigged the wires between the time you opened the door this morning and the time your friend touched the door tonight."

Chapter 24

I shivered at the thought. Someone had gained access to the carriage house during my absence. Actually, two people had—Jacquie and this unknown person who crossed the wires. But no one could have known she would be sneaking in for food. She had known about the security guard, so she must have been watching and waiting for him to leave.

The person who intentionally caused a short in the refrigerator must have planned ahead. Whoever it was couldn't have known Jacquie would be the one who opened the door.

My pulse raced. That dangerous door was meant for me.

"Should you check the other appliances and the ones in the mansion?"

"Might be a good idea."

He handed me a laminated card. "This was behind the refrigerator. Probably a previous tenant."

I recognized the face on the card immediately—Emily Branscom, the local author and historian. It was a gym membership card, dated this year. I thanked him and tried to hide my surprise.

Had Emily lived here? Perhaps she had been a guest and had dropped it. What had Zsazsa said about her? She was having an affair. An affair so discreet that no one knew the identity of her lover. I had a feeling I knew who he was now. Maxwell.

I fetched my purse and located the phone number Jonquille had given me.

Despite the late hour, he sounded wide awake when he answered the phone. He had wanted concrete evidence, and I had it. "Something suspicious has happened here. Could you come over? There's someone I'd like you to talk to."

"Are you at the store?"

"No. I'm at home, in the carriage house."

"I'll be right there."

While I waited for him, I debated what to say. I had already told Alan that a friend was here. I couldn't backtrack on that. Jonquille might push me on it. Should I tell him it was Jacquie Liebhaber? She had said she was counting on me and that it was a matter of life or death.

I had a desire to keep her secret. Even though I didn't know her, I had read her books and felt a kinship to her. Like she was a friend. It was entirely irrational. Authors were just like everyone else, and it was possible that she was peculiar. Could she be carrying out some kind of personal drama? She hadn't given me that impression. No one could fake that kind of fear. Could they?

Or maybe I felt I owed her an allegiance because she had been married to Maxwell. That made no sense, either. Delbert had been his nephew, and I had no allegiance to him whatsoever.

True to his word, Jonquille arrived in fifteen minutes. I introduced him to Alan, who explained what he had found.

Jonquille gazed around. "Where's your friend?"

"She left."

He turned his attention to Alan. "There's no possibility that the wires were crossed months ago and it only now became dangerous?"

"This wasn't some frayed wire that was rubbing on something and getting progressively worse. This was cross-wired,"
said Alan. "It had to have been done recently."

"Now do you believe that the burglary of the mansion was
connected to Delbert's death?" I asked Jonquille.

Jonquille took a deep breath. "Who would want to kill you?"

I stared at him with annoyance. "No one!" But my heart
still raced, and a wave of queasiness washed over me.

"Where was the guard? I'd like to speak with him or her.
Will you be okay here with Alan?" he asked.

"Maybe I should go with you."

We walked over to the mansion. I didn't need to use my
key because the back door was unlocked.

Jonquille wiped an impatient hand over his brow and shook
his head. He marched into the kitchen and very politely spoke
with the nurse and the guard, asking what time they went on
duty. Both of them had been there since seven p.m.

I knew for a fact that the guard had been lounging comfortably in the kitchen since I came over to call Alan. Had I
been braver, I would have pointed that out. But it turned out
that I didn't need to.

Jonquille asked, "Which one of you ordered the pizza?"

Each of them pointed at the other.

"Oldest trick in the book," said Jonquille. He lifted the box
top and read the name on it. *Pizza Man.*

The guard seemed nervous. "Listen, I need this job. So I
messed up. I thought—"

Jonquille interrupted him. "No you didn't. You didn't
think at all. You're lucky no one was killed."

While Jonquille called his buddy at the security company
for a replacement, I slinked back to Mr. DuBois's room to look
in on him.

I cracked the door to a dark room.

DuBois screamed. "Help me. Someone help me!"

I flicked on the light. He was sitting up in bed holding the covers in his hands pulled up to his chin.

"It's just Florrie, Mr. DuBois." I strode to his side. "What are you so afraid of?"

"It's his meds. Happens to old folks," said the nurse from the doorway. "Nothing to worry about."

I reached out for Mr. DuBois's hand and clutched it in mine. "Would you prefer to sleep with a night-light? Would you feel safer?"

Some of the fear in his eyes melted away.

"What if I read to you for a while?" I switched on a light and checked out titles on his bookshelves. How about a Jacquie Liebhaber book?"

Jonquille looked in on us as I settled into a chair next to the bed, opened the book, and read.

I never dreamt that I might find myself on the wrong side of the law. Up to that moment, I had always done the right thing. Had been a devoted wife and doting mother. But I hadn't met evil. Hadn't understood that sometimes, the only way to save oneself was to eliminate the Earl of Darkness.

Wearing black clothes and a dark scarf covering my copper curls, I pulled the oven forward and crossed the wires. . . .

Jonquille seized the book from my hands. He scanned the first few pages. "This is like a blueprint for what happened at the carriage house!"

It was worse than that because the woman who had written it was the one who had been injured. Unless it had all been a hoax. It couldn't have been, though, because Alan confirmed that the wires were crossed. What had she said? They would kill her and make it look like an accident. I was torn about whether to tell Jonquille about Jacquie's visit.

She needed help. But there wasn't anything Jonquille could do for her now that she had left. And knowing that she had been here wouldn't change anything, either. I had promised her, and for the time being at any rate, I couldn't see the benefit in spilling her secret. For all I knew, it could somehow make matters worse for her.

When we returned to the carriage house, Alan had finished methodically checking the wiring of the major appliances.

"You're sure we're safe now?" I asked.

"Positive. Everything else was perfect. It was just the refrigerator that was wired wrong."

I let Peaches out of her carrier. If Jonquille hadn't been with me, I would have been tempted to go over to the mansion to do some snooping. Something was going on that I didn't understand. Maybe I could find a clue there.

When Alan left, Jonquille said, "If it's okay with you, I'd like to sleep on your sofa tonight. They're sending a different guard out, but I would feel better if I were here with you."

My head reeled. Okay, so he had the most amazing blue eyes in the world. He was still something of a stranger to me. On the other hand, I would probably sleep better if I knew he was downstairs. It was very late. I could still drive out to my parents' house but they were surely sound asleep by now, and it would wake them if I arrived.

Jonquille tilted his head. "You're not saying anything."

I took a deep breath. "I'm not used to things like this happening to me. It's all a little strange. I'm used to being a bit of a bore."

Jonquille laughed aloud. "Florrie Fox, you are anything but a bore."

"Could I offer you a glass of wine?"

"Ordinarily I would say yes. However, I'd prefer to be on the ball tonight. Just in case. Don't look so worried! I don't think anything will happen. But I'd rather err on the side of caution. How about a soda or some water?"

I poured sparkling blackberry juice into glasses for both of us. We settled in the great room, with Frodo at my feet, and Peaches prowling.

"I don't really know anything about you," I said. "Did you grow up around here?"

"I'm from Paris."

I blinked at him.

"Paris, Virginia." He smiled. "That never gets old. It's a tiny place not too far outside DC. My mom is an artist and my dad is a chef who has a restaurant out that way. They live on a pretend farm with unruly goats, chickens that lay eggs with yolks the color of orange marigolds, a couple of rescued cows and horses, five cats, and a one-eyed dog named Jack. I have two brothers and two sisters, and that's about it."

"A pretend farm?"

"They don't actually farm, except for one section of farm-to-table veggies that my dad serves. Mostly they just collect animals who need homes and run up extravagant veterinary bills."

"They sound like wonderful people."

"I'm fairly fond of them," he said with a twinkle in his eyes. "But I'm worried about you."

"Me, too. I don't understand why anyone would want to harm me. I had nothing to do with Delbert's murder."

Jonquille quizzed me about who might be angry with me. I had no answers.

I was beat and we both had work in the morning, so I reluctantly went up to bed sooner than I'd have liked. It was late and I was exhausted, but wired by Jonquille's presence and the horrible thought that someone had now targeted me. I snuggled on the bed with Peaches and Frodo, and sketched Jacquie's face with colored pencils. She was probably in her seventies, but her face was remarkably unlined. Either she'd had work done or she took very good care of her skin. I ought to take a cue from that. She hadn't worn a stitch of makeup but still looked good.

In every photo I had seen of her, she had worn her blond hair in a perfect shoulder length bob. But when I saw her today, it was wavy and unruly, as if she hadn't blown it dry. Maybe that was her usual look when she wasn't blown dry, styled, and primped for being photographed?

Her clothes had been unusual, too. She had been dressed in a snow-white oversized man's button-down shirt with the sleeves rolled up, and a pair of cutoff jeans that didn't fit her well, with high-heeled shoes.

As I added details to the sketch, I reviewed what I knew for sure about Jacquie, which was precious little. Trying to sort what she had claimed from what was verifiable, I drew as I thought it all through.

I doodled the lock on my door because she was able to gain access to the carriage house while I was out. Next to it, I drew a key. Would she still have one? Maybe the lock had never been changed? Maybe there had been a key in a hiding place somewhere that I didn't know about?

She'd said she was looking for food. I sketched the refrigerator and a sandwich with frilly lettuce sticking out of it. I believed her story because the burn on her hand proved she had touched the refrigerator door handle.

And finally, I knew she was "missing" and that a private investigator had been hired to find her.

To me, it all added up to one thing. She was on the run, hiding from someone. She had said she was safe here. And she didn't want me to call her husband. Was he the person from whom she was running? But hadn't she said *they*—plural?

I was sorry she had left. Not because I wanted to attract whatever trouble was following her, but because I hated to think of her out on the street, dodging between shadows lest she be seen. I hoped she had another safe place to take refuge.

It was two in the morning before I had calmed down enough to try to sleep. Even then, I lay awake for a long time, thinking about Jacquie. She appeared to have a great life, but under the surface, something was very, very wrong.

Despite the late night, I was up early in the morning, eager to get going. After a shower, I dressed for work in a simple coral top and a full skirt that reminded me of an impressionist painting of huge blooms in corals, pinks, oranges, reds, and a splash of turquoise.

I smelled coffee as I was walking down the stairs.

"How do you like your eggs?" asked Jonquille.

"I like them every way possible. But you don't have to cook me breakfast."

"Scrambled it is. Are you one of those people who doesn't eat breakfast?" he asked.

"No, I always have a bite to eat in the morning." I pulled out the wild blueberry buns and placed one on each of the two plates he had set out.

"I'm glad you were up early. I have two hours to zoom home, shower, and get to work."

After feeding Peaches, I carried the plates out to the garden. Jonquille followed me with mugs of coffee.

Birds twittered in the trees, and the sun glinted on the goldfish in the pond. Frodo roamed, probably sniffing out squirrel tracks.

"I can see why you like living here. Most of us peons who live in the city don't have any outdoor space. My apartment is fine but it's not much more than a place to sleep, shower, and do laundry. On the other hand"—he grinned—"it's very close to work."

"I would say you're welcome to come over here and enjoy the garden, but I think I'll be bunking with my parents for a while."

"You're afraid to live here?"

I hated to admit it, but I nodded and sipped the coffee. I didn't back off from a challenge, but I wasn't gutsy like Veronica and my mom. Besides, this was different. "It sounds terrible, but when Delbert was murdered, I thought I could relax and enjoy this place. But those switched wires on the refrigerator"—I paused and considered my words carefully so I wouldn't imply that Jacquie had been here—"mean that someone gained access to the carriage house while I was out. Even with a guard on duty. And here's the bigger thing—why would anyone want to kill me? Honestly, Jonquille—"

He interrupted me. "You can call me Eric."

I smiled at him. "Honestly, Eric, I'm no angel, but I haven't done anything that would agitate anyone. I'm actually a very quiet, uninteresting person." As I said that, an image of Delbert's mother Liddy shouting at me in the mansion foyer jumped into my head.

"You're anything but uninteresting, Florrie." Jonquille finished the last bite of his eggs. "Here's the thing. I think you'll be safer here. What if the person who is after you follows you to your parents' house? What then?"

I hadn't thought about it that way. I would feel safer at home with my parents, but would I be leading someone there and putting my parents in danger?

"Don't look so dismayed. Felipe will be here shortly. I'm calling the guard service again this morning. They need to understand that this isn't just a babysitting job where the guard can sit around in the kitchen and flirt with the nurse. I don't mean to sound crass, but is there a way Maxwell could pay for some cameras? This is a big place, but there are some very cool and uncomplicated video cameras we could set up around the property. All we need is an iPhone or an iPad to hook them up to. That way we can watch more areas at one time."

This was sounding very appealing. "I think I can talk Maxwell's attorney into something like that. Plus, if the guy comes back, maybe we can identify him from the video."

"Call me when you get the okay, and I'll have a buddy of mine set it up. And, if I'm not being too forward, I can sleep over on the sofa for the time being."

It took a lot of willpower not to jump up and hug him. But from the grin on his face, I gathered my expression had conveyed my gratitude. "Thanks, Eric."

"In the meantime, I'm going to show you a little trick that private investigators sometimes use."

Jonquille rose and strolled through the garden. He returned with the dried stem from a spent flower. "We need thirteen of these."

I roamed the garden with him in search of the straw-like material.

When he placed a tiny bit of straw in the hinge side of one of the French doors, I understood what he was doing.

"This was in a mystery I once read. I should have thought of it myself." In the story, a private investigator marked doors with a bit of straw to know if someone had entered while he was watching the other side of the house. The straw wasn't very noticeable unless someone was on alert for it. If a door was opened, the straw would fall, and on his return, the missing straw would alert him that someone had entered or left the house.

Jonquille and I carefully placed them where they wouldn't be noticed in each of the French doors.

With Peaches in her carrier, and Frodo on his leash, we marked the front door. I left for work, and Jonquille went home to shower.

Jim was already on his bench when I arrived.

"You're early again today, Florrie."

"I have a lot to do. I'll be back shortly with some cupcakes and coffee."

"Everything okay? You look troubled."

"Busy day, that's all," I lied.

As soon as I was inside the bookstore, I let Peaches out of her carrier, unlatched Frodo's leash, and pulled Detective-Sergeant Zielony's card out of my purse. To my great surprise, he answered the phone when I called.

"Good morning, Detective-Sergeant Zielony. I was wondering when I will be able to enter the third floor. I have some business matters to take care of in the professor's office."

The words flowed out of my mouth so smoothly that it frightened me. Was I turning into a liar? My heart pounded in anticipation of him catching me in my fib, though it wasn't entirely untrue. I did need to look around for bills that needed to be paid.

"Yeah. I think we're done there. I'll send someone over to remove it."

Feeling courageous, I added, "And for your information, I would like to clarify that I am not involved in a romantic relationship with Professor Maxwell." There! I had said it. I felt much relieved and very bold.

There was a long moment of silence on his end.

"Then who are you seeing?"

"No one."

"Florrie, you'll get a lot farther with me if you tell me the truth. I know otherwise."

I was stunned. "Then you're wrong."

He snorted and said goodbye.

I was on the verge of shaking. Why did that man make me so nervous? Probably because he had jumped to conclusions and socked the professor in jail.

Peaches mewed and pawed at me.

I stroked her, taking comfort in her purrs. "Thanks, Peaches, we're going to get to the bottom of this."

I plucked a dried stem off a plant in the store and hurried to the back door, where I inserted it in the hinge, just as Jonquille and I had done at the carriage house. I returned to the front of the store, grabbed my purse, and headed out, taking care to lock the door behind me so Peaches and Frodo would be safe.

"Hey, Jim! Keep an eye on the place, will you?"

He gave me a little salute.

I almost jogged down the block in my hurry. But at the end of the block, I spied Sugar Dreams Cupcakes. I pushed the door open and stepped inside. The shop had that sparkling new look. "Hi! So this is where you moved. I'd like two dozen assorted cupcakes, please."

The clerk opened a box and proceeded to fill it. "We love the new location. The old shop was okay, but the bank was taking over the building, and we were a little nervous about a new owner, so the time seemed right for a move. Sometimes it's a good idea to get ahead of these things."

"Welcome to the neighborhood. You'll be seeing me a lot."

She handed me the boxes. "I hope so!"

I walked back as fast as I could.

When I reached the steps of Color Me Read, Jim shouted to me, "All's well, *capitan!*"

I waved at him and opened the door, wondering where he picked up the European version of *captain*. Frodo waited for me at the door, with his tail wagging, but Peaches had made herself at home on a high shelf.

I selected two cupcakes I thought Jim would like and poured a cup of coffee to take to him. Leaving the door unlocked, I carried them out to him.

He inhaled deeply. "Coffee and fresh cupcakes. I'm a lucky guy."

I watched him curiously. How many homeless people on a bench would consider themselves lucky? I exchanged a few words with him before hustling back to the store.

I checked the back door to be sure the straw was still in place. With both doors locked, I did something completely out of character for me. I walked up to the second floor, tore off one end of the crime scene tape, and dared to walk up the stairs to the spot where Delbert had been murdered.

Chapter 25

I paused at the landing. The carpet was still pulled back, revealing the door in the floor. I would have to call a carpet installer to fix that as soon as possible.

Shivers ran along my arms just to think of what had happened there. I trudged up the remaining stairs and along the hallway, trying not to think about the blood on the carpet.

Maxwell's office was a mess. If I hadn't known the police had gone through everything, I would have thought someone had ransacked it.

I searched for a carpeting person on my cell phone and made an appointment for someone to come in at one o'clock in the afternoon to replace the hall carpeting and tack down the carpet on the landing. That done, I immersed myself in the job of searching for anything that might be useful in defending the professor.

Bit by bit, I set about restoring order. It was slow going to organize it all and put papers, notebooks, and fascinating maps back where I thought they belonged. I read or flipped through each item in search of anything that might help the professor.

Three hours later, I had nothing. No leads, no clues, nothing suspicious or even interesting. He had a lot of maps, in-

cluding curious hand-drawn maps, no doubt for locating treasure. Could someone have been after a particular map and happened upon Delbert in the bookstore after hours? I perused
them, but even though some had tempting words like *tesoro* on
them, I wasn't knowledgeable enough about the professor's lat-
est quest to know if one of them was especially important or
rare.

I rose and stared out the window. What had happened
here? Had Delbert been searching for something when I
caught him in Maxwell's office? Had he found a key and used
it to let himself in later that night? He had departed in a hurry.
Had he returned later to look for something in particular?
Maybe he'd had a new scheme in mind and needed some kind
of maps or documentation to make it seem real to his next
victims.

Across the street, a man in a dark business suit stared at the
bookstore. He gave me chills for a minute. I scolded myself.
Maybe he had heard about the murder or intended to shop
here. Everything and everyone was beginning to look sinister
to me.

I sat down at the desk, found a red pencil in the top drawer,
and drew the layout of the office, the hallway, and the secret
hatch in the stairs. I drew little drops of blood in the hallway.
Unless I missed my guess, the gouge on the floor might indicate that the spear had landed inside the hatch. Someone
threw it in there. To get rid of it? Or was it aimed at someone?

It must have been retrieved by the killer, who drove it into
Delbert. Perhaps he had staggered along the hallway, bleeding,
in an effort to get away. Or maybe he died immediately and
was dragged to the hatch to dispose of his body.

I crammed my diagram in the top drawer and went downstairs to open the store for the day. I flipped the CLOSED sign to
OPEN and unlocked the front door.

Bob bounded in, full of enthusiasm. While I opened a box

of cupcakes and set out napkins, I listened to him chatter, and wished I could confide in him about Jacquie. While he babbled on, the man whom I had seen from the window walked in.

He had a receding hairline and his body leaned toward being very well fed. His gaze fell on the stairs immediately, and almost as though he was drawn to them, he slowly walked up.

"Florrie, are you paying any attention to what I'm saying?" asked Bob.

"Yeah. I'll be right back." I sprang up the stairs and found the man staring at the trapdoor. "May I help you?"

He turned weary eyes toward me. "My son died here."

I gasped, embarrassed to have done so. My hand flew to cover my mouth. "Mr. Woodley?"

He nodded, seemingly in slow motion, as though he had no energy left.

"I'm so sorry."

"Not many people are sorry," he murmured. "They say they are, but they don't mean it. It's terrible to know that people are relieved that your child is gone. Even worse to feel some sense of relief yourself."

I had been guilty of that feeling. I could hardly take my eyes off the man. It was terrible to lose any loved one, even the ones who brought more difficulty than happiness to one's life. "It must be very hard for you."

"Are you Florrie?"

"Yes."

"I apologize. On behalf of my entire family, I apologize for their behavior."

"You don't have to apologize."

"My wife told the police that none of this would have happened if you hadn't moved into the carriage house." He eyed me briefly. "You're a good bit younger than Maxwell. He usually goes for women his own age."

"I manage his bookstore. I'm not his concubine."

A glimmer of a smile crossed his lips but vanished in an instant. "You didn't know Delbert, did you?"

"I only met him very briefly."

"I did everything I could to turn his life around." He covered his eyes with one outstretched hand. In the barest whisper, he said, "I didn't like my own son. And now I have to live with that knowledge. There will never be a chance for redemption or reconciliation. I can never take back the last things I said to him."

I didn't know what to say. I couldn't imagine a parent not liking his own child.

He continued speaking, but I wasn't sure he actually meant to talk to me. It was more like a stream of his thoughts. Maybe he needed to work through his guilt but didn't have anyone to whom he could admit the truth.

"It began when he was just a child. Friends, family members, and doctors said he would outgrow his conniving behavior. But he never did. And what began as small, inconsequential ugliness grew into full-fledged deceit. He cared about no one but himself. You can't imagine the sleepless nights and the dread of anticipating the next horrific chicanery."

"I'm sure he had some redeeming qualities."

"You'd think so, wouldn't you? He was always on the lookout for the next scam. I knew he would come to a tragic end. I just wasn't prepared for it to happen so soon. He was young. He had time to change his evil ways. But if I'm being realistic, I suppose he never would have."

I had to throw some hope his way. He was grieving and beating himself up. "Maybe Delbert would have changed and become more like his dad."

He looked at me as though he had just awakened. "Thank you. Good luck to you, Florrie." He turned and walked down the stairs, a sad, stooped figure.

For no good reason, I followed a few steps behind and

watched from a window when he left the store. He walked along the street, just another weary businessman in a good suit. No one would ever guess the pain he carried in his heart.

Bob was busy with a customer and another petted Frodo, while patiently waiting to pay for five books. I rang them up. When I was done, I located two items in my purse—the phone number for Ms. Strickland, and Emily Branscom's health club membership card. I slid the card into my pocket and called Maxwell's lawyer.

"Good morning," I said. "Any news on the professor's case?"

"The autopsy results are back. I had hoped Delbert might have been on a psychedelic drug that caused him to hallucinate. Unfortunately, that was not the case. The spear was the cause of death, but I guess we knew that."

"Any indication of the time of death?" I asked.

"I'll spare you the gory details, but they're speculating between eleven at night and nine in the morning."

"That's a broad window of time."

"That's what I think. How's Mr. DuBois?"

I told her about his confusion at night, and then segued into the crossed wires and the likelihood that it had been done intentionally. "One of the police officers suggested that we buy a number of outdoor cameras since the estate is so large. They can be monitored on an iPhone or iPad, giving the security guards the ability to see more of the estate at one time."

Happily, Ms. Strickland was all for the proposed setup. We made financial arrangements for it, and I hung up, feeling much better about everything.

I texted Jonquille to let him know just as Zsazsa waltzed into the store. She breathed deeply, enjoying the scents of the store, smiled, and helped herself to coffee and a lemon cupcake.

"I've been waiting for you."

"Oh? Has something happened?" Her eyes widened with eagerness.

"Hey Bob," I called. "Cover for me? I'll be back in a few minutes."

"Sure." He ambled over and snatched a cupcake. "Gotta get the chocolate-iced ones while I can."

Zsazsa followed me upstairs to Maxwell's office. I closed the door behind us. I felt slightly guilty for sitting in his chair like I was the boss, but it was the most private place to talk.

"Last night, as far as we can ascertain, someone broke into the carriage house and crossed wires in the refrigerator to shock me. The refrigerator had to be pulled away from the wall and in the back, this was discovered." I withdrew Emily Branscom's gym club identification card and held it out to Zsazsa.

She pulled on reading glasses covered with sparkling rhinestones and frowned at the card. "You think Emily broke into the carriage house?"

"No. I think Emily might have been a regular visitor there."

Zsazsa blinked at me. Her eyes widened so far that the tips of her fake eyelashes touched her eyebrows. "The mysterious man in her life is Maxwell?"

"I don't know. That's why I wanted to talk to you. I can't imagine that she broke in to create a short in the refrigerator. She certainly has no reason to want to harm me. The only thing I can conclude is that she must have lost the card there before I moved in. It was probably swept under the refrigerator by mistake."

Zsazsa stared at the card. "It was renewed recently." She tapped the card against the desk. Her lips, the color of a ripe tomato, drew into a sneaky smile. "You have come to the right woman, Florrie. I believe a few carefully placed inquiries may yield some useful information. But I am quite concerned about you. Would you like to stay with me?"

It was such a generous offer that I was taken aback. "You're too kind, Zsazsa. But the police are making arrangements for better security. I'm not worried."

"Would these police happen to include a certain Sergeant Jonquille of the most amazing blue eyes?"

"As it happens, yes."

She clasped her hands together in joy. "I hoped so. You must bake for him. Something special."

"His father owns a restaurant. I hardly think he'll be impressed by my baking."

"It is a gesture of love, my dear. The tender flakiness, the soft crumb, the delicate sweetness. These are things that speak to the heart."

"It's not like that, Zsazsa. He's just helping me out. That's all."

"Very well." She smiled as though she didn't believe me. "I am still glad that he is looking out for you. Love blooms in the strangest of situations. Now, I shall take this interesting identification card and do a bit of sleuthing."

"Thanks, Zsazsa."

We walked down to the main level, where I noticed that she checked in with her pal Professor Goldblum before she left the store.

Color Me Read was doing a brisk business. I hated to imagine that the publicity about Delbert's death and the professor's arrest was bringing in new customers, but that appeared to be the case.

The carpet layer showed up promptly at one o'clock. When he saw the stair landing, he asked, "Is this where that guy was murdered?"

"I'm afraid so. Can you tack this all back into place?"

"Sure. Sure I can."

He followed me up to the third floor. "Any chance that you can match the maroon of the carpet in the hallway?"

"No problem."

"Florrie!" I knew Veronica's voice without looking.

She stepped up the stairs in ridiculously high heels and an elegant suit.

"How can you walk in those?" I asked.

"You get the hang of it. You should try a pair."

"I'd snap my ankle in a matter of minutes."

"But they look so great, don't you think?"

The carpet layer piped up. "Nothin' like a great pair of heels on a lady."

I motioned to Veronica to follow me downstairs. "What are you doing in Georgetown in the middle of the day?"

"Can you take a quick break?" Veronica's forehead wrinkled with worry.

Chapter 26

"Sure," I said. "I haven't had lunch yet."

I let Bob and Helen know I was going out. Bob promised to keep an eye on Peaches. I took Frodo along on his leash.

Veronica chattered on the way to a restaurant with outdoor seating where Frodo was welcome. We lucked into a table in the shade. Veronica ordered a salad, but I went for a juicy burger without onions, which I promised to share with Frodo.

When unsweetened iced teas were sweating in front of us, I asked, "What's going on, Veronica?"

"I lost my job."

"No! What happened?"

"I was sabotaged by an idiot who wanted my position. He spied when I logged into Twitter, got my password, and started sending inane tweets. He said the most awful things about the company and my boss. To make matters worse, he picked fights with people online—all in my name!"

"That's not your fault. Didn't you explain that to your boss?"

"Of course! But people were complaining to the company about those tweets. They were afraid of losing clients. It was a nightmare."

"Why didn't you tell me? Do you need money?"

"I was so embarrassed. Fired, Florrie. I was fired! I thought if I could get a new job right away, I could pretend I had made the move on purpose. You know, like I was moving up. Mom and Dad don't know yet. Oh, Florrie! I've never been fired before. It was awful."

"Veronica, you know we'll all love you no matter what. Especially since you were wronged."

"So I got a new job not too far from here—"

"That's great!"

"—that I loathe. I hate every minute. I can barely face each day. It's a horrible place. I like everyone. Right? I'm a friendly person. Right? I don't know what's going on there, but they're all angry and tense. No one wants to cooperate. There's all kinds of backstabbing going on. I spend my days huddled in my cubicle, afraid to speak or even send emails to coworkers. I reread all my emails obsessively before I send them because I'm terrified of starting some kind of in-house antagonism toward me."

Our food arrived. Frodo immediately offered me a paw to earn his share of the burger.

I cut off some pieces for him. "I'm sorry, Veronica. That's the kind of thing you can't know until you actually work somewhere."

"I want to quit."

"I don't blame you."

"But I feel like I can't because I don't have another job lined up."

"I have some money saved from the sale of my coloring books. I can help you stay afloat for a little while."

"Thanks, Florrie. I'm not on the street yet. But is it awful of me to quit? Am I being a big baby? What will I say when I interview for other jobs?"

"You could tell them the truth. Say that you left because it was a hostile work atmosphere."

"Oh right. If I were interviewing people for a job and someone told me that, I would peg her as a diva who isn't satisfied with anything. A troublemaker and complainer."

"Do you want to work at Color Me Read for a while?"

"Could I?"

"Sure. Bob, Helen, and I work long days. We'd love a fourth regular so we could get a little more time off. And I'd like it because I know I can trust you."

Veronica finally picked at her salad with a fork. Her shoulders relaxed and her relief was obvious. "You're a lifesaver, Florrie. That would prevent me from having a gap on my resumé. Thanks." She toasted me with her iced tea. "I don't know what I would do without my big sis."

"What are you going to tell Mom and Dad?"

"Ugh. I know they'll be understanding, but I shudder at the thought of Mom calling all her friends to ask if they're aware of any openings. As if her buddies even understood what social media marketing is." She pierced a slice of avocado with her fork. "Florrie, promise me you won't tell them? I'll do it eventually, but for now, I'd rather they didn't know."

At that moment, I couldn't help thinking of Jacquie Liebhaber. Life was so much easier when you could depend on someone. Jacquie wasn't my sister. She wasn't even really an acquaintance. But if she was telling the truth, the stakes were much higher for her than anything I had ever experienced. Imagine the guilt if I told someone about her being in the carriage house and then she was murdered. I couldn't live with myself. I was more determined than ever to keep her secret.

Veronica's natural cheerfulness returned during lunch. When I picked up the check, she said, "I'm going to stop at the jewelry store to have my pearls restrung, then I'll head straight to work to quit. After that I'll come to Color Me Read. Does that work for you?"

"Perfect timing. We're having a reopening celebration tomorrow. Emily Branscom is coming to sign books. And we're having contests for children and adults, in which they can win coloring books and colored pencils."

"Ohhh! Perfect. I can start social media buzz about the events at the store. This will be fun!"

After lunch, I was busy organizing the store for the next day. Helen grudgingly helped arrange displays. Bob and I set up extra seating and low tables so kids could color in the children's room. Then we brought up folding chairs from the basement for adults to sit in while they listened to Emily Branscom talk in the parlor.

True to her word, Veronica showed up two hours later. She hustled me into a private niche and whispered, "It was awful. I don't think they cared one bit. I wonder if someone quits every day. There was no fuss at all. My boss just said 'okay' and took a phone call, like I wasn't even standing there in front of her."

"I think you're better off out of that place."

It turned out that my gregarious long-legged sister was a natural saleswoman. She didn't know much about books, but she enthusiastically rang up sales and signed people up for our newsletter.

Bob had a new crush, and Helen appeared to be annoyed by Veronica's presence.

At ten that night, I turned on the alarm and locked up. "Want some dinner?" I asked Veronica. "I thought I'd stop by that Peruvian rotisserie chicken place."

"Sure. I can wait outside with Peaches and Frodo."

Thinking Jonquille and his buddy might be at the mansion installing the security cameras, I bought two chickens, a large pan of flan, and doubled all the side dishes. The scent of the chicken, black beans, platanos, and three different sauces was incredible. On the way home, Frodo kept sniffing the bag, and Peaches mewed nonstop.

I had to give Veronica credit. In spite of her high heels, she kept up a good pace and didn't complain once about her feet hurting.

About one block from home, Veronica said, "Don't look now, but I think somebody is following us."

Chapter 27

"Where is he?" Adrenaline pumped through me.

"Opposite side of the street. He's back a bit. Let's test him."

My first instinct was to protect Veronica. She had no idea what she was walking into. I should have warned her. But I followed her lead when she stopped walking and pretended to have a pebble in her shoe.

I positioned myself sideways, head down as though I was helping her, but I gazed back and saw the man on the other side. He had quit walking and just stood on the sidewalk, as if waiting for us to resume our pace. In spite of the streetlights, I couldn't make out his face.

I should never have put her in this situation. "Veronica, there are a few things I should have mentioned to you. But for now, let's just walk really fast. We're almost at the mansion."

We picked up speed, striding so fast it was just short of a jog.

Veronica looked back. "He's still there!"

We turned up the driveway at a run. "Felipe!" I shouted.

Jonquille and another guy were outside. They jogged toward us.

"We're being followed." My breath was ragged.

"I see him," said Jonquille, who dashed toward the sidewalk, a few steps ahead of his buddy.

"Police!" Jonquille shouted. "Hands in the air!"

The guy on the sidewalk complied immediately.

Jonquille exchanged words with him for a moment. "Florrie! Do you know someone named Goldblum?"

I hurried back toward them. Sure enough, poor Professor Goldblum's little round face peered at me in the dark. "I am so sorry! What are you doing following us? You scared me half to death."

"You can lower your arms," said Jonquille.

"I wasn't going to let you walk home alone after someone tried to kill you," said Goldblum.

Veronica shrieked. "Is that true? Why didn't you tell me?"

"I have two chickens and a ton of side dishes," I said. "Why don't we all go inside and have some dinner?"

"You are just like Dad," hissed Veronica. "Let's have a nice dinner, and oh, by the way, did I mention that someone shot at me?"

"No one shot at me."

Jonquille and I both bent to check the status of the straw in the front door of the carriage house. We grinned at each other because it was still there.

"Is this some kind of house-entering custom that I don't know about?" asked Veronica.

Jonquille's buddy explained the straw method to her while we all entered the carriage house.

"Wow. I never heard of that." Goldblum was impressed. He crossed the room and checked each of the French doors. "They're all intact! No one has been here."

Veronica and Jonquille helped me carry the food out to the dining table in the garden. I wished I had taken the time to put up fairy lights. Candles would have to do. I fed Peaches and Frodo and brought cold drinks outside to the others gathered at the table.

I couldn't help noticing that Veronica had discarded her impossibly high-heeled shoes in the house. Not that I blamed her. I wouldn't have lasted half an hour in those things.

Jonquille introduced his buddy, Cody Williamson. "Cody used to be on the force with me but he started his own security firm."

While we ate, we told them the story of the burglar, the crossed wires on the refrigerator, and the plan for surveillance.

Goldblum held a chicken leg in his hand. "Surely this can't all be related to the murder at Color Me Read?"

"Jonquille and I have different opinions about that, but I think he's beginning to see it my way. I always thought there was a connection between the burglary and Delbert's death." I savored the piquant sauce on the smoky chicken.

Veronica shot me a frightened look. "Why would anyone want to kill you?"

"I truly don't know. Delbert's mother seems to think her son's death is my fault because I moved into the carriage house. But I can't imagine that she would want to kill me for that."

Goldblum licked his fingers with smacking noises. "It's because you're getting too close to the truth!"

"That *can't* be the reason," I said. "We have nothing to go on. I'm at a total loss. Delbert hurt so many people that there's a decent field of suspects, but so far, we haven't been able to tie any of them to the murder."

"The burglary sounds like someone was looking for something," said Cody. "But the refrigerator ruins that theory. Unless it was two different people with two different objectives."

"The person who crossed the wires must have been watching the houses because he knew there was a guard. He sent a pizza to distract the guard so he could enter the carriage house," said Jonquille.

The way he put it chilled me to the bone. I shivered in spite of the warm summer night.

"Florrie," said Veronica, "I can't believe you didn't tell me all this. I've been yammering at you about my petty problems, and all the while you've been going through sheer terror."

"I'm feeling much better about it now. Did you get the cameras set up?" I asked Cody.

"This is the safest house in town that doesn't have the Secret Service guarding it," he bragged.

We cleared the table, Veronica served the flan, and Jonquille refilled drinks. When we reassembled, Cody turned on an iPad to show us where the monitors were and what was happening.

"Looks pretty quiet all around the property," I observed.

"So why didn't you see Professor Goldblum?" asked Veronica.

"That's a slight problem because of the location of the mansion. Traffic and people go by on this street all the time. Most of them are completely innocent. We couldn't tell that Goldblum had been following you, only that he was walking along the sidewalk. For all we knew, he might reside on this street or on the next block over."

Goldblum helped himself to more flan. "I consider my inadvertent participation to be an excellent trial run, which pointed out this minor flaw in your system. But what if the guard is on the opposite side of the property when he sees someone sneaking up the driveway?"

"An excellent question, professor." Cory grinned. "We've timed it from the farthest spot of the property. He can cut through the mansion and be on this side in two minutes."

"What would have happened had I stopped and lurked

across the street, observing the comings and goings at the house? I take it the guard would have noticed?" asked Goldblum.

"Exactly. And it will be taped. So if the person takes off, we'll be able to watch the tape to see if we can identify him," said Cody.

It was late and everyone was exhausted, so we called it a night.

Before they left, Goldblum teased, "Zsazsa will be furious that she missed this!"

And Veronica raised an eyebrow and whispered, "Is that Sergeant Jonquille's overnight bag I saw?"

"It's not the way it looks."

She winked at me. "It never is."

I woke the next morning, refreshed and determined more than ever to find Delbert's killer. My sketch pad and pencils had landed on the floor during the night. I had fallen asleep wanting to draw but was too tired.

After a quick shower, I studied my closet. It would be a long day. Given all the bizarre things that had happened, I felt the need to look pulled together and in charge, even if I was squirming on the inside. I pulled on a blood orange dress. Flat white sandals, a gold necklace, and dangling earrings set with blood orange stones of coral completed the outfit. I sucked in a deep breath and loped down the stairs.

Eric was busy at the stove again.

"Good morning. Did your father teach you to cook?" I asked.

"Absolutely. My mother is so spoiled by leftovers from the restaurant that I don't think she has cooked anything for decades. I hope it's okay that I used some of your cheese and spinach leaves in a couple of omelets."

"Of course it's okay. It smells wonderful. I'm feeling very

spoiled. We're having a book signing at the store today. Usually I like to bake something to serve but I haven't had time." I opened the freezer. "There's not even anything to warm up except two bagels." I pulled them out and popped them into the oven.

"You've been a little bit busy. Florrie, I went by Pizza Man yesterday to ask some questions. They're not sure they remember the pizza order but they recalled a kid coming in to buy a pizza. He paid from a little wad of cash in his hand. They thought his mom probably sent him in, but I suspect someone paid him to buy the pizza and deliver it here."

"To divert the attention of the guard?"

"Sure. Do you know anyone who wouldn't take the pizza into the mansion and stick around for a slice or two?"

"It's so simple. Almost too easy. But if a kid brought a pizza to your door, wouldn't you tell him there must be some mistake?"

"The perpetrator probably gave him some line to say. Something like, 'Your boss sent it as thanks for your hard work.' Or maybe he said it was from a neighbor for DuBois."

I could see someone buying that explanation. "Any activity last night?" I asked.

"Not a thing."

"Does that mean he gave up or that he thinks I'm dead?" I poured coffee for both of us.

Jonquille folded the omelets with a practiced hand. "Probably neither. It would be easy enough for him to find out if you went to work. I have a feeling our guy isn't stupid. If he were, we'd have caught him already."

"So you think he'll try again?" I swallowed hard but tried to act nonchalant as I added the bagels to our plates.

We carried our breakfasts and mugs out to the garden table. It was so peaceful that I could hardly believe any of this was happening to me.

Jonquille looked me in the eyes. "I hope not, Florrie. I wish we could catch this creep. But we don't really have anything to go on. You can't remember arguing with anyone? Or ticking someone off?"

I bit into the warm eggs and melting cheese. My mouth still full, I murmured, "So good!"

"I'm glad you like it. Seriously, isn't there anyone who is upset with you?"

I sipped my coffee. "Delbert. But he's gone. Delbert's mother. I'm not the type to tell people off."

"I heard you let Zielony have it yesterday morning."

My mouth full of omelet, I blinked at him. I swallowed and said, "Oh. That. He was under the crazy impression that Maxwell and I are lovers. I *had* to clear that up!"

"So you're not?"

"You thought that, too?"

He avoided my eyes. "I kind of hoped it wasn't the case."

I put down my fork. "I admire the professor. He has done fascinating things. You don't meet people like him every day. I spend most of my time reading about places or drawing them. But he's a real-life adventurer. He has an incredible mind. Most people just try to get through their days. They're thinking about their jobs, or how to get a job, or what's for dinner, or whether their kid flunked his math test. That's life and it's normal. But the professor speculates about whether ghosts exist, and what's beyond the universe, and what happened to the Ark of the Covenant. I love him." I hastened to add, "In a platonic way, because he's so interesting. But I have no romantic interest in him. I suspect Delbert's mother put that thought in Zielony's head. I'm lucky he hasn't arrested me yet."

Jonquille didn't even try to hide his amusement. "Zielony's a stubborn guy. That's for sure. And I'm sorry to say that he does have a compelling case against Maxwell. When the DNA tests come back, it may even be a strong case."

"If Maxwell murdered Delbert, and a random professional thief burglarized the mansion believing no one was living there, then why did someone enter the carriage house to cross the wires on the refrigerator?"

Jonquille's eyes met mine. "We're going to get to the bottom of this, Florrie. I promise."

Veronica pulled up at the carriage house just as Eric and I were leaving. We planted the straw in the hinge side of the door again. Such a silly thing, really, but it gave me such comfort!

"Good morning! Do you think the professor would mind if I parked here?" asked Veronica.

"Probably not." I shrugged. "He's not here anyway, so you have my official permission."

We said goodbye to Jonquille and set off for the bookstore with Frodo and Peaches.

"No kiss goodbye?" asked Veronica.

"I told you. It's not like that. He's sleeping on the couch."

"You're kidding! I was already imagining a double wedding. You are coming to Mom's cookout, right?"

"I wouldn't miss it. I have to meet this special guy of yours."

"He's adorable and so good to me. You'll love him."

I was happy for Veronica. But I'd heard that before from her—more than once. She was quick to fall in love and just as fast to dump her beaus.

The store wasn't open yet, so I left Veronica to pump up the social media about the store while I bought pastries.

The morning air was crisp and blessedly cool as I strode up the street to Heinrich's Bakery. Through the glass window, I could see beautiful Sonja wrapping a box with a thin gold ribbon and handing it to a customer.

A bell on the door rang when I pushed it open. "Hi, Sonja.

You're up early for someone who worked into the wee hours of the morning."

She looked up and gasped. "Florrie! I don't go to bed on Friday nights because I have to be here at three in the morning on Saturdays to help my aunt start baking. It's a very long day, but I'll get a nap this afternoon before I tend bar again." She tilted her head. "Do you believe in kismet?"

"A little bit, I guess."

"This meeting was meant to be. I was thinking of you just yesterday. The girl you were asking about walked right by the window. Of course, by the time I ran out the door, she was gone. But it was definitely her."

"The one who was so angry with Delbert?" I dug in my purse for something to draw on. I found an envelope that contained a bill I needed to pay, and an emerald-green crayon. "Can you describe her for me?"

She gestured toward her own features as she described the woman. "Long blond hair worn straight. It came halfway down her upper arms. Sort of a square face, I think. Her lower jaw was angular, emphasizing her cheekbones. A straight nose. Not too long but not pug or ski jump."

I slowed down as I drew because the face was beginning to look all too familiar to me.

I handed her my drawing. "Imagine that she's not actually green." I held my breath.

"You have captured her quite well."

I'd hoped I hadn't. The face on the envelope bore an uncanny resemblance to Veronica.

Chapter 28

I swallowed hard and tried not to show my distress. "I'll keep an eye out for her. Thanks, Sonja. But I didn't come here for that. I need cookies for children and elegant pastries for adults, please."

We decided on chocolate chip cookies, sugar cookies, and oatmeal cookies for the kids. Choosing the pastries would have been such a pleasure if I hadn't felt sick about Veronica. Pointing to the items in the case, I bought far too many mouthwatering treats—apples peeking out of puff pastry, chocolate croissants, lemon tarts, glistening fruit tarts, and creamy cannolis.

Sonja packaged them all and promised to let me know if she saw the woman again. I thanked her and left, moving slower than molasses.

It couldn't be Veronica. It just couldn't! There were thousands of beautiful blondes in Washington, DC. Many with square faces and high cheekbones. Surely there were hundreds in Georgetown on any given day. But Veronica had been in Georgetown yesterday. And someone at her old job had sabotaged her. It sounded like the kind of thing Delbert had done to people.

What was I thinking? No, no, no. It was all a coincidence. I knew Veronica better than that. How could I suspect her for even a moment?

When I reached the bookstore, it was teeming with children and their parents. I didn't know whether it was publicity from the murder or Veronica's professional social media push that brought people to Color Me Read. But they came in droves. One mom brought the six children who were attending her young daughter's birthday party, along with their mothers. Seven moms and seven kids, all shopping for themselves. I thought the cash register might overheat.

Zsazsa made her way through the crowd. She poured herself a cup of coffee as she always did, but she stood beside me behind the counter, gazing around in awe. "Are you giving away free puppies?"

"It seems like it."

I rang up three of my coloring books and a box of colored pencils for a woman. "I hope you enjoy these."

"I have information," Zsazsa whispered into my ear.

She had my full attention.

In a soft voice, she said, "I visited the gym yesterday to inquire about a membership for myself. I told them my friend, Emily Branscom, raved about the place. Ugh." She drew her mouth down and pinched her nose dramatically, holding her pinkie in the air. "It reeked of sour socks. I'll never understand the attraction. At any rate, I asked if Emily had found her membership card yet."

"You didn't."

"How else can one obtain information? Of course I did. She had it with her on Tuesday. It was only when she arrived yesterday that she couldn't find it."

"Are you certain? That would mean she was in the carriage house while I lived there. And after Professor Maxwell was in jail!"

"She must have a key," reasoned Zsazsa.

"But there was a guard. Of course, he didn't notice the guy who crossed the wires, either. There are only a few possibilities. Either she let that guy in or she crossed the wires herself."

Zsazsa placed her hand on my arm. "Or she thought she left her favorite earrings on the nightstand and arrived at an opportune time when she happened to miss both the guard and the wire changing person." Zsazsa wrapped her arm around me. "There could be a very reasonable explanation."

Unlikely! "She just *happened* by when the guard wasn't watching? She had a key and let herself in to look for something she thought she had left there? She somehow dropped her gym membership card and accidentally knocked it under the refrigerator, which she apparently did not touch because she would have gotten shocked?"

"Well, when you put it that way . . ."

"There's one thing I can do right now. Bob!" I beckoned to him. "Can you man the cash register? I have a little problem I need to take care of."

I grabbed my purse and left before anyone could ask questions. Guilt pummeled at me for leaving the store when it was so busy. But my survival was more important.

Hurrying, I returned to the chic hardware store. The cost of new locks for the front door and all the French doors put a nice dent in my budget. But it had to be done. Who knew how many of Maxwell's women had kept a key to the carriage house?

I carried my purchase home, trying not to think about how busy the store was. I located a screwdriver and swapped out the lock on the front door. If I hadn't felt guilty for abandoning the store, it wouldn't have been a big deal. But guilt had a way of making me drop things and jab myself with the screwdriver. An hour and a half later, all the locks had been changed, but my hands looked like I'd been in a fight. I heaved a sigh of satisfaction. I, Florrie Fox, was independent and capable. And I was going to find Delbert's killer so my life could return to normal. All I had to do was use my little gray cells.

I returned to the store feeling much better about the situation. I had told Zielony off. It appeared that Sergeant Eric Jonquille might be smitten by me, and today anyway, the store was a booming success.

At five o'clock, Emily Branscom arrived. In the animal world, she would have been a chipmunk. Petite, with round cheeks and a perky attitude, she had a ready smile for everyone. She wore a crimson dress that clung to her tiny figure. Around her neck hung a dramatic turquoise pendant set in silver.

It was impossible that this woman wanted to kill me. Zsazsa's theory that she had left favorite earrings behind began to seem more likely. I chatted with Emily, and told her how sorry Maxwell would be to miss her talk and signing.

"I can't believe the poor man is in jail. From what I hear, they have a rather good case against him. They say he told people he was going to rid himself of Delbert. Of course, there's also the problem of the trapdoor. Not many people know that they exist in these old houses. That certainly narrows the field of suspects."

"But you know about them," I said. When I realized it sounded like I was accusing her, I quickly added, "Have you written about them in your books?"

"Naturally. Prohibition was a fascinating time in our history. People did all kinds of clever things to hide their hooch. Too many of those hiding places have been closed up or torn down in remodels. It's a shame when we let those marvelous historic quirks go. Have you heard the dead man's ghost yet?"

She caught me off guard. "You mean Delbert? No."

"Interesting. I had assumed he would be here. Do you mind if I wander about a bit? I'm quite sensitive to their presence, so I might be able to feel his energy."

"Yes, of course. Please feel free to be sensitive." Was that what one should say? I had no idea.

She ambled away, gazing about.

Fifteen minutes later, she approached me. "Florrie, you have several spirits here. But I'm only picking up one dark spirit."

"That would be Delbert," I said drily.

She tilted her head and studied my face. "Have you been experiencing troubling events in your life?"

And now she was freaking me out. Should I play as though nothing was wrong or should I confront her? I looked her straight in the eyes. "I'd call Delbert's murder and Maxwell's incarceration troubling."

"Oh definitely, but I meant on a more personal basis."

I played dumb. "I'm not sure what you mean. Looks like it's time to get started." I led her through the seats to the front of the room.

"Ladies and gentlemen," I said, "thank you for coming today. I am so very pleased to introduce Emily Branscom, whose books about Washington, DC, always cause us to look at things a little bit differently. Emily?"

Polite applause welcomed her. It was standing room only.

Emily spoke without a lectern or notes and moved about as she talked.

"Ghosts are nothing new in Washington. I'm sure many of you know that Abraham Lincoln and Andrew Jackson are said to haunt the White House. There are many well-known ghosts in Georgetown, too. What I pursued in my book are the many ghosts that few speak of. The ones that"—she gazed up at the ceiling and around the room—"exist among us in our everyday lives."

She paused for dramatic effect.

"How many people here live in a building that was built before 1930?"

Many of the people in the room raised their hands.

Without moving her head, Emily shifted her eyes to scan the room in a way that was positively scary. "Then chances are extremely good that a dead body was in your home for several days."

A number of people gasped. One man laughed and said, "Nonsense."

She spread her hands wide. "When you leave here today, notice how many old buildings you pass. Washington is loaded with them. And, of course, Georgetown was founded in 1751, so we know there have to be many ghosts here."

She walked across the room to the show window at the front of the store. "You see, once upon a time, people didn't just die in hospitals like they typically do today. Most of them died in their own homes. The family would place the body in the parlor, in a room much like this one, and receive their bereaved friends and relatives there. So you may well have had a corpse on display in your living room!"

The crowd murmured. I hoped no children were listening. They would have nightmares.

"Of course, they required someone to transport the bodies to the graveyard. Certain members of the community handled that task. As time went on, they undertook other matters regarding the dead, as well, hence the name *undertaker*."

More murmurs from the audience. They were captivated.

Bob leaned over to me. "Did you know that?"

"No. She's very interesting."

"Some homes were even built with a coffin corner, a special nook where the coffin would be placed. Take yourselves back in your minds to the days before embalming. The days when doctors cared for patients in their homes. The days when a horse-drawn carriage delivered the body to the graveyard for burial. It begins to make sense, doesn't it?"

She paused and smiled at them.

"There were no nursing homes or assisted living for the elderly. They stayed at home or lived with relatives until they died."

She roamed the room. "Another interesting term came from that time, as well. Not everyone had a fine room in which to receive guests when the body was in repose. Consequently, some people began to offer their front rooms for the task, and their houses were called *funeral homes*."

At that point, Bob and I hustled to the cash register because people were lining up to buy her book.

Emily wrapped up her talk and spent the next two hours chatting with readers and signing books. When I thanked her for coming, she said, "Florrie, you need to do something about Delbert's spirit before he ruins your life."

Zsazsa stood nearby listening. In a hushed tone, she said to Emily, "We know about you and Maxwell."

"What about us? Is Maxwell a sensitive, too? I would not have guessed that."

Speaking in a low voice, I got right to the point. "We found your gym membership card."

"Wonderful! I have looked everywhere for that thing. Where was it?"

"In my house."

Chapter 29

"How could that be?" asked Emily. "I don't even know where you live."

"I live in Maxwell's carriage house."

Her eyebrows shot up. "Really! I had no idea. I've heard that it's quite lovely."

She was beginning to annoy me. How could she look at me with that innocent expression? "Emily, how did your gym card come to be under my refrigerator?"

She blew me off by turning to collect her things. "Sweetie, I have no idea. I'm just glad that you found it."

She slung her handbag over her shoulder and smiled at me. "May I have it?"

Zsazsa nudged me with her elbow. "What were you doing there, Emily?"

"What are you implying?" asked Emily.

"Look," I said, "why don't you just tell me what you were doing in the carriage house?"

"How many times do I have to say this? I have never been in Maxwell's guesthouse."

Zsazsa piped up. "We will keep the secret of your affair with Maxwell. We just need to know a few things."

Emily took a step back. "My affair with Maxwell? That's preposterous."

"We understand that you want to keep it quiet," I said. "That's fine with us. But for my peace of mind, could you confirm that you had a key and let yourself in?"

"I did no such thing. I have never had a key to the carriage house or to the mansion, for that matter. I have never stepped foot in the carriage house, and now I most certainly do not want to. I have never had an affair with Maxwell, and I think the two of you are complete lunatics. May I please have my gym card?"

"No," said Zsazsa firmly.

"No?" Emily held out her hand. "It's my card, and I would like it back, please."

"It is better if we give it to the police."

Zsazsa surprised me when she said that. I played along. "We wanted to spare you the embarrassment of having to reveal your affair with Maxwell to the authorities. We know how quickly that kind of thing gets around, but since you don't want to tell us what happened and why you were there . . ."

Emily fingered her turquoise pendant. "How do I know that you actually have it?"

Zsazsa still had it in her possession. I glanced her way afraid there might be a tussle for it.

But Zsazsa was on top of things. She moved out of arm's reach before she pulled it out of her pocket and held it up.

Emily's lips bunched in anger and her eyes narrowed.

And that was the moment when Sergeant Jonquille walked up in his uniform with his shiny gold badge displayed on his chest. He couldn't have timed his appearance better.

Emily blanched and licked her lips nervously. "You called the police?"

"What's going on here?" asked Jonquille.

Zsazsa handed him the membership card.

In front of Emily, I said, "The night that Alan repaired the refrigerator, he found this underneath it."

Jonquille examined it. "Okay."

Zsazsa piped up. "She used it at the club on Tuesday, but she had lost it by Thursday."

Jonquille's head snapped up. He clearly understood the implication that Emily had gained access to the carriage house. "Excuse us, please?"

Zsazsa and I retreated to the busy desk where stragglers still bought books. After a few minutes, Emily marched out, but not before she threw me an ugly look.

Jonquille hung around while we closed the store and locked up. Bob was going to get Chinese takeout. Veronica, Jonquille, and I went along, but it did not escape my notice that Jonquille was very quiet.

When Bob and Veronica were in the garden and Jonquille and I were in my kitchen, he asked in a very calm tone, "Why didn't you tell me about the gym membership card?"

"We thought she was having an affair with Maxwell. According to Zsazsa, Emily's husband has made it very well known that she's seeing someone, but she has kept her affair very quiet. No one knows who it is that she's seeing." I fed Frodo and Peaches.

"You didn't think I should know about this?"

"You didn't think it was important, either, until Zsazsa told you it was lost after Maxwell was incarcerated."

"That's true. But don't you realize that you can get into a lot of trouble running around playing sleuth? If you come up against the wrong person . . ."

He didn't have to finish. I understood what he meant. He was trained and armed and knew how to defend himself. I would be clobbered.

"You're right. I didn't expect it to turn out this way. How did she explain it to you?"

"She claims she doesn't know how it came to be here."

"That's what she told us."

Jonquille's mouth shifted to the side. "Bear with me here, Florrie. I know you said you're not having an affair with Maxwell."

"Not that again!"

"What if *she* thinks you are?"

That stopped me in my tracks. "Noooo! I never considered that. You mean she was jealous, so she let herself in and booby-trapped the refrigerator to get rid of me?"

Veronica barged into the kitchen. "Where's the food? I'm starved!"

We joined Bob outside. Mostly the topic of conversation was ghosts, which led to a lot of laughter. But in the back of my mind, I was thinking about Emily.

Joking about how we no longer had the energy to work all day and stay up all night, Bob and Veronica left. Eric helped me clean up the kitchen, then we stepped outside to talk with the guard.

On the monitors, the day had been as uninteresting as the night before. While they chatted and reviewed tapes from the cameras, I went over to the mansion with Frodo to check on DuBois.

Given the late hour, it wasn't surprising that he slept. He looked peaceful and his respiration appeared to be regular. I longed to touch his hand lightly but didn't want to wake him.

On my way out, I stopped by the kitchen to talk to the nurse who confirmed that he had been given a sedative to help him sleep.

"Is he still seeing things?"

"Every night."

"When will that stop?"

"Depends on the person," she said. "He's still very weak.

What happened to him was a big shock to his system. It takes time to recuperate at that age. I'd expect to see progress in a month or so."

I thanked her and returned to Jonquille and the guard. They wrapped up their conversation, and we said goodnight.

Inside the carriage house, Frodo, Peaches, and I headed up to bed, but I couldn't sleep. I envied Frodo, who snored, and Peaches, who curled up and drifted off immediately.

I opened my sketchbook and looked through it. Mostly meaningless doodles of pearls and shoe prints and faces. I sketched one more face, that of Emily Branscom. Her face was tiny and delicate, not unlike a doll. She wore her hair shoulder length. It had been so perfect that it must have been shellacked with a good amount of hair spray. She had a little heart-shaped mouth, and a tiny nose that almost seemed to come to a point at the tip. She was petite and sweet, yet there was a bitterness around the outer edges of her eyes and in the wrinkles around her mouth.

There was one other person who knew for sure whether she was having an affair with Maxwell. And that was Maxwell, himself. Would he tell me? Or would he be a gentleman to the death and never admit it out of some archaic sense of decency?

I turned the page. It wasn't really Emily Branscom who was keeping me awake. It was my own sister. I tried to focus and think it through. Sonja had seen the mystery woman at Club Neon. Was there a way to discreetly find out whether Veronica had been at Club Neon the night Delbert was murdered? Assuming she had been, that still didn't make her the mystery woman or the killer.

Some guy at work had been very rotten to her. Maybe there were a lot of people like Delbert. Just because I hadn't met them didn't mean they didn't exist. Lots of people took credit for other people's ideas and stabbed them in the back. Offices were notorious for that kind of behavior. All I had to do was ask her the name of the guy who sabotaged her. Very simple. Nonthreatening. It could come up in conversation, and she wouldn't know that . . .

And then I saw the pearls I had doodled and my heart sank. Why was Veronica having her pearls restrung?

What was I thinking? This was my sister! I knew her better than just about anyone. Okay, she was athletic and perfectly capable of throwing a spear, but her heart was pure gold. She could get angry, especially at injustices, but there was simply no way that she would kill anyone. I was being completely ridiculous. The stress of Delbert's murder must be skewing my logic. I was so desperate for answers that I was imagining my own sister as a suspect. Nonsense and rubbish! I was officially the worst sister in the world.

It was a good thing the next day was Sunday. It had been one week since Delbert died. I fell asleep and dreamed of a faceless person chasing Delbert down the hallway with a spear. And now he was chasing me in my dreams.

I woke shamefully late the next day. The sun streamed through the window. Peaches lay on her stomach, enjoying the warmth.

I bounded out of bed. Poor Jonquille! He had probably been waiting for me to rise for hours. Instead of showering, I pulled on a skort and a sleeveless button-down shirt and ran down the stairs barefoot.

He still slept. Even with his remarkable blue eyes closed, he was lovely to look at. He had a square jaw, like Veronica and the mystery woman, but his rounded nicely to what was surely a stubborn chin. A pair of round tortoiseshell glasses lay on the floor next to a book about the psychology of murder.

It was the day of Mom's cookout. I debated briefly whether I should take Eric along after all. Maybe not. Eric would detract from the attention Veronica craved. She had brought home at least a dozen guys whom she thought were *The One*. I, on the other hand, had introduced my parents to exactly one guy whom I had dated. And I probably wouldn't have if they hadn't shown up unexpectedly at my apartment. It would be better if all eyes were on Veronica and the new beau.

I had arranged for Helen to fill in for me so I could have a day off, but I hadn't shared the new burglar alarm code with anyone yet, so I would have to go over to open the store and to close it.

And I had promised Mom I would bring dessert. I wandered into the kitchen and took butter and eggs out of the fridge to warm up for two strawberry sponge cakes.

"Hey! You're up!" Shoving his glasses on, Eric strolled toward me, barefoot and adorably tousled. "Man, it was great to sleep in this morning after the long days we've had."

"I hope you're off today."

"You bet. You, too?"

"Sort of. I changed the password for the alarm on the store, and I'm the only one who knows it, so I'll have to go over to open and close." I started the coffee brewing.

He leaned against the kitchen island. "Is there a reason you haven't shared it with the other employees who open and close in your absence?"

"Not a *good* reason, I guess. Whoever murdered Delbert had the password. As it turned out, a lot of people knew what it was, including some of the regular customers. It seemed prudent to keep it a secret for the time being. Just until we figure out exactly who got in and what happened that night. I guess I feel safer that way, and it's better for the bookstore."

He smiled. "Smart move. Do you suspect Helen or Bob?"

"Not really. Apparently, Helen followed some guy around at her last job and was fired for it. That doesn't make her a murderess, though I suppose it puts her judgment into question."

"And Bob?"

"Bob wouldn't hurt anyone. He's a big lovable teddy bear."

"With a crush on your sister."

"And on Helen! He obviously goes for tall, leggy types."

"I know your sister is seeing someone. How about Helen?"

"She's been chasing some guy she met at the store. Sounds like he might have dumped her, though."

"Your sister is popular. My friend Cody wanted to know about her relationship status."

I nodded as I fed Peaches. "Men are always attracted to her."

It bothered me a little bit that I was so comfortable with Eric. We walked the dog around the neighborhood, admiring the other mansions. On our return, he whipped up eggs Florentine for breakfast, while I baked the torte for my mom's cookout.

When we ate breakfast in the garden, Eric said casually, "I noticed that you changed the locks on the carriage house."

"I was stupid not to do it sooner. Having the guard gave me a false sense of security. Plus Delbert was dead, so I didn't anticipate anyone else wanting access to the carriage house."

"No one expected that someone else would want to break in. Not even me." He glanced up at me. "I noticed your sketchbook the other day."

Startled, I met his eyes.

He held up his palms. "Hey, I'm the son of an artist. I know better than to look in it, but I'd like to see it. Any chance I could have a peek?"

I deliberated. "Sure. Why not?"

I left the table. Frodo accompanied me in my dash upstairs to retrieve it. "We're going to see Mom and Dad today. You'll have fun running around without a leash again," I promised him. The garden was beautiful, but there wasn't room for a dog to run at top speed.

I returned to the table and said, "I'm feeling a little guilty about keeping Frodo so long. And I'm feeling awful about imposing on you to babysit me every night."

"Are you saying you don't want Frodo and me here anymore?"

"No, I love having both of you here. But Frodo is probably much happier running in his big yard at home. And you have a life. I'm sure there are things you need to do that you have put off because of me."

"A few. But I've been enjoying it. Sitting out here is like being in a park. It's a treat. And the company has been very enjoyable."

I handed him my sketchbook. He laid his glasses on the table and opened it. "Delbert."

Chapter 30

"Delbert was on my mind even before I found him with a spear in his back. Gosh, has it only been a week? I had never met him before and the next day he was dead."

Eric's eyes opened wide. "This is me!"

"That was the day we discovered Delbert's body. You were kneeling on the floor and looking down at me."

"Thanks for making me look better than I do. Aha. This is Delbert on the floor. It's like a timeline of what happened. Cool! You even drew the shoe print and the notch in the floor."

"Don't you think that was from the spear?" I asked.

"Probably. I know Delbert wasn't the nicest guy, but the blood in the hallway and the gouge in the floor indicate that there was some kind of altercation. Whatever happened to him was horrific."

"That's what I think. Someone threw the spear at a person who was probably standing or kneeling in the space."

"And there's the pearl."

I was afraid of his answer, but I asked anyway. "Do you think that means it was a woman? Men don't often wear pearls. In tie tacks, maybe, but not many men wear those anymore."

"It's possible. Or it could mean that a woman was present."

"It was drilled through," I said. "So I think that means it came from a necklace or a bracelet."

He flipped the page. "Helen? So you did suspect her?"

"In the beginning, I thought it must be someone with a key to the shop who knew the code to turn off the alarm. That narrowed the field of suspects. But then I learned how easy it is to bump a lock and that a number of people knew the code to disarm the alarm."

"So you no longer suspect her?"

I winced. "She bought new fake pearls. Clearly, that in itself is meaningless. A totally innocent thing. But one wonders if she did that because her other pearl necklace broke. . . ."

"Lance Devereoux? You know him?"

"Bob and I paid Lance and Scott Southworth a visit. Lance told us about Delbert ruining his career."

"I see. You certainly have gotten around." He flipped the page. "Who is this?"

I inhaled sharply and hoped he didn't notice. "Jacquie Liebhaber. We talked about her before. She's a women's fiction author who was once married to Maxwell." I wondered how I could put it without breaking my promise to her. "A private investigator came here looking for her."

Eric raised his eyebrows. "Curious. Why would he have thought she might have returned to her ex-husband?"

"Maybe she felt safe with him?"

Eric studied me. "How does she fit into Delbert's murder?"

"He reprinted the contents of some of her books under his own name as e-books. She's not the only author to whom he did that. And I thought it peculiar that she went missing around the time he was murdered."

"Aha. That *is* a sign of guilt." He sighed. "If Maxwell did murder Delbert, she might have been present."

I didn't want to consider that possibility.

As if he knew what I was thinking, he said, "We have to go where facts take us."

"So far, they haven't taken me anywhere. I seem to go in circles, suspecting everyone."

"And we finish with Emily Branscom, who is hiding something."

"The identity of her lover."

"Because she's still married. That's a good reason."

"I would hope they have separated by now if she's really sleeping with someone else."

He flipped through the sketches one more time. "You're very good. The detail in your work is fantastic. Like the crinkles around the eyes. You capture a person's character."

"Thanks." The alarm went off on my iPhone. "I need to go over to the store to open it."

Eric offered to walk with me. We took Frodo along and strolled toward Color Me Read. Families were enjoying the warm weather. Couples were headed to brunch. It was hard to remember why I had ever been fearful.

I unlocked the door as Helen arrived, one hand digging in her purse. "I'm glad you're here. I always keep the store key in the zippered compartment of my purse, but I don't see it."

I looked at Jonquille, but he was busy watching Helen.

"No matter. I'll find it before Bob and I have to lock up tonight," said Helen.

I swung the door open, and we walked inside. How could I word this so it wouldn't sound like I was accusing her of something? While I punched in the code to disarm the alarm, I said, "I hate when that happens to me. Why don't you look again? Maybe it's in another compartment?"

This time Jonquille shot me a look of approval.

I tried to urge her a little bit more. "Those big bags just swallow things whole. It drives me crazy."

"But I love them," said Helen. "They're so chic." She

reached her arm down into it and pulled out four lipsticks, a wallet big enough to be a small purse, and a makeup bag. "Voilà!" she cried, triumphantly holding up the key.

I breathed a sigh of relief. At least it hadn't been stolen. I was feeling bold with Jonquille present. "You're not wearing your pretty pearls today."

She frowned at me. "I thought you wanted the day off. What are you doing here?"

So much for that. "I'm leaving. I just wanted to be sure everything was going well here."

Jonquille, who was holding Frodo's leash, turned and headed for the door.

Helen caught my elbow and whispered, "Out of uniform, that guy is cute! I don't blame you for not waiting for Maxwell's release. Bankhouse says he could be in the slammer for the rest of his life."

I was saddened by the disdainful way she spoke about Maxwell's incarceration. It might be a good thing that it wasn't my natural inclination to lash out at people. "Have a good day, Helen," I said, walking out the door.

As we walked back, Jonquille asked, "Are you sure you'll be okay by yourself this afternoon?"

"Of course. I can't expect you to be my personal body-guard."

"You have my number. Call me if anything happens, no matter how unimportant it might seem."

He reached for my hand and clasped it in his. I looked into his eyes and thought I might melt.

"Just call me. Okay?" he said.

We walked up the mansion driveway, where Felipe stood guard. I was delighted to see him because I had more faith in him than some of the other guards.

Eric grabbed his gym bag and took off.

I bolted the door and frosted the tortes with whipped cream.

The strawberries I had bought at the farmers' market were huge and had a saturated deep red color like wild strawberries. I sliced them in half and decorated the two tortes with them. When they were in the fridge, I cut some of the leftover strawberries, placed them in a bowl, and sprinkled them with a little sugar. Then I added a generous dollop of leftover whipped cream on top.

I pulled back the bolt and stepped outside with Frodo on his leash. I exchanged greetings with Felipe. "Keep an eye on the place, will you?"

"Sure thing."

We headed straight to the mansion where I delivered the strawberries to Mr. DuBois.

He was sitting in his wheelchair, looking frail. He ignored the berries to reach for Frodo. He massaged Frodo's ears and motioned to me. "Come closer." I bent over but that wasn't near enough for him. He gripped my shoulder and whispered, "I'm no longer swallowing those mind-numbing pills. I hold them under my tongue and when the nurses leave the room, I flick them into that plant."

The leaves of the poor plant were turning brown along the edges. "I don't think it likes your meds."

"Bah! I didn't, either. The plant is giving its life to save mine. I want you to take me upstairs."

"Can you walk?"

"Don't be daft. It doesn't become you. There's an elevator."

Of course. It made sense that a big house like this would have an elevator. "All right. Are you ready to go?"

"Quick! Before Nurse Ratched comes back."

I smiled at his reference to the tyrannical nurse in *One Flew Over the Cuckoo's Nest*. There was nothing wrong with his brain. I propelled the wheelchair forward.

"Faster!" he hissed. "She'll find us if you don't move it!"

"No one said you have to stay in your room, did they?"

"I don't care if they did or not. They stick me in there. Get me out of here. Hang a right. Quick!"

I pressed a button and the elevator door opened immediately. It was just large enough to accommodate the wheelchair, Frodo, and me.

"Press the button for the third floor," he said.

I did as he asked. In a minute, I was backing the wheelchair out into a hallway.

"We'll start on that end."

I rolled him into a bedroom that connected to a second bedroom through a Jack and Jill bathroom.

He leaned forward, scanning everything.

"What are we looking for?" I asked, glad to have a chance to snoop.

"I hear things. They always say I'm hallucinating, but I'm not. Next room."

"Wouldn't you be hearing sounds from the second floor?" I asked.

"Of course. I want to see what they've done to my house."

I pushed the wheelchair into a sewing and craft room. At the end of the hall we visited a large attic that was used for storage. Most of the windows were dormers that jutted out of the roof and gave me a better overview of the property. From where I stood, I overlooked the roof of the two-story garage, the swimming pool behind it, and a garden that extended back probably as far as the garden of the carriage house. The grounds were lovely and well tended.

"Ready for the second floor?" I asked.

We took the elevator down one floor.

"Start on that end." He pointed toward the rooms over his.

I indulged him, but truly thought we were unlikely to find anything of interest. The sounds he heard were probably the nurse, the guard, or traffic. Still, I was enjoying my tour of the house, and if we stumbled across a clue, then that was all the better.

The bedrooms on the second floor were beautifully outfitted with luxurious fabrics and antique furniture. I couldn't help wondering how many of Maxwell's ancestors had slept in those same bedframes. It was sort of comforting to think that the same family had lived in this home for more than a century.

We turned right to a newer wing with modern furnishings. I peeked out of a window and realized we were over the garage.

The only thing that piqued my interest on that floor was that someone had cleaned up Maxwell's room. The clothes and items that had been unceremoniously dumped out of his dresser by the burglar had disappeared. I presumed they had been folded and put away in drawers.

"Turn me around so I can see." Mr. DuBois eyed every detail in the room from the contents of the bookshelves to the placement of the throw rugs. "Needs to be dusted," he grumbled.

"Are you satisfied that no one is up here?" I asked.

"No. I am not deranged. I know what I heard."

What I was hearing was the nurse calling Mr. DuBois in a panic. "I think we'd better return."

He seized my hand. "Take me to the carriage house with you."

Instead of arguing, I thought I'd get farther with him by pointing out the problems. "There's no elevator in the carriage house. You'd have to sleep on the sofa."

"Bah! You may recall that I did that once for two hours. I didn't get a wink of sleep on your uncomfortable furniture. But they could move the bed in."

Clearly his brain was working well. "The nurses would still come to care for you. In fact, because there are no walls on the main floor, they would be with you all day and all night."

He leaned to the side to glare at me. "I resent your logic."

Trying to ignore the fright in the nurse's tone as she continued to call his name, I squatted beside the wheelchair. "For two hours? So you did not sleep in the carriage house after Delbert tried to break in?"

"I tried. Couldn't do it."

So no one knew where the professor had been during that time. "Did you tell the police you were with Maxwell all night?"

He lifted his chin in defiance.

I was pretty sure that meant he had lied to the police to protect Maxwell. I still didn't think Maxwell was guilty, but he didn't have an ironclad alibi for much of the night.

The poor nurse shouted, "There's no way he could be upstairs."

"He's with me," I yelled.

"Young ladies of good breeding never shout," Mr. DuBois declared, as if I were his pupil.

"Then I guess I just showed my lowly roots." I pushed the wheelchair into the elevator.

"Take me to the basement," said DuBois.

"I think it's time for you to return to—"

He clenched my arm with a great deal more strength than I could have imagined. "The basement," he hissed.

I punched the button marked B and seconds later, the doors opened to a dank cellar. The walls were mostly brick. It appeared to me that the ceiling of wood slats had been bolstered by steel columns and beams.

A few ladders and other unwieldy items like sinks and mantels had been stashed there. An ancient furnace that was large enough to walk into took up a significant amount of space. Hot water heaters and a counter with a sink lined one wall.

"There's certainly nothing to see here," I said, eager to leave.

We ascended only to be met by the agitated nurse.

"I almost called 911! Where have you been? You have no right to remove him."

In the calmest tone I could muster, I explained that we had visited the bedrooms above Mr. DuBois's quarters so he could see for himself that no one was there.

The nurse was speechless for twenty seconds. "I would appreciate it if you asked permission before rolling him about. It's time for his pill and a nap."

She all but pushed me out of her way and wheeled poor Mr. DuBois back to his room.

Chapter 31

I returned to the carriage house and phoned Ms. Strickland. "Any news on Maxwell?"

"He no longer finds jail quite as fascinating as he did in the beginning."

That wasn't surprising.

"But we finally have a little break. A key to the bookstore was in one of Delbert's pants pockets."

"They're just telling you that now? Seems like they would have known that immediately."

Ms. Strickland sighed. "I totally agree. It's not enough to spring Maxwell, of course. Anyone could have planted the key in his pocket, but it does open up the possibility that Delbert went there on his own that night."

"I wondered if that could be the reason he was pawing through the professor's desk!" It wasn't much, but it was good news. "I know I'm not next of kin, but I'm wondering if you could get the doctor's instructions regarding Mr. DuBois. They seem to be pumping a lot of pills into him."

"It's highly unlikely that we could obtain anything like that due to the patient privacy act. Still, I'll make an inquiry and see what happens."

I thanked her and hung up. After a quick shower, I stood in my closet wrapped in a towel, looking at my clothes. What did I own that was the most Norman repelling? He liked grass, so green was out. Turquoise was probably too close to green. Ohh. Dead grass. Why didn't I have drab brown clothes? I settled on a sundress the color of a hazy blue sky, almost verging on gray. I had bought it because I loved the white polka-dotted fabric.

For my peace of mind, I marked the French doors with straw like Jonquille had shown me. As an apology for leaving Peaches behind, I filled her bowl with her favorite, tuna and duck.

I had mixed feelings about returning Frodo. I had enjoyed his company, even if he would have welcomed an intruder by licking him. I packed his dinner bowl, bed, and toy into my car, asked Felipe to keep an eye on the place, marked the door with straw, and drove to the suburbs with Frodo in the front seat and a strawberry cream torte safely away from him in the backseat.

When I opened the door for Frodo, he bounded out of the car and ran in joyful circles on my parents' lawn, delighted to be home.

The air felt balmy and summer-like on my bare arms, and cooler than in the city. The scent of meat searing on the grill hung in the air.

Carrying the torte, I walked around to the gate on the side of the house and let Frodo into his fenced backyard.

The first person I saw was the last person I wanted to see—Norman. He waddled toward me.

Frodo, who loved attention from everyone, sped past him like he didn't exist, and ran to the cluster of people hanging around the grill on the patio. I wished I could do the same.

"I'm sorry about your boyfriend, Florrie." Norman smiled at me, sending up goose bumps on my arms.

Oh no! My parents must have told his parents that the relationship with Jonquille was over. Aargh! I reminded myself that there were plenty of other people to talk to. It wasn't a date, and at worst, it would only be a few hours. I could always bail early if he was too annoying.

"Hi, Norman." I kept walking toward the patio, but he kept pace with me.

"Maybe I can ease your broken heart," he said.

An opening! How could I use that to my advantage? I looked away and said, "It will take a long time before I'm ready to even think about another man." Good, good! I looked down at the ground and bit my lip to stop myself from grinning. I would have pretended to wipe a tear from my eye if the torte hadn't required two hands to carry it. I didn't like that I was getting better at lying, but it was coming in handy.

"Florrie!" Mom hustled toward me. She held out her arms, and when she took the torte, she whispered, "The Spratts think your romance with the cute cop fizzled and died."

"Gee thanks, Mom."

"This is beautiful! I could use your help in the kitchen. Excuse us, Norman."

I liked this better already. All I had to do was pretend to be busy.

When we were in the kitchen and safely out of earshot of any Spratts, Mom said, "I'm sorry, dear. The Spratts are such old friends of ours. Your father and I thought it best if we just kind of erased your lie by saying you weren't seeing Sergeant Jonquille anymore. Unless you are?"

I hoped I might be sometime in the future, but it seemed unwise to fuel the fire under that lie again. "No, Mom. But if Norman becomes a pest, you'd better rescue me."

"Stick with your dad and me. We'll save you. I promise. One more thing, sweetie, if you don't mind."

"Sure."

"Let's not talk about murder tonight. I don't think the Spratts would understand. Iced tea?"

I spooned ice cubes into the tall glass and poured the dark amber liquid. "Is there anything I can do to help?"

"Not right now. I prepared most of it in advance."

I walked to the sliding glass door and looked out. The Spratts were there with my dad and Norman. Veronica was wearing crazy-high heels again and someone had his arm wrapped around her waist. Mr. Spratt appeared to be discoursing on something. Veronica's friend turned his head slightly to listen to him. I blinked. Surely I wasn't seeing right.

"Mom, what's the name of Veronica's new boyfriend?"

"Scott. Scott Southworth. You'll love him. He's very smart. His dad is that big builder. I've seen the Southworth name on a lot of construction signs. And you won't believe who his stepmom is."

"Oh?" I watched him with Veronica, my heart sinking.

"Jacquie Liebhaber!"

Chapter 32

"I can't wait to meet her. You like her books, too, don't you, dear?" asked Mom.

"Yes. I do." My head was spinning. How on earth did Veronica get involved with Delbert's roommate? And Jacquie's stepson, no less. He had been nice enough to Bob and me the day we paid them a surprise visit. But I couldn't forget that he had also been going out with Helen.

"Florrie, would you take these appetizers to the guests, please?"

"Sure." I picked up the platter and carried it outside. I greeted Mr. and Mrs. Spratt.

Veronica said, "Scott, this is my sister, Florrie."

"Hi, Scott. We met before at your house. How's Lance?" I asked.

Scott's sandy hair was almost the same shade as Jonquille's. Just like Bob had said, it stood up on the top of his head in a wave from his forehead. Both sides were cut close. He wore a short mustache over a pretty mouth, but he hadn't shaved in a couple of days. It was a popular look. Very trendy, but not my style.

"The poor guy lost his job for good. He's a mess right now. If Delbert were still alive, he might be tempted to do him in."

"I'm so sorry to hear that. He seemed like a nice guy. I hope he lands on his feet."

"Who is this you're talking about?" asked Norman.

"My roommate." Scott helped himself to a crostini with pancetta on it.

"And I was horrified to hear about your stepmother. You must be worried sick."

Scott swallowed a bit of the crostini. "We tried to keep it quiet, but she missed a couple of engagements and word got out."

"What happened?" asked Veronica.

"We don't know where she is. But she has done this before. My dad says all fiction authors are prone to drama. Hopefully she'll show up again soon."

"Your private investigator hasn't turned up any leads yet?" I asked.

He stopped eating. "What private investigator?"

"You didn't hire one? He came by asking if we had seen her. A lanky guy with a narrow face?" I watched Scott's expression change to concern. "I can't recall his name, but I have his business card at home. I could call and let you know.

"I'd appreciate it if you did that. It's somewhat worrisome. I think Dad would have told me if he had hired someone."

Mrs. Spratt edged over toward us. "Your mom says your little romance with the police officer didn't work out, Florrie."

Veronica tilted her head. "You said there was nothing going on."

Ugh. How many times would that lie raise its ugly head again? "There isn't anymore," I said through clenched teeth, hoping Veronica would get the message.

"She's not ready to date anyone else yet," Norman informed everyone.

Dad looked uncomfortable. He was probably worried

someone would say the wrong thing and my lie would be exposed.

"I hear you live at the Maxwell mansion," said Scott. "Must be a beautiful place."

Thank heaven he changed the subject. "Actually, I live in the carriage house in the back of the property, not with the high society in the mansion."

"My stepmother, Jacquie, is always talking about the grand parties they used to have."

"I can imagine. My mom said everyone knew about the Maxwells when she was growing up."

And then Norman edged closer to me.

I passed the platter to Norman to hold and excused myself, saying, "Looks like Dad needs some help at the grill."

He didn't, of course, but I was relieved to get away from Mrs. Spratt and Norman. When we sat down to eat, I made a point of helping serve so that I could see where the Spratt family was sitting before I joined everyone.

I should have brought Jonquille. For the next hour, I dodged Norman, who swapped seats with his dad to be closer to me. Meanwhile, Veronica beamed and snapped selfie after selfie of herself and Scott. I wanted to think he was a nice guy, but I couldn't help worrying about his relationship with Helen. It sounded like he had dumped her but I wasn't sure.

When I cleared the table, I noticed that Scott had walked deeper into the yard to take a phone call. He put his phone away and rushed back, his face ashen.

"Excuse me for leaving early. There's a problem with my dad."

Veronica stood up. "Is he all right?"

He appeared to be at a loss. "I don't think so. Please thank your mom for me." He left at a jog.

Veronica stumbled after him in those impossible heels. "Scott! Wait up."

We all heard him say, "Maybe Florrie can give you a ride

home. I need to go straight to his house and possibly the hospital." He planted a quick kiss on her and then he left Veronica standing there, watching him go.

She took off her shoes and walked back to the table barefoot and looking dejected. "I hope everything is okay with his dad."

Mrs. Spratt said, "My, but you girls have melodramatic relationships. Florrie, you will be so much better off with Norman than with that policeman."

I smiled as sweetly as I could. Veronica was the actress in the family, not me. But I had read enough books to know how to do a fairly decent Scarlett O'Hara type. "I don't believe I'll ever be able to love again after Eric."

Mom scowled at me.

Veronica seemed surprised. "I can't blame you, Florrie. Sergeant Jonquille is very cute."

Mrs. Spratt's nostrils flared. "Norman has a new haircut. Isn't it handsome?" She bestowed a loving smile on her son.

Veronica's eyes met mine. I had to look away quickly before I broke into uncontrollable laughter.

Happily, the torte was a huge success. Light and sweet, the perfect ending to our meal.

I slipped into the kitchen to wash dishes when the Spratts were departing. I didn't think I could take any more of Norman.

He ruined my plan by sneaking into the kitchen and planting a smooch on my cheek. It was more slobbery than Frodo's kisses. I danced away from him, holding up my soapy hands to defend myself. "Goodnight, Norman."

"I'll call you." He waved and left.

When Mom returned to the kitchen, I said, "We have got to find Norman a girlfriend. That's the only solution."

"I understand now why you don't want to date Norman. Honey, the next time you lie to spare his feelings, I promise I'll back you up. Just let me know in advance so we're all on the same page."

Veronica handed Mom the dessert plates. "Did you take your pearls to the jeweler I recommended?" asked Mom.

"He's stringing them now."

I was afraid to ask, but I had to know. "What happened?"

"It was so embarrassing. My pearl necklace practically exploded. I didn't know they could do anything like that. Pearls sprang and rolled all over the floor."

"They're supposed to be double-knotted so that won't happen," said Mom. "The most you'll lose is one pearl. All I can think is that they weren't strung properly to begin with."

Dad joined us in the kitchen to ask about my safety. I told him about Jonquille and Cody setting up cameras, and how I had installed new locks. I didn't mention that Jonquille was sleeping over nights. Even if he was staying downstairs on the sofa, I figured it wasn't the kind of thing one's father probably wanted to hear.

My mother had other concerns. She smiled at me doubtfully. "Maybe you can bring that nice Sergeant Jonquille with you next time?"

I tried to act casual. "Maybe."

There was no mistaking the hope in her eyes. "Did Veronica send you the selfie she took with Scott? They make such a nice couple." Mom picked up her phone and flipped through pictures. "Your dad gets mad at me when I say things like that. They haven't been seeing each other long, but one of Veronica's relationships has to finally work out, and Scott is adorable." She held out her phone to me.

Veronica always took a great photo, even close up in a selfie. I hoped Scott wouldn't end up hurting her.

Chapter 33

"Florrie! Is something wrong?" asked Mom.

"A little bit." I emailed the photo to my phone. "I met him once before. He was Delbert's roommate."

"The dead boy?"

"The very same."

Mom looked over my shoulder at the photo. "How sad for Scott to lose his roommate."

I wasn't sure how much to tell her. It would come out eventually. "Would you be sympathetic about his other girlfriend? He's been seeing Helen, too."

Mom clapped her hand over her mouth. "What a scumbag! Veronica will be devastated."

"I think I have to tell her, don't you?" I handed Mom her phone. "He hasn't called Helen in a couple of days, so maybe he chose Veronica over her."

Mom hugged me. With a sad expression, she said, "Veronica has to know. Maybe it won't be so bad. They're not married or engaged. I don't even know if they have a mutual understanding yet."

She knew as well as I did that Veronica would be crushed if Helen were still in the picture.

To make matters worse, I was mighty irritated with my sister because she hadn't mentioned that she was dating Delbert's roommate.

I hated to leave Frodo with my parents, but he was their dog, after all. I might have kept him longer if I hadn't seen how much he loved being home. I went to hug him and thank him for being my sidekick for a few days, but he was already sacked out in his dog bed, snoring.

I would have gladly stayed longer once Norman was gone, but as it was, I had to close the store. Armed with a cooler filled with more leftovers than four people could possibly eat, I hopped into my car and Veronica joined me for a ride home.

I tried to keep the annoyance out of my tone when I asked, "How come you didn't mention that Scott was Delbert's roommate?"

"I didn't know until tonight."

"How is that possible?"

"Who is Sergeant Jonquille's roommate?"

"He doesn't have one." At least I didn't think he did. Had he said that he lived alone?

"Then that doesn't count," said Veronica. "I didn't interrogate Scott about who he knew."

"Seems like he might have mentioned that his former roommate was just murdered. That has to be a pretty traumatic event. You never went to his house?"

"Not yet. He usually picks me up and takes me somewhere when we go out."

"Speaking of which, thanks for the information about how to dress for Club Neon."

"Did you have fun?"

"It's not exactly my kind of place."

"Florrie, you can't always stay home and draw or read a book. Besides, that's where I met Scott, so now that Jonquille isn't working out, maybe you should go once in a while. You might meet someone nice, too."

"Were you there Saturday night a week ago?"

"I think that was the night my pearls exploded. Can you imagine how hard it was to find them on the floor in that dark place?"

"Did you see Delbert there that night?"

"I wouldn't know Delbert if he came up and said hi."

The muscles in my jaw relaxed. I hadn't realized that I had been clenching my teeth in fear. "You never met Delbert?"

"Not that I know of."

She wasn't the woman Sonja had seen at Club Neon. What a relief. "So who was the guy who sabotaged you at work?"

"Ugh. Why did you have to bring him up again? I've been trying to forget Berto Woodley."

"Are you kidding me? What did he look like?"

"You think you know him?"

Good grief. Now I felt sick to my stomach. "Possibly."

"I don't know. He had a strange face."

"Strange how?"

"I don't know. Just different. Why are we talking about him anyway? He's out of my life forever." She switched on the radio.

My thoughts were all jumbled. I needed my sketch pad to help me make sense of everything. All I knew for sure was that I didn't want Veronica to have been involved in Delbert's murder and that I felt incredibly guilty for even thinking she might have been.

The local news came on the radio.

The car of beloved local author Jacquie Liebhaber has been located partially submerged in the Potomac River. Liebhaber, author of dozens of bestselling women's fiction novels, has been missing for over a week.

Tragically, upon hearing the news of the discovery of her car, her husband collapsed and is now in serious condition in a local hospital.

Veronica screamed.

I almost drove off the road. It was a good thing I-66 was clogged with Sunday afternoon traffic as residents returned to town, so I had been driving slowly.

"Which hospital? Did they say?" asked Veronica.

"I don't think so."

Veronica pulled out her cell phone. "I'm texting Scott right away. I can't believe I let him go alone. I should have gone with him."

All I could think was that Jacquie's fears came true. The people she was running from had found her.

Tears welled in my eyes. It was my fault. I had promised Jacquie that I wouldn't say anything about seeing her. But if I had, maybe this wouldn't have happened. Maybe Jonquille and the police could have helped her.

It was a brutal lesson. Sometimes keeping promises was a bad idea. I didn't want to learn this lesson. Not this way. Not at Jacquie's expense. What had happened to her after she left the carriage house? I hoped she hadn't suffered. How stupid of me. Of course she had. She had been so afraid, and now her fears had come to fruition.

"Veronica, I don't know how to tell you this, so I'm just going to come right out and say it."

"Oh no. This is a lecture, isn't it? You are not the boss of me, Florrie."

"Scott is dating Helen."

"Why would you say something like that? Is this some kind of weird sibling jealousy? That was just hurtful."

"I'm so sorry, Veronica. I know how much you like Scott. But it's true. Even Mom agreed that you have to know."

"You told Mom?" she screeched. "That was so mean. Now Mom and Dad will hate him. Let me out of the car."

"Don't be silly. I can't let you out on the highway."

"How would you feel if I told you Jonquille was seeing someone else?"

"It wouldn't make me happy. But I would be glad I knew the truth about him."

"Oh sure. That's easy to say when it's only hypothetical. Did Helen tell you this?"

I felt slightly better. She was beginning to consider that it might be true. "Yes."

"You know she doesn't like me. I don't know why you would believe her. Scott has been a perfect gentleman. Everything I could ask for in a man."

Veronica was still seething when I dropped her off. Nevertheless, I asked her to keep in touch about Scott's dad.

The roads were horribly congested, so I took back roads to Key Bridge. When I pulled into the mansion driveway, Jonquille was there waiting for me.

I was running late. I parked and stepped out of the car. "What are you doing here?"

"I thought I'd walk over to the store with you."

I couldn't help smiling like a fool. Maybe this would turn into a relationship after all. We rushed over to the store, and I completely forgot to keep a vigilant eye out for anyone sinister. On the way over, I filled him in on Scott, Jacquie Liebhaber's car being found, and Scott's dad collapsing.

We hurried up the steps to the front door and walked inside just in the nick of time. The music had been turned off. Bob and Helen were getting ready to leave. Both Bob and Helen wondered why I had come. I had to fudge a little bit.

"It was recommended that we change the alarm password after Delbert's murder. After all, someone broke into the mansion, as well. We didn't know if the killer would come back here. If I'm the only one who knows the code, you guys are in the clear if anything else happens."

"Are you saying that we're suspects in Delbert's murder because we knew how to disarm the alarm?" Helen was indignant.

"The person who killed him knew how to cut it off. As it happens, the password was fairly well known, so that theory didn't really pan out," I explained, hoping to sooth her.

"This is all so annoying." Helen grabbed her purse. "Excuse me. I'm in a rush. I barely have time to change before I meet Brian."

Brian! Scott had used a different name with Helen. "Just a second, Helen." I looked for the selfie of Veronica and Scott on my phone and handed it to her.

Helen's mouth opened, but she didn't say anything. She didn't take her eyes off the picture. Finally, she choked, "What is Brian doing with your sister?"

Bob peered over her shoulder and muttered, "Uh-oh."

"So that *is* Brian? Your Brian?" I asked just to be absolutely certain.

Jonquille took it all in, his brow furrowed.

"Why is he posing with Veronica?" Helen's delicate skin had flushed with anger.

"His real name is Scott Southworth. It looks like he's been dating both of you."

"No! No, no. Why are you doing this to me? There's no date on this picture. It could have been taken months ago."

"I'm sorry, Helen."

She shot me a dirty look and stormed out of the store. But she turned around and came right back. "Bob, do you have plans for tonight?"

"I thought I'd get a pizza."

"How would you like to help me get to the bottom of this?" Helen smiled at him.

"When did you hear from Scott last, Helen?" I asked.

"Around three this afternoon."

"I think he's at a hospital with his dad."

"Which one?" she asked.

"I have no idea."

"Come on, Bob," she ordered. "Brian . . . Scott is going to need a hospital when I'm through with him."

Good-natured Bob jumped at the chance. He handed me the bag of cash to be deposited at the bank and grinned like his wishes were coming true. Wiggling his eyebrows, he said, "See you tomorrow morning, Florrie."

I hoped Helen wouldn't break his heart. But that was useless wishing. Poor Bob.

With their departure, the store lay quiet. As though it had been put to bed.

Jonquille gazed around. "It must have been like this when Delbert let himself in the night he was murdered. I wish we knew what he was thinking that night."

He didn't seem capable of rational thought. Did he think he would empty the cash register? Steal a treasure map?

I stood at the bottom of the stairs. "Someone else was here that night, too. Why aren't I psychic? I wish I could see the two of them sneaking about the store."

One of them had opened the hidden door under the stair landing. And one of them had retrieved the spear from the professor's office.

"Two people up to no good. But who?" asked Jonquille.

I set the alarm, we stepped outside, and I locked the front door. Jonquille and I stood in close proximity on the stoop. "I didn't want to believe this, but I am reluctantly coming to the conclusion that there might have been three people present that fateful night. And one was a woman."

Chapter 34

"The pearl," said Jonquille.

I had picked up the pearl and examined it. "One of the people who broke in must have brought a woman along. Either Delbert or his murderer."

"Delbert? From what I've heard about him, that seems unlikely."

"I talked to a bartender from Club Neon who said he was popular at the nightclub. Maybe he meant to impress her. He probably bragged about inheriting the store one day."

"Or did the killer bring a girlfriend? Maybe they planned some kind of heist together and were surprised when they discovered Delbert in the store?" suggested Jonquille.

"I wonder if he tried to call the police?" I said.

"Maybe not. He wasn't supposed to be in the store, either. Or maybe they were friends of his, people who didn't frighten him."

"You mean all his bragging might have led to his death? He might even have brought them with him or opened the door for them. And then her pearls broke in the ensuing fracas. And one sole pearl remained behind, caught under the carpet."

I breathed a little easier. It hadn't been Veronica! Her pearls broke at Club Neon.

It was the dinner hour and Georgetown was slowing down. Fewer cars, fewer people. We walked back, thoroughly enjoying summer in the city.

When we reached the carriage house, Jonquille helped me carry in the cooler full of leftovers.

"This stuff smells great."

"I'm sorry I didn't take you along."

"Was Norman obnoxious?"

"It was so uncomfortable that my mother apologized to me and won't force the issue anymore. I think the only way to get rid of him is to find him someone else."

"Now you're going to be a matchmaker? That's a tricky business."

"Especially for a debonair guy like Norman."

Jonquille poured sparkling lemonade for the two of us, and I fetched my sketchbook.

We sat in the garden while Peaches prowled in her jungle.

"Are you feeling the need to draw?" asked Jonquille.

"Always. But right now, that pearl really bothers me."

"You said Helen bought new pearls."

I flipped the sketchbook to the page with Helen.

"Wait. Not so fast. I was concentrating on the players you drew the other night. What are all these other things? Like this feather?"

"The bartender at Club Neon had a huge plume in her hair. She was afraid of some guy with a butterfly tattoo." I pointed to the butterfly.

"I understand the spear and the shoe print. Those were at the site of the murder, but what about the clock?"

"Seven minutes before three Sunday morning a week ago, Delbert tried to open the French door of the carriage house."

Jonquille chuckled. "I don't have to ask how you knew that. I've never seen so many clocks in a home. But it's key because it means he was still alive then, and that the murder occurred after three in the morning. And this?" He pointed to a necklace.

"The famous Maxwell emerald and diamond necklace."

"Which is probably what the burglar was after," said Jonquille. "And what's with the two martini glasses and the cupcake? Wistful thinking?" he teased.

"On Monday, after the professor was arrested, Mr. DuBois was washing two martini glasses. I don't know if Mr. DuBois and Maxwell are in the habit of having a martini together. I assume it's more likely the professor had a guest the night before. Probably Emily Branscom. And the cupcake is meaningless. Scott and Lance had a box from Sugar Dreams Cupcakes when I visited them. A bank took over the building and the store moved."

Jonquille sat back in his chair. "I've been trying to figure out why Emily Branscom's name is so familiar to me."

"You've probably seen her books around town. Or maybe you read about her in the newspaper. She's pretty popular."

Jonquille glanced over at me. "Would you be okay here by yourself for an hour or so? I'd like to check her out at the police station."

"You're going to bring her in for questioning?"

"No. I just want to check some paperwork is all."

I walked him to the door, where he had a word with the guard.

But instead of going back into the carriage house, I marked the door with straw, locked it, and popped in on Mr. DuBois. A different nurse had arrived. She held a finger up over her lips. I tiptoed back to his room.

He slept peacefully. I sat down in the chair next to his bed. What had he been looking for in our little tour of the house? I leaned back, kicked off my sandals, and curled my legs up under me. Closing my eyes, I listened.

Birds still twittered outside, something crashed in the kitchen.

The air-conditioning hummed softly. I didn't hear anything coming from the bedrooms upstairs.

I decided to return later, after dark, to listen again. I stretched and ambled out to the kitchen, where my gaze fell upon a row of martini glasses inside a cabinet with glass doors.

I ran back to Mr. DuBois's room and flicked on the light on the nightstand. "Mr. DuBois," I hissed. Gently, so I wouldn't alarm him, I shook his shoulder.

He opened one eye and his mouth.

"Who visited Maxwell the night of Delbert's murder? Who had a martini with him?"

"Professor Maxwell isn't home at the moment. I shall tell him you called." He closed his eye.

He was drugged to the gills again. Giving up, I went home.

The guard wasn't outside. I hoped he was around somewhere.

A man shouted at me from the driveway.

Large and muscular, he lumbered toward me holding the largest bouquet of roses I had ever seen. The sun glinted off his bald head. A huge black mustache covered his upper lip. He fit the description of the man who had frightened Sonja at Club Neon.

My heart pounded. Where was the guard? A person could hide a large gun under all those flowers. I jammed my key into the lock of the carriage house.

"Florrie Fox?" he asked. "These are for you."

I braced myself for the bullet. He handed me a giant vase filled with red roses.

As he turned to leave, I spotted a butterfly tattoo covering his arm just above his elbow.

"Wait!" I cried. "Who are you?"

"Jerry. I work for Mr. Woodley."

"Why were you asking questions about Delbert at Club Neon?"

He appeared surprised. "You know about that, huh? Mr. Woodley wanted to know what Delbert had been doing and with whom."

"Mr. Woodley doesn't believe that it was Professor Maxwell who murdered Delbert, does he?"

"Naw. He feels pretty bad about that."

"Thank Mr. Woodley for the flowers."

"Sure thing."

Even though my hands were full, I checked for the straw in the door. It was still there when I unlocked it, assuring me that no one had entered that way. But when I stepped inside, I found Jacquie Liebhaber holding Peaches in her arms.

Chapter 35

We screamed at the same time.

"Hush!" Jacquie slapped a hand over her own mouth. "The guard will be in here any minute."

I peered at her in disbelief. "Jacquie Liebhaber?"

"Please don't give me away to the security guard," she begged. "I'll explain everything."

What was I supposed to do? The woman was famous around the world. I didn't think she was a threat to me or anyone else.

She was dead on about the security guard, though. There was a rap at the door.

"Miss Fox? Is everything okay?"

Jacquie looked a lot more terrified than I felt. I flicked my hand at her as an indication she should hide. She retreated up the stairs.

I opened the door, still holding the roses. "I feel so stupid. It was a spider. I'm a little queasy about them." Where the devil had he been when a huge man walked up the driveway?

He gazed around. "You sure?" In a whisper, he said, "If somebody is in here and you're pretending everything is all right, tug on your left earlobe."

I burst out laughing. "Thank you. That was very clever of you. But everything is quite fine."

"I'm just outside if you need me."

"Thanks. I feel much better knowing you're there." That was a fib. If he was on the ball, Jacquie wouldn't be in the house at all, and he'd have noticed the man with the bouquet of roses.

I closed the door, set the roses on a table, and walked to the stairs. "I thought you were dead."

"Dead?" She walked back down the stairs. "Why would you think that?"

I told her about the radio report. "I guess they didn't say you were dead, but I sort of assumed it. Finding a half-submerged car in the river isn't a good sign."

"Sheesh. I cannot believe it took them a whole week to find my car. I didn't even hide it well."

"*You* left your car submerged in the Potomac?"

"That should give you an indication of how scared I am. It's not every day that someone tries to fake her own demise."

"But why?"

"It's a long story."

I figured she was hungry. "How would you like to tell me over a steak and potato salad?"

"Oh yes! Thank you, Florrie. You're just as wonderful as Maxwell told me. I feel like we're already old pals."

"The professor knows you're here?"

"No, but he always speaks of you with such fondness. I'm afraid I gave you a terrible fright when I tried to get into the carriage house."

I stared at her in shock, momentarily speechless as I realized what her words meant. "You? You're the one who jiggled the handle of the French door in the middle of the night?"

"Guilty. I'm so sorry that I scared you. I thought the carriage house was empty and hoped someone had left one of the doors unlocked.'"

So it wasn't Delbert who tried to break in. He might have already been dead by then. "You wanted to hide here?"

"In my books, the heroines never go home to hide because that's the first place people would look for them. I guess my current residence is where they would expect to find me, but this property feels like home to me, and I haven't lived here in so long that no one would suspect I was here. Have you heard anything about Maxwell?" she asked. "How's he holding up?"

"*As well as can be expected* is what they tell me. His lawyer says he has limited phone access, so I haven't spoken with him."

"Florrie, I have a huge favor to ask of you. And then, how about we share a bottle of wine from Maxwell's cellar with that steak?"

"I think I have a bottle of wine in the kitchen."

Jacquie smiled broadly. "Oh, you're a goody two-shoes. No raiding the wine cellar. I love you even more. The nurse has stocked up on the most dreadfully bland foods at the mansion. It's a wonder DuBois is getting better at all. If I hadn't managed to intercept a delivery from the grocery store before the nurse put everything away, I would be starving."

"You've been living here?"

"I wouldn't exactly call it living, but yes, I've been hiding out here. It's a wonderful place, isn't it? I built this carriage house as my office when I was married to Maxwell. I used to come over here every day to write. In the summer, I sat out in the garden, and in the winter, when there was snow on the ground or the wind howled, I would build a fire. He updated the kitchen considerably since then. Wife number three probably did that. The garden looks fabulous. So lush! These are lovely roses. From your police admirer?"

"Oddly enough, they're from Delbert's father, Mr. Woodley."

"Really? Maxwell was never fond of him. Said he was far

too vulgar. It's been years since I saw him. Looks like he has learned to be more gracious."

"He came to the store to see where Delbert died. It was very sad. I think he feels like he failed as a father."

"I can understand why. Delbert was always bad news. I'm no shrink, but I suspect the best parent in the world couldn't have changed his predisposition to wreak havoc."

I unpacked the food and fixed her a plate of steak, beans, potato salad, and an ear of corn.

"It's been so long since I had a cat," said Jacquie. "Peaches is just lovely. She's been such a blessing to me."

A blessing? I could hear Peaches purring. "So that's why Peaches was always tired when I came home. She played with you during the day."

"I suspect it was the goldfish that tired her out. I hope you don't mind. I've been so relieved to be able to get out in the fresh air. It did a lot to calm my nerves. Did you notice the cat fence that runs across the fence around the garden? It's made so that they fall back into the garden if they try to jump out. His third wife must have been a cat lover, too. I'm sure DuBois hated that."

I set a wineglass and a bottle of my favorite red wine on the coffee table and brought her the plate I had prepared.

"Oh lovely! Thank you, Florrie!" Jacquie ate like she hadn't seen food in days.

"You've been here on the estate since the night you tried to get in?"

"Why do you think I'm dressed like this?"

I had no idea where to start. I knew it was a rhetorical question on her part, but I thought it was as good a place to begin as any. "Why *are* you dressed like that?"

"Because I can't go home, and I certainly cannot go shopping! This is Maxwell's shirt. I took the liberty of cutting the legs off a pair of his old jeans. I was somewhat horrified to find the waist isn't too large for me."

"Did you clean up Maxwell's dresser?"

"Wasn't that an awful mess? DuBois certainly couldn't do it. Maxwell wouldn't have cared. He was never one to be tidy. But I don't like messes."

"You weren't afraid someone would notice?"

"Not that. Who complains when somebody cleans up? All the nurses probably thought a different nurse did it. If they even went into his bedroom."

"Aside from the creepiness factor, I'm pretty impressed that no one except DuBois knew you were here. And he thought you were a ghost."

"Crumbs, my dear. In my books, villains always carelessly leave crumbs. I made sure that I didn't."

Would it be rude of me to ask why she couldn't go home? I decided it wasn't. After all, she was hanging around in my home, sneaking food, and cutting up the professor's clothes. I dared to ask.

Between bites, she said, "The short and horribly boring truth is that my husband has a gambling problem, and I'm through with him. The longer answer is somewhat more hair raising."

I sipped a glass of sparkling water and stroked Peaches while Jacquie ate.

"This potato salad is superb. I love the pickles in it. Anyway, on Friday afternoon a week ago, I received a text from my credit card company. I have one of those thingies where they notify me if someone tries to charge more than a certain amount. My husband was away on business, so I thought it must surely be a fraudulent transaction. I'm sorry to say that it was my husband trying to get cash from a machine at a casino." She dabbed her mouth with the napkin and sucked in a huge breath. "I've known about his problem for a long time. But I truly thought he had it under control. He's been seeing a shrink who was helping him overcome his compulsion."

She sipped her wine. "After days alone, you have no idea how wonderful it is to talk to someone." She took a deep breath. "So, you know how sometimes things just occur to you out of the blue? One thing happens and it leads you to other random thoughts? I went home to check on my jewelry and it had been ransacked. Gone, gone, gone. All my beautiful sparkly things and some sentimental items from my mother and grandmothers. That bothered me the most. Those heirloom items weren't very valuable. But losing them is a crushing loss to me."

Jacquie interlocked her fingers and held them tight. Her hands trembled slightly. "We had been through it all before— the promises and the tears and the discussions. We've lost an enormous amount of money. Just wasted! Gamblers always think they're going to win it back. They keep pumping money in, certain they will win big."

She shook her head. "Creditors were calling, and he was getting foreclosure notices on his properties. And still he wouldn't stop. I couldn't take it anymore. The next morning, I rose early and moved all my funds into other banks. I don't have Maxwell-type money, of course, but if my husband knew where it was, he'd have wangled a way to get at it. You can't imagine how terrible it is to live with a gambling addict. In the evening, I came to see Maxwell for advice."

She smiled. "Maxwell, for all his reckless adventures, is actually quite wise and very kind. His concern was the life insurance policy that my husband holds on me. If I die, he gets five million dollars. Maxwell was right. I had to leave for my own protection. My husband was out of town, so I hurried home, intending to pack a few things. But when I entered the house, I could hear him speaking with someone. The number *five million* was mentioned so clearly that I can still hear him saying it today. I didn't dare stay a second longer. I left immediately. I was afraid to be alone in a hotel somewhere, so I dumped the car to mislead anyone searching for me and came back to Maxwell. And now, he's not here but I am."

"He didn't see you the night you tried to get into the carriage house?"

"I don't think so. All the lights came on, and I was terrified that I had triggered an alarm. I fled into the mansion and up the stairs to his bedroom. Early in the morning, I could hear DuBois running about, so I hid. Then Maxwell left and later on the police swarmed the place. At first I thought they had come to search for me. I didn't know about Delbert's murder at the time."

She studied her hands. "Florrie, my life is at risk if anyone finds out that I'm here. No one else can know. Maxwell pointed out to me that my husband probably borrowed against his real estate holdings from some unsavory types who would think nothing of helping him knock me off."

"Did you have a martini with the professor?"

"How did you know?" she asked.

"So you're his alibi!"

"But I left. I wasn't with him all night."

"He was in his office when I left Color Me Read that night at ten o'clock. What time did you get here?"

"Ten thirty. I parked in front of the store, met him at his office, and we walked over here."

"Did you see Mr. DuBois? It would be great if he could confirm this."

"No. He tends to retire early because he rises early to make breakfast."

"So the professor made two martinis and you talked about your problems."

"Actually, *I* mixed the martinis. Maxwell likes them very dry with a green olive. He says no one but me ever gets them right."

"What time did you leave?"

"Around midnight. I walked back to the store, drove home, panicked, ditched my car, and walked here. It's a long walk from the river. It seemed so close by car. I was exhausted, mentally and physically. Can you imagine how draining and frightening it is to know that someone wants to murder you?"

My heart went out to her. I couldn't imagine being in her shoes. "You can't live this way forever."

A soft smile lit her face. "No, I can't. Here I am revealing my whereabouts and trusting you to keep my secret. Although, I'm not so sure I wouldn't enjoy hiding for a longer time. With some clothes and decent food, I could live like this for quite a while. If I weren't so doggoned scared for my life, it would be like a writing retreat."

"I changed the locks. All of them. There's no way you have a key." I watched her expression carefully. "And I marked the doors. No one opened the front door while I was gone. How did you get in?"

"There's a passage from the mansion."

"I hope you'll excuse me for saying so, but it's really creepy that you were able to enter without my knowledge."

"I apologize for that. I never did it when you were here. Not at night or when you were home. Actually, I've been using that scenario in a new book that I'm writing. I do understand the ghoulish factor."

"How did you know when I was home?"

"I've been spying on things from the rooms over the garage. I figure if someone enters the property, I'll hear the commotion and can hide fairly quickly."

"Where is this passage?"

"It starts at the mansion, runs under the garage, and comes

over here. It's actually a fascinating story. Georgetown was a major stop on the underground railway for escaping slaves. The Maxwell family had some crazy members, but one of them was a remarkable man who helped a lot of slaves on their way to freedom. When I moved into the house ages ago, I discovered the place where the slaves hid. Ugh. I guess when you're escaping a nightmare, you'll take refuge anywhere. It was a dark, dank pit far under the house, accessed through a hidden door in Maxwell's bedroom. It came up out here in what was once a stable. When I found it, I had Alan install lights so it wouldn't be so dark and terrifying. I shiver when I think that they probably only had candles to light the way. It must have been horrific."

"Where does it open in here?" I glanced around the room in search of a well-hidden door.

"It's best if you don't know."

"I think I have a right to know. Is there a way to lock it?"

"Whoa! Keeping me out, are you? You can throw a bolt from the inside. I was never concerned about anyone sneaking around. After all, it was just family. And . . ."

Her voice trailed off. She swallowed hard and looked away. "After our little girl was kidnapped, Maxwell and I thought it would be smart to have a safe room in the house. The Maxwells were very prominent and known for being wealthy. You can lock both ends from the inside."

"I'm sorry about your daughter."

She nodded and stared at Peaches. "I still think about Caroline with every breath I take. She must have been so scared. My poor beautiful baby. I can only hope that her death wasn't painful or brutal."

"Did they ever find her?"

She shook her head. "To this day we don't know what happened to her. But I know what happened to us. Maxwell and I fell apart. Maxwell and I saw Caroline's face when we looked at each other. Each of us was a daily reminder to the other of the daughter we had lost. It's a pity really. I don't think we ever stopped loving each other. And now, the only thing that makes the fear of dying more bearable is the knowledge that I'll be with Caroline again."

She wiped her eyes and bent forward toward me. "I see some of my books on your shelves. I'll let you in on a little secret. The character of Harrison is based on Maxwell."

I jerked back. "No kidding? Of course! Why didn't I make the connection? The intrepid explorer. He's always such a gentleman even in the most unexpected circumstances. By the way, I spoke with your agent."

"Aww. Jessica's a dear. I hate to worry her. I just haven't been able to figure out a way to contact anyone without leaving a cyber trail. You can't imagine how hard it is not to have access to a computer or a laptop. I've been writing in longhand, something I haven't done in ages. Which brings me to the favor I must ask of you."

Chapter 36

I was wary and held my breath.

"It seems to me that the obvious thing to do is cancel the life insurance policy on my life. I don't even know if that's possible, do you?"

"I have no idea."

"Me, either. But it seems like I ought to be able to since I'm the insured. This must have happened before. When people get divorced, it could be dangerous to allow one to carry insurance on the other. Right now that policy is a five-million-dollar bounty on my head. Once I'm not worth five million bucks as a dead woman, then I'll be free to live my life again. I expect I'll have to hide out a little longer, though, just in case some of my husband's more vulgar creditors still think my demise means they'll get paid."

"On the other hand," I said, playing devil's advocate, "won't the insurance company call your husband? He's the one who paid for the policy." I thought about it more. "But it doesn't seem right that he could continue to insure you against your will."

"Exactly. It's all quite confusing, isn't it? As the insured, I hope I can cancel the policy he paid for."

"So what's the favor you need?"

"I'm being very careful not to disclose my location. I'm sorry to say that I've learned a few unpleasant tricks from writing my books. If unscrupulous people are looking for me, they'll have tapped the phones of the people I'm likely to call. I'm sorry to say it's not that difficult to do with modern technology. I don't dare log onto any computer or use any of my passwords. That means I can't use my email programs, or text. So, I was hoping you might allow me to use your phone to call the insurance agent. I would do it from a phone in the mansion, but that pesky nurse and guard are always roaming about. And there's a good chance that phone has already been tapped anyway."

"Yes, of course. That's not a problem at all. It's the least I can do. There's one problem, though. My name will show up on the caller ID. Once they know that, it's only a skip from me to you."

Jacquie gasped. "How stupid of me. Can you buy me one of those phones that can't be traced? What do they call them? Disposable? I'll pay for it." She pulled out a wallet and handed me two hundred dollars in cash. "That should cover it, don't you think?"

"I imagine so. Eric will be here later, so I'll dash out to the drugstore to buy one right now. That way you won't lose any time calling the insurance agent in the morning."

"No! Go in the morning, when more people are around on the streets. I would be sick if anything happened to you. I don't want to draw you into my problems."

"I appreciate that. I'll pick up the phone before work tomorrow. How's your hand?"

"It hurt like the devil. I'm doing better now. I saw that Alan came."

"You had a similar setup in one of your books." I hoped I hadn't sounded accusatory.

"That worried me. *Everything* worries me. The slightest sound, even branches rustling in the wind. I'm always on edge, terrified that someone has located me. I understand your point about my book. I considered it, too. I've had far too much time to think. It seems unlikely to be a coincidence, but nothing else happened after that."

"Maybe the person thought you died from the shock. If he didn't know that I lived here, he might have thought no one had found your body yet."

"I just can't imagine how anyone could know I'm here."

"There is the possibility that I was the target. In which case it may have been Emily Branscom because she's the only person who could want to harm me."

"Emily Branscom? What does that strumpet have against a sweetheart like you?"

"Apparently a number of people thought I was having an affair with Maxwell. It's simply not true. Alan found Emily's gym card behind the refrigerator when he repaired it. Sergeant Jonquille speculated that Emily might want to get rid of me so she could have Maxwell all to herself."

Jacquie sat up straight. "That wicked woman! It's not enough that she's seeing my husband? She had to have Maxwell, too? How many men is she sleeping with?"

"*Your* husband?"

Jacquie flipped her hand. "She's welcome to him. We had a good run for a few years. But his gambling brought our marriage crashing down. And after this, there's no hope of reconciliation. I could never go back to him under any circumstances knowing that he planned to kill me. But Emily—two men! She's such a tiny, innocent-looking woman. I wouldn't have thought she had it in her." Jacquie crossed her legs and tapped a manicured nail against her knee. "You see what she was doing? By mimicking a scene from my book, she was trying to cast suspicion on me. Diabolical! I must use that in a book."

"That's turning lemons into lemonade."

Jackie laughed, a full-throated, warm chuckle. "Honey, there's nothing that happens in life that won't turn up in some author's book. People are the most fascinating creatures you can imagine."

My phone pinged, indicating a text from Veronica. I picked it up.

At hospital with Scott. His dad has been beaten to a pulp. Almost unrecognizable. Horrible.

I debated whether it would be wise to tell Jacquie. Deciding that honesty was always the wisest course, I said, "My sister is dating your stepson, Scott."

"Really? I'm glad to hear that. He never wanted to talk with me about his love life. I always asked, and he always gave me some kind of idiotic reply."

"Jacquie, she's at the hospital with him. Your husband was beaten very badly. I'm so sorry."

"Oh no." She sagged against the sofa and hid her face in her hands. "When you borrow from unscrupulous characters and you don't pay up, they send their goons after you. Will he live?"

I texted her question to Veronica.

Don't know. Very bad shape.

"She doesn't know."

Jacquie walked to the French doors. "I hope they don't go after Scott."

"Why would they? He didn't do anything, did he?" I hoped Veronica hadn't fallen for a gambler.

"Those people have no conscience. They know that threatening family members will force the debtor to cough up money."

How had Veronica managed to land in the middle of this? I comforted myself with the thought that they were safe at the hospital. No one would attack them there. But I had to warn her. I texted:

Stay in public areas and be alert. The people who beat him could be dangerous to Scott, too.

Jacquie glanced at her watch and walked over to the kitchen. "We'd better get this place cleaned up before your sweet gentleman friend arrives. I find his presence very comforting. What with the guard outside and a cop staying over at night, I don't think I could have found a safer place."

"You don't have to wash your dishes. I'll do that."

She winked at me. "Crumbs, my dear. Never leave crumbs. Your boyfriend is trained to find them."

"Jacquie, why don't you stay and tell him what's happening? I'm sure he could help you."

"You're so sweet and naive, Florrie. He would take me to the police station where I would be interrogated. They would take a statement and let me go. And I would be dead in twelve hours." She clasped my hand. "Promise me. No matter how deep and lovely his eyes are. No matter how your toes tingle or your heart melts. You will not tell him about me. Promise?"

Dead in twelve hours was a fairly strong selling point. "Promise."

I put away the bottle of wine, and when I turned around, she was gone. Out of sheer curiosity, I wandered the room in search of a hidden door. I examined it top to bottom but could not find any sign of a door or a latch to open it.

I smiled a little. I might have been reluctant to disclose the location, too, if my life depended on it being hidden. I longed to tell Jonquille about Jacquie. Oh, the guilt! But she would come out of hiding soon. She just had to call the insurance company and cancel the policy. What would happen if the insurance company had to have her husband's permission to cancel the policy? What if he was in a coma or unable to talk or sign a document?

I sat down on the sofa with my sketch pad and leafed through it. Starting with my newest doodles, I worked backward. It was sort of like connecting the dots in a drawing for children. A lot of people appeared to be connected to each other. I doodled a circle.

Emily Branscom was having an affair with Jacquie's husband. Jacquie's husband was in dire financial trouble, desperate enough to murder Jacquie. His son was dating Veronica and Helen, apparently simultaneously.

I longed to install Delbert in the middle, but that didn't work because he wasn't connected to them all. But someone was.

I flipped the page and began again. This time, Scott went in the middle. He was his dad's son, Jacquie's stepson, and the son of Emily's lover. He was dating Veronica and Helen. And Delbert had been his roommate. Scott was the link between them all.

Could he have murdered Delbert? Or was I jumping to conclusions? Lance had kicked Delbert out by that time, so it seemed unlikely that Delbert would have invited Scott to the bookstore. Delbert was probably angry with Scott. It could have been some kind of revenge.

On the other hand, Scott used a fake name when he met Helen at Color Me Read. That screamed guilt. Why had he visited the store? To scope it out? What was he looking for?

Were he and Delbert there searching for the same thing? Did one of them find it?"

I didn't want to think that Veronica had been with Scott at the store the night Delbert was murdered. Surely she would have dumped Scott or been hysterical if she knew he murdered Delbert. Of course, she hadn't told me what happened to her at work. Even if she didn't come forward with the truth about that night, she wouldn't continue seeing a killer, would she? But there was that pearl. I doodled it again with a broken strand of pearls. It grated at me because it tied my sister, who was kind and gentle and sweet, to the murder.

I shivered to think that Veronica was with him at that very moment. I had to get her away from him. She was already miffed with me for telling her he was seeing Helen. This would be tricky. He might be able to see her phone, so a text could be dangerous. Maybe a phone call would be better.

I pressed her number on my phone and listened to it ring.

Chapter 37

My call rolled over to Veronica's voice mail. Why didn't we have some kind of secret code that I could text to her to indicate trouble? I had to be very careful what I said.

Veronica, call me as soon as you can. I have a big problem.

I hoped that wording wouldn't make it sound like I was onto Scott, just in case he overheard my message when she played it back.

A text came in from Veronica.

Seriously? Now? I'm in the ER with Scott, whose dad may not make it through the night. Can't it wait until morning?

I kept my response simple.

No.

She didn't text back.

My phone rang and I jabbed the accept button.

"Hi, Florrie. It's Mom. Is Norman with you?"

"Thankfully, no."

"He hasn't come home yet, and his parents are worried sick."

"Mom, Norman is thirty years old. He doesn't have a cur-
few. Maybe he went to a movie."

"You're right. His mother always talks about him like he's
ten. Thanks, honey."

I hung up and called Bob. "Did you find Scott?"

"You bet. I just witnessed the catfight of the year. I'm not
sure, but I think your sister won. Helen is pouting, and Scott
departed with Veronica."

"They left the hospital? Where are they going?"

"I have no idea. But . . ."

"Tail them! Can you follow them?"

"It's too late for that. What's going on, Florrie?"

"I think Scott killed Delbert. We have to get Veronica
away from him."

"Whoa! Not the answer I expected. They've got a big
head start. It would be a fluke if we saw them."

"Let me know if you do."

I hung up. Where was Jonquille? I was about to call him
when my phone rang. Veronica was calling. Thank heaven!

"Veronica! I was worried when I didn't hear from you.
Everything okay?"

"Listen carefully, little Florrie." I recognized Scott's terse
voice. "Veronica is with me. Bring Jacquie to the tow path on
the canal, and you can have Veronica."

My heart raced but I tried to play it cool. "I have no idea
what you're talking about."

"Don't play stupid with me. I know Jacquie is there."

"You mean Maxwell's second wife? I haven't seen her." I
could hear my blood pounding in my ears.

"Then say bye-bye to your sister."

Someone near him made muffled sounds. He must have
gagged her!

"Wait! I'll find Jacquie, but I don't know where she is. I need some time."

"Well played, Florrie. But I'm not giving you time to call your cop friend. If a single police officer or cop car shows up, it's curtains for Veronica."

He hung up.

My hands were shaking when I phoned Jonquille.

"Hi, Florrie! I'm on my way."

"I think Scott murdered Delbert. He has Veronica and wants to trade her for Jacquie."

"Slow down. Where is Scott?" Jonquille sounded calm but serious.

"In his car. He said to meet them on the tow path."

"That doesn't make any sense. How are you supposed to find Jacquie?"

"He thinks she's here. And if any cops show up, Veronica is dead."

"Listen to me, Florrie. Let us handle this. There's nothing you can do. Stay put, okay? It will only make things worse if you're running around down at the tow path."

In my heart, I knew he was right. But I didn't want to wait at home wringing my hands like some maiden in distress. "Eric? You'll save her, won't you?"

"I'll do my best, Florrie."

I ended the call feeling helpless. I barely had time to pace to the French doors and back when I heard a knock at the front door.

"Florrie?"

That was Veronica's voice!

"Florrie, let me in. Ugh."

I peered out. Veronica stood on the other side of the door. Where was the guard? I was 100 percent certain that she wasn't alone. Scott must be with her. I had to let her in. But before I did, I tucked a chef's knife into a partially open kitchen drawer where I could reach it easily.

The second I unlocked the door, Scott pushed it open. Veronica stumbled inside, one high heel on, the other missing. Her eyes expressed her terror.

I shoved her behind me and backed away from Scott. While his frantic gaze darted around the carriage house, I backed slowly toward the fireplace. Keeping my eyes on him, I gently prodded Veronica to shuffle backward. My hope was to reach the French doors and escape into the garden. The odds of us getting out of the gate to the driveway were slim, but I didn't see any other way.

Veronica sniffled behind me, murmuring, "What are we going to do? We need time to find Jacquie."

That gave me an idea. It was a long shot at best.

"Jacquie, run!" I screamed, hoping he would turn long enough for us to hurry out through the garden.

He fell for it and ran to the door, his back to us. He paused, and my hope faded. But then he dashed outside, and I knew I had to get Veronica out of there.

But as I turned, a hand reached over my mouth and tugged me backward.

Jacquie's voice whispered in my ear. "Don't make a sound. Hurry!" She pushed me into a tiny space, and I found myself climbing down a ladder. Jacquie closed the door above, and I heard the latch slide in place.

It was a tight spot for the three of us. Jacquie Liebhaber placed a finger over her lips in a signal not to make any noise. Veronica looked terrified. Peaches was nonchalant.

I made the universal *okay* symbol by making a circle with my thumb and forefinger so Veronica would know we were safe. At least I hoped we were. I untied her hands.

We could hear Scott roaring. Books flew. I suspected some of my beloved clocks crashed to the floor.

He stomped up the stairs, screaming, "You can't outfox me. I know you're here." Moments later, he pounded down them. "Jacquie told me about the hidden passage. Come out, come out," he sang. "You have two minutes to produce Jacquie. Two minutes."

There was silence. Jacquie, Veronica, and I gazed at one another.

"Time's up! Send Jacquie out or die in flames."

Seconds ticked by.

"Okay, so that's how you want to die. You see, I don't have to produce Jacquie, all I have to do is make sure she's dead. With all this wood, the place ought to go up in flames very quickly. I'll look the hero for trying to rescue you. And it will save me the trouble of killing you individually."

I turned to Jacquie and pointed back. It seemed like a good time to head through the tunnel to the mansion.

But at that very moment, we heard music. More specifically "Love Me Tender," sung badly off-key to a strumming guitar.

If our situation hadn't been so dire, we would have been trying to stifle laughter.

And then it stopped.

We waited for an eternity that was probably only minutes. I sniffed the air fearing Scott had started a fire and left. But I didn't hear crackling or smell smoke.

The next sound was truly music to my ears. Sergeant Eric Jonquille called, "Florrie! Florrie! Are you here?"

Jacquie winked at me. When we heard Jonquille dashing upstairs, Jacquie urged Veronica, Peaches, and me out of hiding.

Jonquille ran down the stairs, swung me up in his arms, and held me tight. "I thought I'd lost you," he breathed into my ear.

It wasn't until he released his grip on me that I saw Scott through the open door.

He lay on the ground outside, being handcuffed by a cop, while Norman and Jim looked on.

I scooped up Peaches so she wouldn't run out to the street and walked outside clutching her in my arms.

"Norman? Jim? What are you doing here?"

Jim beamed at me. "I sure am glad to see that you're all right."

Norman appeared somewhat confused.

A cop helped Scott to his feet. Scott wasn't my type to begin with, but I couldn't help thinking how much anger distorted his face. If Helen or Veronica had seen him like this, neither one would ever have been attracted to him.

Veronica walked up to him. "How could you do that to me? I thought . . . I thought you were special. Did you only go out with me because my sister worked at Color Me Read?"

Scott said, "I thought I would marry you."

"Oh please!" she cried. "Did you intend to carry me off to the altar bound and gagged?"

Scott sounded sincere when he said, "Delbert told Lance and me what he did to some woman at work using her social media accounts to bad-mouth people and get her fired. He thought it was brilliant of him. One night we were at Club Neon, and he pointed you out to me. I couldn't believe he would be that cruel to someone so beautiful. I bought you a drink, and we hit it off. I didn't know anything about your sister."

"You thought I was beautiful?" asked Veronica in a wistful voice.

Was she nuts? "Veronica! He was going to kill you! You never mentioned to her that Delbert was your roommate?" I asked.

"I'm not stupid! She never would have gone out with me if she knew that."

"What I'd like to know is why you and Delbert went to

Color Me Read that night. What did you want there?" I
asked.

"Jacquie used to talk about the emerald and diamond necklace that she wore when she was Mrs. Maxwell. She said it was
like being royalty. I found an old picture of her wearing it. It
looked to me like the stones would be worth a lot if I broke
down the necklace and sold them individually. Plus, they
would be impossible to trace back to the necklace. I was planning to use one of the diamonds in an engagement ring for
Veronica."

"Aww," Veronica cooed. "How romantic."

"A stolen diamond. That's what you find romantic?" Good
grief! I hated to think what might have happened if Veronica
had married Scott.

Scott continued, "And then when I lived with Delbert, he
bragged about that necklace and how he would inherit it
someday. He thought it was worth millions. I talked to my dad
about it, and he thought it was probably hidden in the hooch
hatch in Color Me Read. His company did some work there a
long time ago and he remembered it. So I stopped by the store
to scope it out and met Helen. It was easy to get her a little
loaded at a bar and swipe her key to make a copy. I figured
there was a code to shut off an alarm, but after a little wine, she
blabbed that."

"You fought with Delbert over the necklace?" I guessed.

"No. It wasn't that way at all. That night, I dressed in black
and let myself into the store. I found the hatch and opened it. I
jumped in, and suddenly, a spear barely missed me." He shook
his head.

"It was really close. It was almost my corpse you found
there. The tip stuck in the floor. For a second, I thought the
professor had booby-trapped the place until I turned around
and saw Delbert above me. Lance and I had kicked him out of

the house, and I knew he wasn't going to have a beer with me and laugh about finding me there. He was holding a vicious-looking hatchet."

Looking at Jonquille as he talked, Scott said, "He pulled his arm back like he was going to throw it, and I instinctively grabbed that spear and let it fly. It was me or him. I knew it was a fight to the death. Delbert was seriously crazy. At the precise moment that I threw the spear, he turned to run, and it hit him in the back. He screamed and kept going up the stairs and along the hallway toward an office. He was bleeding something awful. He fell face-first in the hallway, moaning. I took the hatchet away from him, wiped it off, and put it in the office. When I came back, he was dead. By that time I was panicking. I dragged him to the hatch, threw him inside, and tried to tuck the carpet back in place. I got out of there in a huge hurry." He sniffled.

"I didn't know what to do. Dad had gone out of town to try to win enough money to keep the creditors at bay. Gambling is addictive, and he was sick. He thought it was the only way he could get back on his feet. He had mortgaged everything, hadn't made payments in months and months, and he was so desperate that he was borrowing money from scumbags. That's when I got worried. They started coming around demanding payments of usurious loans. They took advantage of him and were charging 50 percent interest. It's impossible to pay back that kind of loan. I had to do *something*."

He locked his eyes on Veronica. "I was a little hysterical. I mean, I never killed anyone before. Dad had come home early because he lost again and had nothing more to bid with. He hoped I had found the necklace, but I had messed up big-time. And then a really nasty guy came by to collect what he was owed. To get rid of him, Dad told him about the five-million-dollar insurance policy he had on Jacquie. The guy said he'd do the job, but he'd better get the money he was owed. Jacquie never came home that night. We were afraid he had kidnapped her and killed her."

Scott took a deep breath and released it slowly. "The next day, Dad went online and found out Jacquie had emptied bank accounts. She had wiped them clean. We didn't know what to do. Did she take the money on her own? Or did someone force her to take the money? So I started nosing around her desk and found her book of Internet passwords. I logged on as her and used Find My iPhone. Surprise, surprise. Turned out she was at the Maxwell mansion."

"So you knew where she was?" I asked. "Then why did you hire a private investigator?"

"We didn't. Things were getting worse and worse for Dad. We didn't even have the money to hire a decent PI. When Dad's girlfriend was visiting, I borrowed her car and drove over to Georgetown. I figured Jacquie was staying in the carriage house in back of the mansion. She loved that place. I got rid of the guard by paying some kid to deliver a pizza to the mansion, bumped the lock, and switched the wires on the refrigerator. Then I waited to hear if she was dead."

Chapter 38

"So it was just plain greed?" asked Jim.

"Don't you understand? It was never about the money," said Scott.

Jonquille and I shared a look.

"It wasn't like I was greedy or needed to be super rich. The money was only a vehicle to save my dad. Like Veronica wound up as a commodity that I could exchange for Jacquie. I didn't want to hurt Veronica. But I had a hunch that Florrie would do anything to save her, just like I would have done anything to save my dad. But I wasn't able to protect him from those goons. When Dad called me this afternoon, he could barely speak. I drove to his house and found him on the floor, beaten to a pulp. He was barely recognizable, but still breathing. I called the ambulance, and while I was at the hospital, I knew what I had to do. There was no choice. I had to strangle Jacquie and dump her into the river. It was the only way I could get that kind of money."

An ambulance arrived to whisk the guard to a hospital.

"Is he going to be okay?" I asked Jonquille.

"I hope so. Apparently Scott pretended to be your friend, and when the guard walked to your door, Scott choked him

from behind. But he only succeeded in knocking him uncon-
scious."

The ambulance backed out of the mansion driveway only
to be replaced by a police car that took Scott to the station.

Jonquille ushered us all inside.

I couldn't help myself. I boiled water for tea to soothe our
nerves and brought out the strawberry cream torte while Jonquille tried to piece everything together.

He pointed at Veronica. "I think this story probably starts
with you."

"I should have listened to my big sister. I went to the hospital
to be with Scott. His father was a mess. I've never seen anyone
look like that. They're not sure if he'll survive the night. So we
were there in the waiting room when Helen and Bob found us. I
didn't want to believe Florrie when she told me Scott was dating
Helen. Well, Helen was furious and gave him an earful—in the
waiting room in front of everyone! Scott said we were leaving,
but when we got in the car, he bound my wrists and put a gag
over my mouth."

She closed her eyes and heaved a heavy breath. "I thought
it was the end. I was so scared. When we got here, he took the
gag off, but told me if I screwed up, Florrie would be dead. He
choked the guard and forced me to ask Florrie to let me in."

Jonquille gazed at Norman. "Who are you?"

"Uh, I didn't know anything about any of this," said Norman. "I just came to woo Florrie." He gestured toward the
guitar he brought with him.

Jonquille smiled. "So *you're* Norman Spratt."

Norman blinked repeatedly as though he was having trouble figuring out what was happening.

Jim stopped eating for a moment. "I was walking along the
sidewalk when I saw Scott drive by with Veronica gagged and
looking scared. He turned up the mansion driveway. Never
trusted that guy. He always looked shifty to me. I eased up the

driveway pretty slow because I wasn't sure what was going on. And then Norman came along with his guitar, and I thought the whole thing kind of peculiar, so I followed Norman. I spotted the guard lying on the ground right away, so I knew something was up. Then old Norman here ignored the guard and commenced to playing his guitar and singing 'Love Me Tender'! I stood next to the door, expecting Scott to open it to see who was singing, and sure enough, he did just that. I jumped him and punched him in the head a few times to take him down."

"What were you doing up this way?" I asked. "I thought you always headed for the canal at night."

"There's a bakery a few blocks away that gives away all their stale bread on Sunday nights. I never miss it."

I looked at Jonquille. "How did you know to come here instead of going to the tow path on the canal?"

"I'd like to sound brilliant, but I didn't know. We put everyone on alert and sent extra cops down that way. But I had a feeling Scott was craftier than that. He knew you would call me. When you said the name *Emily Branscom,* I knew it rang a bell. I went over to the district police station tonight and did a little digging. I wrote Emily a ticket for parking in a no-parking zone right down the street."

I shrugged. "So?"

"It was on the day someone crossed the wires of your refrigerator."

"So it was her?"

"Not exactly. She was also issued a parking ticket the night of Delbert's murder."

"I don't understand," said Veronica.

"Scott drove the car of his father's mistress when he committed crimes. That's also why he stole her gym club membership and left it behind the refrigerator. He was trying to make her look guilty."

"So Emily wasn't involved at all?" I asked.

"Looks that way," said Jonquille. "And now, I'm sorry to have to do this, but I need statements from all of you."

We piled into cars and drove to the police station. It was a long night with terrible coffee. But I was determined to spring Professor Maxwell as soon as possible. I phoned Ms. Strickland and woke her with the good news that an arrest had been made in the murder of Delbert Woodley.

While we sat around at the police station, I sidled over and sat down next to Jim. He smelled a little rank, but I took his hand into mine anyway. "Thank you. If you hadn't been looking out for us, there's no telling what might have happened to Veronica and me."

"It was nothing." He squeezed my hand. "You've been watching over me for a long time. It was the least I could do."

I had no idea how to begin. Subtlety clearly wasn't one of my strengths. "Jim, what happened to you? Why do you live on the street?"

"It's a boring story. Life sometimes twists in directions that you don't expect, and you can't do anything but go along."

"Don't you have any family who could help you?"

He shook his head. "Not anymore. Don't worry about me. I'll be okay."

I tried to prod him a little bit. Surely there was someone who cared about this man. "Are you married?"

He massaged his ring finger. "She passed."

"I'm sorry." Why wasn't Bob here? He would know how to coax information out of Jim. "What was her name?"

"Sue. We met in high school. She used to say that we were meant to be together. We weren't anybody special, but ours was a true love affair."

I believed him. Even his voice became gentle when he spoke about her. "What happened to Sue?"

"Early onset Alzheimer's disease. I lost a little bit of her every day." He closed his eyes as if the mere memory of it was still fresh and raw.

"Jim, I'm sure she wouldn't want to see you living this way."

"No, she wouldn't. She would be horrified. We had good jobs. Sue was a registered nurse and after a stint in the army, I went to work as a recreation director. But as she declined, I had to stay home and take care of her. People told me to send her to a facility, but I couldn't bring myself to do that to her. And they're very pricey, too. I sold the house and that kept us afloat for a while. Then the car"—he looked down at his hand—"and then our wedding rings."

"Didn't you have friends who could help you?"

He examined my face. "Folks have their own lives to lead. They start off being wonderful, but after a while they taper off, and you're all by yourself. All alone with the most precious person in the world to you."

I heard sniffling and turned around. I hadn't realized that Veronica was listening.

She wiped her eyes with her fingers. "That's such a sad story. We'll help you, Jim. Won't we, Florrie?"

"Jim," I said gently, "would you like a job?"

Jim patted my hand. "Nobody would hire me. I've asked for jobs sweeping stores and bagging groceries. Nobody wants a ragged fellow like me hanging around."

Veronica hugged Jim. "We'll help you. For Sue."

Jim and Veronica bawled, and my eyes grew misty.

Jonquille showed up just then. "What's going on? Why is everyone crying?"

"It's true love," wailed Veronica.

Joquille was thoroughly confused. "This ought to cheer you up. Ms. Strickland must have pulled every string she had at her disposal because the professor is about to be sprung."

At three in the morning, Professor John Maxwell walked out of jail. We were all waiting for him. Everyone except Jacquie.

A cheer went up along with applause. He had been sorely missed. Much to my surprise, he looked pretty good in spite of being incarcerated.

He hugged me to him. "I knew I could count on you, Florrie."

"Don't give me too much credit. A lot of people were involved."

"Jailhouse rumor has it that you're dating a cop now. Will I like him?"

"You would believe a jailhouse rumor like that?"

"He'd better be very special for my Florrie."

None of us got any sleep that night. In the morning, Veronica and I went to work as though nothing had happened. We were dog-tired, but still wired from what had happened to us.

I brought the last piece of strawberry cream torte to Jim for breakfast. He sat on his bench entertaining an audience of reporters. I handed him the torte.

"Cake for breakfast?" he asked.

"Sponge cake. It has a lot of eggs in it."

He laughed and said, "Thanks, Florrie."

Unfortunately, the mere mention of my name turned the attention of the reporters to me.

To escape them, Veronica and I hurried to the bookstore, where Bob waited at the door.

"Are you ever going to tell me the alarm code?" he asked.

"FreeMaxwell," I said.

"I should have guessed."

There was a long awkward moment when Helen arrived. She and Veronica stared at each other, and we all froze in place.

Finally, Veronica said, "I'm glad you told Scott off last night. If I'd had any sense, I would have dumped him on the spot. I should have realized that you and Florrie weren't lying."

Helen held out her arms to Veronica for a hug. "I'm just

glad that you survived. How could two smart women like us have fallen for such a terrible man?"

Bob sagged with relief and gave me a thumbs-up.

The bookstore was swamped from the moment we opened for business. Veronica kept the social media buzz going. Who'd have thought a murder would be good for business?

Mom and Dad showed up at ten minutes past ten.

"Why must we always hear about our daughters' exploits from the Spratts?" demanded Mom. "Mrs. Spratt phoned an hour ago to inform me that Norman is not allowed to play with my girls anymore because they are indecorous and risqué and put her Norman in mortal danger. Apparently Norman called his parents from the police station in the wee hours of the morning! Then your poor father nearly had heart failure when he opened the newspaper this morning and learned that Veronica was dating a murderer whom she brought to our home yesterday!"

I was a little ashamed by the way Veronica and I laughed when our parents were so serious. But I was very relieved to be done with Norman, even if it was a little embarrassing that his mommy thought I was a wild woman.

Each of us took a quick coffee break to chat with Mom and Dad and assure them that all was well with us.

Maxwell walked in around eleven followed by members of the press.

It did not escape my attention that Helen had her eye on a particular reporter who bore a striking resemblance to Scott.

I nudged Veronica. "Leave the Scott lookalike alone."

She glanced up from her work and spotted him in the crowd. "I could never date anyone who resembled Scott. I'd fear for my life the whole time. No thanks. I'm done with that type. I'm looking for someone totally passive and boring."

"There's always Norman," I said, "but we've been banned from playing with him."

That set us off in fits of uncontrollable laughter.

Maxwell held court in the parlor. He smiled, posed for pictures, and regaled reporters and shoppers with tales of his incarceration, which began to sound more like a trip to a concrete jungle than the misery that it probably was. His buddies Zsazsa, Goldblum, and Bankhouse hovered nearby, drinking it all in.

Jonquille stopped by to say hi. He looked bushed and was on his way home for much needed sleep. I hated to admit to myself that I would miss seeing him every day.

I worked until ten that night, ate leftovers from Mom's cookout, and fell asleep with Peaches next to me.

Even though the sun streamed through the windows when I rose the next day, morning didn't seem as sunny without Jonquille.

In the hope that he might feel the same way, I showered in a hurry and dressed in a delicate blouse and a flared melon-colored skirt that always made me feel very feminine.

I was making coffee when someone knocked on my door. I grinned. Hoping it would be Jonquille, I threw the door open wide.

Jacquie walked in.

"What? You're using a door like a regular person? Have you come out of hiding?"

"Almost." She pointed outside. "I have my own bodyguard now. For the time being at least."

I looked out the door, and Felipe waved at me.

"That's probably a good move." I fetched my purse and returned her two hundred dollars. "I assumed you didn't need the disposable phone anymore. If anyone were listening in, you would want them to know the bounty was off your head. It is, isn't it?"

She nodded. "Maxwell took care of that for me right away. Isn't that just like him? He wasn't even home twelve hours before he started taking care of me when he's the one who ought to be pampered."

"Does that mean you two might reconcile?" I asked.

"Could be. We'll have to give it some time."

"I guess you'd like your carriage house back to work in. I can look around for another apartment," I said reluctantly.

"Maxwell and I want you to stay. I always thought Caroline might live out here when she was about your age. She never got the chance, but your presence here brings me joy. If things work out between Maxwell and me and I move in, I'll renovate something to suit me. Maybe the third floor of the mansion. I always dreamed of writing in a cozy French-type garret with huge windows on a slant in the roof and a little balcony with French doors."

"I didn't know how to reach you yesterday, Jacquie. I want to thank you for saving Veronica and me. I honestly think one of us would be dead if you hadn't pulled us into hiding. I intended to run out to the garden, but Scott would have caught one of us for sure."

Instead of being happy, she wiped tears from her eyes. "I wasn't able to save my own child, so it means a lot to me to have been able to save someone else's."

I hugged her. "I'm so sorry. You would have been a very cool mom."

"Thank you, Florrie." She sniffled. "So the real reason I came over here was to invite you, Veronica, Sergeant Jonquille, Norman, and Jim to a party for Maxwell tomorrow night. I hope you'll come."

"I wouldn't miss it."

"Wonderful. Can you invite Jim? I'm not sure where to find him."

"I would love to. Jacquie, does your husband own the building where Sugar Dreams Cupcakes used to be?"

She seemed surprised. "How did you know? I guess he

doesn't own it anymore. The last I heard, the bank was taking it over."

She left with Felipe.

I sipped my coffee and realized that clues to Scott's desperation had been there from the very beginning. I just hadn't made the right connections.

The following evening, we gathered around the pool of the Maxwell mansion. Mr. DuBois was still in a wheelchair, but he was back in his element, bossing the caterers around.

Zsazsa wore dramatic eyeliner and an eye-catching low-cut dress. Goldblum was his jolly self. Bankhouse admitted to everyone that he had feared Helen might be involved.

Jonquille came with his friend, Cody, who could hardly take his eyes off Veronica. At least we knew Cody was a decent and law-abiding sort.

Jacquie was resplendent in a puffy white button-down blouse with the collar turned up in back and a pair of cropped pants that looked satiny. Her hair had been cut and colored, and she looked like the photo of her in the back of her books.

I knew Jacquie and Maxwell would be a couple again from the way they looked at each other. She would gaze at him from across the pool, their eyes would meet, and there was no mistaking the love between them.

Jim parked his belongings at the carriage house so no one would steal them. I had arranged for a visit to a barbershop, and Veronica had gone shopping for him on her lunch hour. He wore his new khaki trousers and a blue shirt, and mingled with the others comfortably. If I hadn't known, I never would have suspected that he lived on the street.

Norman followed me like a baby duck follows its mother. I began to worry that his mom's warnings about my wicked behavior had actually attracted him to me more.

Jacquie had also invited my parents. I inched toward Dad when I saw him speaking with Jim.

"Florrie and Veronica told me what happened to you," Dad said. "I'm very sorry for the loss of your wife. At the request of my meddling daughters, I have asked around a bit, and found that a friend of mine has been looking for a dependable person to help out at his roller skating rink. If you're interested, I can pick you up and drive you to the interview tomorrow."

Jim hugged my dad like he was the best person in the world. I wasn't the only champion of lost causes in my family. I learned it from my parents.

In spite of the interesting company and the incredible buffet, talk turned to Scott and Delbert.

"There are a few things that I still don't understand," I said. "For starters, if Scott and his dad didn't hire a private detective to find Jacquie, then who hired the man who came here looking for her?"

Maxwell put his arm around my shoulders and whispered, "Follow the money."

"The insurance money?"

"Jacquie is worth a lot to someone else, too," he said.

"Her agent?" I guessed.

"When I disappeared," said Jacquie, "I missed a couple of appearances, which worried my agent, who is a dear friend. She knew that I was having problems with my husband. When I didn't respond to her calls, and my husband didn't have any answers about what might have happened to me, my agent hired that private investigator to find me."

"Scott said he found you by using Find My iPhone. But you were being so careful. You didn't make any calls so they wouldn't find you."

"I don't understand that, either," said Jackie.

Jonquille stepped up beside me. "He found your password.

I tried it out on my own phone last night. A map popped up right away and showed me where I was. Scott located you in seconds."

I eyed my sister. "So you were at Club Neon the night of Delbert's death. With Scott?"

"Right. He was distracted and in the end we didn't stay long."

"That was the night your pearls broke?"

"So embarrassing. They rolled all over the floor."

"Scott helped you collect them?"

Veronica frowned. "He was very much a gentleman about it."

"He must have had one in his pocket that fell out when he was covering up the hatch in the floor," I mused.

Veronica addressed the professor. "What I want to know is what happened to the emerald and diamond necklace? If Delbert didn't have it on him, and Scott didn't find it, then what happened to it?"

Maxwell sighed. "One of them must have discovered it. I never keep it in the safe because that's the first place everyone would look. It's always in a carved-out book on the shelf in my bedroom. It's gone, so Scott must have found it the night he broke into the mansion."

"Oh please." Jacquie laughed. "Did you think I would let some burglar walk off with that necklace?" She gently parted the top of her blouse to reveal it on her neck. Large round emeralds were surrounded by diamonds, and a giant pear-shaped emerald hung from the middle. The diamonds that surrounded it sparkled under the evening sun.

"Have you been wearing that the whole time?" I asked.

Jacquie grinned. "You've heard the expression *over my dead body?* The burglar was going to have to kill me to get it. No two-bit con was going to get this away from me and divide it into unrecognizable pieces! It's a historical work of art. The necklace belongs here at the Maxwell estate."

Jonquille slid his hand into mine and drew me away while all eyes were on Jacquie and the necklace.

He whispered in my ear, "Run!"

Still holding hands, we sprinted across the grass and dodged behind a cluster of rhododendrons and azaleas.

"I thought I'd never get you away from Norman. That guy ought to be a private investigator. Here he comes. There's no shaking him."

Still holding my hand, he leaned in and kissed me on the lips. "I've missed you, Florrie."

My heart beat so hard I was afraid he could feel it. And I was fairly certain that my toes tingled. But I could hear Norman nearing as he called, "Florrie! Florrie! Where did you go?"

"Where's a secret passage when you need one?" I joked. "Breakfast tomorrow?"

"I thought you'd never ask."

Jonquille kissed me again and this time I definitely tingled all the way down to my toes.

When we walked back, Norman fell in step with us and told us all about the grass in the professor's yard.

Jim took the job at the skating rink. My mother found him an affordable apartment nearby, and Maxwell paid the rent for the first year to help Jim get back on his feet. I missed seeing Jim every morning, but there was someone else who brightened my days.

Jacquie dedicated her next book to me. It was the one she wrote longhand while in hiding and featured a coloring book artist who had to go into hiding because her husband held a five-million-dollar insurance policy on her. She called it *Color Me Murder*.

RECIPES

Blackberry Breakfast Muffins

(makes 12 muffins)

Butter for greasing muffin tin
1½ cups flour
½ cup sugar
1½ teaspoons baking powder
¼ teaspoon nutmeg
⅛ teaspoon salt
1 egg
½ cup 2% milk
⅓ cup butter, melted
1 cup fresh blackberries
½ teaspoon cinnamon
¼ cup sugar
¼ cup butter, melted

Preheat oven to 350 degrees Fahrenheit. Grease muffin wells in the muffin pan. Combine the flour, ½ cup sugar, baking powder, nutmeg, and salt in a bowl. Mix well with a fork, and make a well in the middle. In another bowl, whisk the egg with a fork, pour in the milk, and combine, then whisk in the ⅓ cup melted butter. Add the egg mixture to the flour mixture and stir until just combined. It should be lumpy. Do not overmix! Add the blackberries and turn gently to distribute. Spoon into muffin pan, dividing evenly, filling each well about ½ full. Bake at 350 for 10 to 20 minutes. Meanwhile, stir the cinnamon with the ¼ cup sugar. Melt the ¼ cup butter in a small bowl. Remove the baked muffins from oven. While still hot, remove each muffin from the pan, dip into the melted butter, and then dip into the sugar.

Raspberry Quick Bread
with Vanilla Glaze

1 teaspoon vinegar
1 cup milk
2¼ cups flour
1½ teaspoons baking powder
¾ teaspoon salt
¾ teaspoon cinnamon
1 stick butter (8 tablespoons) at room temperature
¾ cup dark brown sugar
½ cup regular sugar
3 eggs
2 teaspoons vanilla
2 pints fresh raspberries (may use fresh blueberries or halved
   small strawberries)

Preheat oven to 350 degrees Fahrenheit. Line a bread baking pan with parchment paper so that it hangs over the long sides. Butter the interior ends of the pan. Pour the vinegar into the 1 cup of milk and set aside. Place the flour, baking powder, salt, and cinnamon in a bowl and mix well. Set aside. Cream the butter with the sugar. Beat in the eggs. On a slow speed, add the flour in batches, alternating with the vinegar-milk and berries. Add the vanilla and beat. Bake around 60 to 70 minutes or until a cake tester comes out clean. Lift out of pan with the parchment "wings." If using a small loaf pan, bake the remainder of the batter as small cupcakes for 16 minutes or giant cupcakes for 20 minutes.

Vanilla Glaze

3 tablespoons melted butter
1 cup powdered sugar

1½ tablespoons heavy cream
1 teaspoon vanilla

Krista's tip: For easy cleanup and application, make this in a
microwave-safe glass measuring cup.

Melt the butter in the microwave for about 30 to 40 seconds. Add the powdered sugar, the cream, and vanilla. Stir or
whisk until thick and smooth. Pour over cooled bread.

Strawberries and Cream Torte

Cake

¼ cup flour
5 slightly heaping tablespoons cornstarch
1 teaspoon baking powder
4 large eggs at room temperature
3–4 tablespoons warm water
½ cup sugar
1 teaspoon vanilla

Preheat oven to 350 degrees Fahrenheit. Grease two 8- or 9-inch baking pans. Cut parchment paper for the bottoms and insert. In a bowl, whisk together the flour, corn starch, and baking powder. Set aside. Separate the eggs into two mixing bowls. Four egg whites go in bowl one. The 4 egg yolks go in bowl two.

Lightly mix the egg yolks with the warm water. Add half the sugar and beat.

Beat the egg whites on a low speed until foamy. Then increase to medium speed. Beat to soft, moist peaks. Add the remaining half of the sugar and beat. Do not overbeat! They should still be a little bit soft.

Stir the flour mixture into the egg yolks. Add the vanilla. Gently fold the egg yolks and egg whites together until the flour cannot be seen and everything is incorporated. Pour into prepared pans. Bake 10 to 15 minutes. When touched, it should be firm but spring back. Remove from oven, place on kitchen towels, and immediately loosen by running a knife around the edges. Place a plate over top, and grip with the towels to flip. Peel off the parchment paper. Flip from plate onto cooling rack. Cool before frosting.

Cream

4 teaspoons of cold water or cold heavy cream
1 packet (about 1 teaspoon) unflavored gelatin
1 cup heavy cream for whipping
¼ to ⅓ cup powdered sugar
½ teaspoon vanilla

Pour the 4 teaspoons of water or heavy cream into a small pot. Sprinkle the gelatin over it. Give it a few minutes to thicken. Meanwhile, beat the 1 cup of heavy cream until it begins to thicken and take shape. Add the sugar and vanilla and whip. Do not overbeat! Place the gelatin over medium-low heat and stir constantly until gelatin is completely dissolved. Remove from heat and cool, but don't allow it to set. (If it should set, try reheating and stirring to dissolve it again.) While slowly beating the cream, pour the gelatin into it. Whip at high speed until it holds a stiff peak.

Assembly

2 to 3 16-ounce packages of fresh strawberries

Set aside 3 or 4 pretty strawberries for the top. Place the bottom layer of the cake on a serving plate. Top with cream and spread. Hull and halve the strawberries (or chop them if you prefer) and arrange on the cream. Place the top layer over the strawberries. Spread cream over top and sides. Ideally, you will have enough strawberries to halve them and place them around the base, point up. If not, then pipe cream at the base and on the top. Add halved strawberries to the top.

Turn the page for a preview
of Krista Davis's next
Domestic Diva Mystery . . .

The Diva Cooks Up a Storm

Coming June 2018
from Kensington Publishing

Dear Sophie,

I met a very cute guy recently. We went out once and now he has invited me to an "underground dinner." He doesn't know where it will be, what will be served, or who else will be there. This sounds very suspicious. I don't want to end up under the ground! Is this a real thing?

Trepidatious in Lick Fork, Virginia

Dear Trepidatious,

Underground dinners, also known as pop-up dinners, are all the rage right now. An undisclosed but well-known chef prepares a surprise menu in a location that isn't revealed until the last minute. Tickets are typically bought well in advance. They're a lot of fun, but you'll have to decide whether this is what the new boyfriend actually has in mind.

Sophie

At ten in the morning on the first day of my summer vacation, a bloodcurdling scream pierced the tranquility of my neighborhood in Old Town Alexandria. My hound mix, Daisy, had been sniffing around my backyard while I enjoyed a mug of coffee.

Daisy barked once and ran for the front gate. Dogs have far better hearing than humans, so I trusted her inclination about the direction of the trouble and followed right behind her.

A man ran toward us on the sidewalk, his gait awkward and ungainly. He waved his hands madly around his head and continued screaming.

By that time, my neighbors Nina Reid Norwood and Francie Vanderhoosen had emerged from their homes.

At first blush, the man appeared to be deranged. But as he

neared, his dilemma became readily apparent. Angry bees buzzed around him and more followed.

I seized his hand. "Quick. Into the house!"

Daisy snapped at the bees as we ran, Nina and Francie bringing up the rear. We rushed into my kitchen and quickly closed the door behind us.

A few bees had made it inside. Nina and Francie grabbed sections of the newspaper and swatted at them while Daisy continued to chase and snap at them.

Meanwhile, I sat the man down. Thirtyish, I guessed. His green T-shirt bore the hound face logo of The Laughing Hound, a local restaurant. His jeans were dusty, as though he'd been doing lawn work in them. He was having trouble breathing. Red welts had already formed on his face.

"Do you have a bee allergy?" I asked.

"Noh. Gihzzy." He opened his mouth for some deep breaths. There was no mistaking the swelling of his tongue.

I grabbed the phone, dialed 911, and handed it to Nina while I wet a kitchen towel with cold water. I had no idea whether that was the right thing to do, but I held it against his face.

Francie seized the beautiful pink begonia from my bay window, pulled it out of the pot, and scooped up dirt in her hands. "Scoot over, Sophie."

She packed the dirt against his face. One of his eyes was swelling shut.

"Will you look at that?" asked Nina. "Bees are still buzzing around your kitchen door."

Some of them were even hitting the glass window in the door.

Moments later the reassuring wail of an ambulance soothed my nerves. Allergic or not, this guy needed medical attention. I opened the front door and they walked inside, calm as a serene lake.

An emergency medical technician asked the man, "What's your name, sir?"

His speech was so garbled that none of us could understand it.

"You ladies know him?"

The three of us looked at one another and shook our heads.

"He came running down the street with bees buzzing all around him," I said.

The EMT felt the young man's pockets for a wallet and extracted it while another EMT asked what was on his face.

Francie beamed when she said, "Dirt. It's an old home remedy. Soothes the stings."

The EMT shook his head in obvious disbelief.

The one with the wallet said, "I don't see any allergy alerts in here. You're Angus Bogdanoff?"

The young man nodded.

"Got any allergies?"

"Noh." He shook his head.

They administered a shot of epinephrine, put him on a stretcher, and wheeled him out to the ambulance. We trailed along, feeling helpless. We couldn't even notify anyone for the poor guy.

When the ambulance departed, Nina, Francie, and I returned to my kitchen. I took lemonade and iced tea out of the fridge to make Arnold Palmers.

"I'd suggest sitting in the garden," said Francie, "but we probably ought to let any lingering bees dissipate."

"Not to mention that it's already getting warm," Nina groaned. "I swear this is the hottest summer I can remember. I try to stay indoors until six in the evening. Thank heaven the underground dinner tonight doesn't start earlier. They'd have people fainting all over the place."

"Everyone is too pampered these days. We didn't have air-conditioning when I was growing up. I remember my daddy sitting outside to read at ten o'clock at night because it was too stuffy in the house. And no one had air-conditioning in their cars, either. We kids sat in the back with the windows rolled down. Mom and Dad made ice cream with an old crank machine and whole milk. It was such fun running around the neighborhood, catching fireflies in the dark. Now that's how summer ought to be."

Nina shot her a sideways glance. "I bet you wouldn't go without air-conditioning today."

She'd caught Francie, who laughed. "I bet I could weather it better than you."

I suspected that might be the case. A true outdoorsy Southerner, Francie had reached the age where she said what she thought, even if it might sting. She made no effort to tame her yellow strawlike hair or hide the wrinkles she had earned from years of gardening and bird watching in all kinds of weather.

"What do you know about bees, Francie?" I asked. "What do you suppose possessed them to chase Angus like that?"

"Bees can be ornery little buggers. They're focused on protecting the hive and the queen. My guess is that Angus accidentally stumbled onto a hive and disturbed it. I've heard they'll chase a person up to half a mile."

Nina shuddered. "I love honey, but bees scare me."

I was handing the refreshing drinks to my friends when someone knocked on the front door. Daisy accompanied me to open it.

Hollis Haberman, who lived on the next block, stood on my stoop. In his fifties, Hollis liked to eat and had long ago given up any sort of exercise. His face was flushed from the heat and the short walk to my house.

"Hollis! Come on in out of the sun. Could I offer you an Arnold Palmer?"

"That would hit the spot. Sorry to disturb you, but my

yard man vanished, and I'm told he was seen headed this way acting kind of strange."

I closed the door behind him. "Angus was working for you? Come into the kitchen. Nina and Francie are here. It was the strangest thing. He was being chased by bees. You'd better be careful in your yard."

Hollis touched my arm ever so gently. "Could I have a word with you out here first?"

"Sure." I frowned at him. "What's up?"

Hollis's belly heaved when he took a deep breath. He lowered his voice to a whisper. "Do you know of a way to test your food at home to be sure nobody poisoned it?"

Connect with

Visit us online at
KensingtonBooks.com
to read more from your favorite authors, see books
by series, view reading group guides, and more.

for sneak peeks, chances to win books and prize packs,
and to share your thoughts with other readers.

facebook.com/kensingtonpublishing
twitter.com/kensingtonbooks

Tell us what you think!

To share your thoughts, submit a review,
or sign up for our eNewsletters, please visit:
KensingtonBooks.com/TellUs.